THE CHEATED WIFE

ALISON IRVING

For Anne, Lesley and Louise

CHAPTER ONE

As I toasted the New Year with my husband Tom and our friends, I smiled prettily and restrained myself from grinding my champagne flute into his handsome face. He grinned charmingly at me in the dim room and his musky heat assaulted my senses as he leaned forward to smooth my long, brunette hair back from my face.

'Here's to a New Year and new beginnings, Vicky,' he sighed huskily into my ear, and caressed my butt with his huge hand.

'To new beginnings,' I repeated sweetly and permitted his hand to linger for a short-lived moment. When I carefully moved away, his mouth hardened and a surly expression marred his good looks as he glanced around to check my withdrawal hadn't been noted.

No one but me would recognise his poor form, but then again, only the two of us were aware I was going off-piste from what we'd discussed before we left home.

'It's crucial we portray a united front, sweetie,' he'd earnestly explained as I'd pulled on my black dress earlier.

Freshly shaved and neatly dressed, he'd sat on the edge of

the bed, and fiddled with his wedding band, as if to draw attention to his commitment. My lip had curled and I'd spun away to struggle with the zip on the back of the dress. Ever the gentleman, he'd stepped over to help without needing to be asked and I'd frustratingly surrendered, shivering slightly as his fingertips caressed my skin.

'I'm not stupid, I'm well versed in how to play the role of the loving wife.' The words shot out and landed full square on him. I could've added I'd had years of training, but bit down on my true feelings, like so often before. In the mirror I'd noticed his momentary scowl, then he remembered his current position and gave a self-deprecating laugh.

'I know you're not stupid, and I really appreciate you coming with me to Annie and Matt's.' He could smoothly flip from irritated to amiable in the blink of an eye, which I'd always found hugely compelling. What remained unsaid, but which hung over us in a dark cloud, was yet another apology for his wayward behaviour.

Later, as I clutched my glass in Anne's living room, I recalled the exchange while *Jools Annual Hootenanny* flickered silently on the television. Tom expected me to act as though everything was hunky-dory, whereas the reality was far from it. But a New Year's Eve party was not the place to highlight the cracks in our marriage, and I smiled tightly at him. He stiffened as I put stale air between him and me, to kiss my friends and their husbands on the cheek.

'Happy New Year,' declared Annie, with a gentle smile. Her husband, Matt, chastely pecked my cheek, terrified to loiter for fear Annie jumped erroneously to the conclusion I was sleeping with him.

'Happy New Year!' squealed Kate, over-exuberant as ever, to compensate for the fact two-fifths of our Book Club were missing. Her husband David beamed as he chinked glasses with me, then moved swiftly onto Tom. Backslaps ensued, like eight year olds on the football pitch after scoring a goal.

No *here's to us* or *to the best friends ever* drivel we'd normally proclaim, for our formerly close-knit friendship group had been crushed into smithereens. Our other Book Club member Laura was holed up somewhere with her hot new man Sam, and Claire... A ripple of hurt as I contemplated Claire, my not-so-loyal friend who'd recently exposed her yearlong affair with Tom, my husband of twenty-odd years.

Obviously I was devastated at their treachery and genuinely grieved the destruction of our friendship group, but secretly a tiny piece of me was less devastated by Tom's behaviour, for this was a well-worn tale of our marriage.

Cheat. Discover. Beg. Forgive.

The never-ending circle of life, or rather the never-ending circle of deceit in the Ford marriage.

My tall, broad, gorgeous husband pecked my friends, the epitome of affability and dependability. The driest of kisses on Kate's pink cheek, the lightest of touches on Annie's bare arm. Meanwhile my hand burned from where he'd clasped it as the bells tolled midnight and our *annus horribilis* at long last drew to its woeful close.

One death.

One affair.

And one visit from the police.

It certainly would be a year none of us forgot quickly.

I quashed those morose reflections as Annie switched on the overhead light, and we drained our glasses as though gasping for sustenance. We'd tried and failed to conceal the unpalatable fact: six was so much more pitiful than ten and the upbeat music clashed with our deflated mood. No volume was loud enough to conceal the gaping void where the others should be.

In years gone by, the ten of us would have crowded into

Laura and her husband James's house for our annual New Year's Eve gathering, not far along the street from where we partied. Now James was dead and Laura had sprinted with indecent speed into a sparkly new relationship with Sam.

We shouldn't have come. I was unsure if I'd said the words aloud or if they'd screeched inside my head.

Poor Annie frantically increased the volume, and encouraged us to dance. Despite her encouragement, the guffaws and copious amounts of alcohol fell flat. As the clock sedately ticked its way to 1am, I'd had my fill of pretence.

'Let's go,' I whispered to Tom when Annie disappeared into the kitchen to replenish the drinks. Matt talked rugby with David on the sofa, and Kate napped on an armchair, glass upended, as Prosecco dribbled onto the carpet.

My tolerance for socialising had bottomed out. I had to leave immediately or the tightening in my chest would obstruct my breath. There was no air in the room; it was suddenly too hot, the atmosphere too heavy.

'We can't leave! It's early yet.' Tom hissed at me, rictus grin in place, anxious anyone might suppose we wouldn't survive his recent misdemeanour. Because I'd implied, although I was distraught at his latest betrayal, I was prepared to forgive him. Now he strove for atonement, superficially at least, half-heartedly at best.

'We're going now,' I spat in his ear, disinclined to keep up the charade any longer.

Annie arrived with more bubbly, but I covered my glass with my hand and refused. 'It's been such a fun night, but we have lunch with my parents tomorrow. I can't risk being over the limit with the police so vigilant at this time of year.' Straitlaced Annie whisked the bottle away from me, the mention of drink-driving causing a flush to stain her pretty face.

'We'd better leave too.' David shook Kate by the shoulder.

Groggily she opened one eye and woke with a start. Saliva rolled sluggishly down her chin, David compressed his lips into a thin line and instructed her to wipe her face. She did so, then rose so fast she teetered slightly on her high heels, black hair flattened from where she'd been lying.

Tight hugs and a longsome goodbye followed and we promised to meet up soon. I hid my exasperation, for naturally we'd see each other soon: we all lived within a stone's throw. Our street was right at the edge of Castlebrook village, hardly twenty minutes' drive from Belfast, but an oasis of calm surrounded by green fields and the undulating Antrim Hills. Fifteen minutes in the other direction and we'd be at the coast.

Blank windows from neighbouring houses kept their silent watch as the four of us made our way down the street. No stars and no moon tonight to welcome the New Year and guide us home. We stopped outside our house and waited as David and Kate made their unsteady way down the street, her heels tapping on the pavement. When they disappeared onto their driveway with a final wave, we stepped onto our own path.

The shriek of a cat, so reminiscent of a crying baby, made me jump. Maybe our cat Keiko was mauling some unsuspecting vermin. Wordlessly we walked to our front door and Tom unlocked it, then moved aside so I could enter first. The still house appeared to hold its breath as it waited to see what transpired next.

More unforgiving words? Slamming doors? Noisy make-up sex?

'Do you want a drink?' Tom asked me, with sincere brown eyes and chastened features.

'Feck off,' I answered, as I slipped off my shoes and coat. 'You can sleep in Alex's bed tonight.' I threw it over my shoulder as I hung my coat in the cloakroom and stalked into the kitchen.

He'd been sleeping in our daughter's bed since I'd learned about his affair.

His shoulders drooped as his gaze dropped sadly to the floor. Plausible, but the penitent act was an ancient one which had played out four other times in the past twenty years. I'd unquestioningly pardoned him the first time, when he cheated with a gorgeous young air stewardess. Fate had thrown them together on multiple long-haul flights after I gave birth to our second daughter Flora, and I'd exposed their dirty messages while my breasts leaked milk. I was too fragile to deny his fervent pleas for absolution then.

The next time I'd walked in on him kissing the neck of the wife of one of his colleagues at a party. I may have presumed it inoffensive if her hand hadn't been down the front of his trousers and her blouse unbuttoned. The memory of her lacy red bra taunted me for some time after.

And so it went on. Time after time after time. Routinely when he was caught, he implored and beseeched, and predictably I forgave him. He hadn't changed in twenty years, but I had.

Perhaps this time I wouldn't accept his behaviour and lame excuses.

For this time he'd chosen my friend, and although I understood her reasons for doing what she'd done, his role was indefensible. A fire created deep at my centre blazed at the memory of Claire and her motive for sleeping with my husband. She'd been my friend for many years and then betrayed me in the worst way possible. Surprisingly though, I forgave her completely, and almost admired the nerve it had taken to sustain it for so long. Nevertheless I'd shared those complex emotions with no one, and was unlikely to.

On the other hand, I was uncertain if I could pardon Tom, the serial philanderer, so effortlessly.

So why would I stay with him? He was devastatingly attractive, though looks wear thin over time. He had a great job as a first officer on an Irish airline and was charismatic, funny and loving. And when he focused his attention on you, he was irresistible, possessing the uncanny ability to make you feel you were the most incredible woman on the planet.

He was also weak, easily bored and a narcissist.

But I adored being Tom's wife, as on paper we were the ideal couple; good-looking, prosperous and universally envied. Privately I'd acknowledged that for years, as I'd outwardly feigned ignorance. Which is why I was so angry with Tom. By choosing a friend to stray with, he jeopardised 'us'.

However there was no question I would leave him.

Did I like what he'd done? A categorical no.

Did I want to make him squirm? Unquestionably yes.

Did I still love him? Possibly.

Was I simply a glutton for punishment?

Overcome with lethargy and unable to dissect that question, I filled a glass with water and tiptoed back into the hall. No sign of Tom, so I went into the sitting room, switched on a corner lamp and reclined on one of the velvet sofas. Tom's heavy footsteps banged overhead in our daughter's room, his tantrum obvious in each slam and thwack. When at last he fell silent, I finally relaxed. The Christmas tree lights twinkled and I studied them, mesmerised. I'd missed the others tonight, and although I'd no fight with Laura, she was consumed by her rekindled romance with her old boyfriend.

Rather perturbingly, I'd missed Claire more. My devious, dishonest friend. I missed her wicked laugh, her quick-witted retorts and had never once suspected what she'd been up to.

What a mistake that had been.

My thoughts wandered, unwilling to dwell on my mortification for long. Instead I lifted my phone from where it lay on my lap, and examined it methodically. I'd been offline for several hours, and could have missed so much. Normally I liked to keep on top of it regularly, but had limited opportunity all evening to scroll through the alerts on my mobile.

Messages from our daughters Alex and Flora, who celebrated in Belfast.

A text from Laura, insulated with Sam in a cottage on the coast.

And then, a notification from the person I dreaded most.

CHAPTER TWO

I fell asleep on the sofa in the early hours of New Year's Day, fully dressed and exhausted. Tom woke me when daylight filtered through the slatted wooden blinds. He carried a cup of coffee, face shadowed, jaw tense. He'd presumed when I'd agreed to attend Annie and Matt's party his penance was over. Arrogant to a fault.

With a muttered thanks, I lifted my mobile to indicate he was dismissed. He hesitated, obviously expecting me to converse normally with him. When I didn't, he loudly cleared his throat.

'Please can we move past this? I've apologised so many times. I'm so sorry. She came onto me and I was flattered. She refused to take no for an answer. Please forgive me.' He knelt on the floor beside me and grasped my free hand. The intoxicating smell of his aftershave teased, and I briefly indulged myself as I stared at his lush lips. I ached to rake my hands through his hair, rip off his shirt and feel the firm muscles of his torso as I lay under his weight.

'Feck off, Tom.' I hauled myself from my daydream. 'Claire said you pursued her and I believe her.'

'She's lying, Vicky, honestly she is. You know the lies she told about you. She's made it up about me chasing her in exactly the same way. She messaged me constantly, demanded we meet and – I'm embarrassed to say – in the end wore me down.' He shook his head as if dismissing the image of him and her doing who knows what, who knows where.

'I'm not going to change my mind. You're not coming with me to my parents today. You can do whatever you want. I hear Will has left Claire, you could go to her house and shag on the carpet.' His face reddened and my stomach curdled at the realisation they had indeed shagged on the carpet in Claire's house.

Nauseated by him, I roughly pushed him away and swung my legs over the side of the sofa. The coffee cup was knocked over in my haste, and the hot liquid splashed over both Tom and the carpet.

'You'd better clean it up,' I spat caustically, as he rose, nursing his hand where the coffee had scalded him. 'Hold your hand under the cold tap.' I softened a little as I hadn't meant to burn him.

Promptly I pivoted away and left him standing in a puddle of coffee as my eyes misted over. To know he and Claire had been intimate in her house, disgusted me. Perhaps this time he really had done the inexcusable. Hastily I climbed the stairs to avoid him seeing how upset I was, and when I reached the sanctity of the bathroom, locked the door and dejectedly stripped off the figure-hugging black dress I'd worn to the party. My lacy black lingerie followed and lay in a crumpled heap on the white tiles, taunting me. I nudged it out of the way with my toe and studied my reflection in the full-length mirror as the bath filled with water.

Today dark circles betrayed my sleep-deprived night and the toll the last few weeks had taken. Objectively though, despite reaching midlife and the accompanying fine lines, I knew I was still attractive. Throughout my life women either resented me for my looks, or conversely wanted to be my friend. Attractive by proxy if you like. Men made no secret of the fact they wanted me, but none of them had come close to Tom.

And yet my husband repeatedly slept with other women, leaving me hollow. My exterior may be immaculate, but my interior was littered with deep flaws. I sighed sadly, added fragrant bath oil to the water and lowered myself into it with a small moan.

Purposefully I put my marriage woes to one side and my attention moved on to more pressing matters. The notification I'd received last night. My stomach which had begun to settle, lurched once more.

While this might be a new year, it appeared there was to be no new beginning.

Usually I was unbothered by envy, as it tended to be harmless. But when it became more menacing, I was inexperienced in how to act or what to do. Anxiety pulsated as I tossed one idea then another around, and pondered what I should do next.

I soaked until the water cooled and by then I'd planned my course of action.

Filled with sudden energy, I heaved myself out of the bath, briskly dried off, then wrapped myself in my fleecy dressing gown. Tom could make his own amusement today, for I needed time apart from him and his hangdog expression. Before we'd left for the party last night, I'd informed him he wasn't to attend my parents' New Year's lunch. He had glowered and asked in a pathetic tone what he should do on his own all day.

'I don't care,' I'd yelled, 'there's bound to be someone desperate enough to want to spend it with you.'

There were many people who'd be happy to have him to

themselves for a few hours. He'd cringed at my words, for I rarely lost control and usually preferred to drip acid rather than pour a river of it over his head.

In the bedroom I searched through the drawers until I found the black cigarette trousers I'd chosen to wear with a loose fitting cream silk blouse. My father was exacting in his view of appropriate clothing for a woman aged fifty, and I never challenged his instructions.

Fifty and still wary of him.

I snorted, slightly embarrassed.

Tom remained downstairs, which gave me time to check social media once I'd dressed. Propped against the headboard, I inspected Facebook and Instagram, as twinges of apprehension caused my heart to race. Photos of fireworks, entwined hands, New Year GIFs. I searched on, lost in an online world and oblivious when Tom walked into the bedroom.

'What time are you leaving?' he asked flatly.

I flipped the phone over and raised my eyes. His were steely now. Coffee hadn't worked its magic, so he'd moved on to the next phase of his act. Contrition blended with antipathy.

'When I'm ready.' I began to rise, but he hampered my way.

'What time will you be home? Alex and Flora will be here by five.'

'I'll be home by then, don't worry. The girls know dinner will be at six.' The steak pie I'd prepared yesterday was in the fridge, ready for our daughters' arrival.

'Please let me come with you. Your parents will ask awkward questions otherwise.'

'If they ask, I'll be honest with them.' He was directly in front of me, which forced me to shimmy down the edge of the bed and slip past him. The air was charged, his annoyance obvious at my lie. He might believe I'd divulge his latest affair to my parents, but there was no chance of it, for I'd never give them a whip to beat me with. It was bravado, nothing more. I stretched into the wardrobe and unearthed a pair of ankle boots. Using the wall for balance, I pushed my feet into them and avoided eye contact.

Tom stood with his hands on his hips.

'Let me pass, please.' My voice was measured, though I longed to bellow my suffering as visions of his body entwined with my friend's ran riotously through my head.

Slick with sweat. Hot words of passion. Barefaced lies.

In an effort to dissolve them, I blinked rapidly. Stubbornly they persisted as he stepped aside and I made my way downstairs. My phone vibrated with a notification, but Tom was on my heels, so I set it face down on the worktop without looking. I studiously took no notice of him, made myself a frothy coffee and popped a slice of bread into the toaster. He slumped heavily onto a stool at the breakfast bar and begged again to go with me, brow knitted. Doubtless he'd believed me when I'd fibbed about disclosing his indiscretions to my parents.

When I reached the limit of my tolerance, I said wearily, 'Don't be bloody stupid, Tom. Do you really think I'd tell Mum and Dad about your affair? You know what their response to that little gem would be.'

He studied his clenched fists, as a muscle twitched in his jaw. For my parents were the golden goose which kept on laying, and the prospect of the bottomless pit of money drying up was guaranteed to stop him in his tracks.

'Thank you, sweetie.' Back to contrition. 'I'll heat the pie later so you don't need to rush home.' He smiled sheepishly at me then disappeared into the sitting room.

His alleged remorse left a rancid aftertaste and I was fully mindful it was the danger of my parents learning his secret which had caused his about-face. My mouth was dry as I nibbled the toast, and even with liberal lashings of marmalade, I had difficulty swallowing. For I was now distracted by another issue.

The newest notification. When I checked it and found it was nothing more sinister than a message from a work friend, my nerves dissolved. Today could be all right after all. Suddenly I was ravenous, my mouth no longer arid, so I brewed fresh coffee and buttered another slice of toast.

As I munched it at the kitchen table, I scrolled through my mobile again, replied to the New Year messages, texted my daughters to remind them not to be late for dinner, then began over.

Checking and double checking everything was as it should be and nothing untoward had been posted. No unwelcome comments nor messages. Simultaneously anxious in anticipation of what I might read, but helpless to stop myself from looking.

Before long, it was time to leave for the lunch at my parents, and I stuck my head around the door to the sitting room to say goodbye to my errant husband. Gloomily he jerked his chin and silently reproached me from the sofa. A spasm of pleasure at his sour expression and I swiftly turned on my heel.

Fresh air buffeted me as I stepped outside and instinctively I glanced around, alert for anything unusual. Satisfied no one was hanging about, I slammed the front door with as much force as I dared. It wouldn't do if a neighbour heard the bang or questioned our marriage.

For appearances were everything. Anything else could be shrouded in haze and obscurity.

What isn't seen, can't hurt you. Can it?

CHAPTER THREE

It was a crisp January day and the winter sun hung low in the sky. Wispy clouds streaked the sky and scuttled towards the coast. As I drove from Castlebrook village towards Belfast, I passed no vehicles on the country roads and a handful on the motorway. New Year's Day was either time for an invigorating walk, or a listless start improved by painkillers and television. The solitude bathed me in temporary happiness, and I used the drive to mull over my circumstances as nineties hits played on the radio.

My irritation plunged with each mile I put between myself and Tom. Before Claire announced his infidelity in mid-December, he'd increasingly irked me by getting under my feet and tripping me up with his hovering presence. Uninvited fingers had slithered over nightly to stroke my bare flesh in bed. Unexpected gifts for me when he'd returned from a work trip. Too late it became clear his saccharine behaviour had been a smokescreen for his affair.

Now I ached to have space without repeated demands for understanding and forgiveness. His interminable begging was tiring and I longed to wake refreshed after a dreamless sleep.

For him to return to work so I could take my time to explore *if* and *why* and *how*.

His new-found remorse and accompanying clinginess intruded into the other facet of my life, which was entirely separate from my family. It fulfilled me in a way my jaded relationship with Tom did not, and had ignited exhilaration, enjoyment and excitement.

Until it didn't.

My stomach sank as I manoeuvred the car along the West Link. The busier city roads needed greater concentration, but my focus was obstinately elsewhere, ruminating about my alternate life which had become a little disturbing.

Always apprehensive for that unwelcome face outside. Each buzz from my mobile caused a flash of nerves. The quiet knock on the door of my consulting room, uncertain who would enter. Persistent checking of my emails, texts and social media. The sad thing was, there was no one I could trust to share the burden of my worries, which sometimes threatened to overwhelm.

For it was unremitting and in spite of what was said, or done, it appeared there was to be no end. What had started so promisingly had disintegrated despite my wholehearted efforts and I'd dealt with it alone when my husband had been occupied elsewhere, breaking his vows.

I scolded myself often, for I should've known it would lead to disappointment.

My mind was consumed with negativity as I arrived at the gates of my parents' house in South Belfast. Thankfully my deliberations were cut short as I swung onto their driveway and parked in front of their garage. A quick glance in the mirror, then I lifted the chilled bottle of champagne I'd fortunately remembered to bring from the fridge at home. My father would've been furious if I'd not extended the courtesy of a gift when visiting them.

The cool air calmed me as I walked across the gravel path and rang the doorbell. My parents' home was not a house which invited an informal hello when you entered without knocking. As I waited, icy gusts blasted and my skin prickled at the whirr of security cameras rotating towards me. The heavy oak door was opened by my mother, faultless in a baby pink silk sheath dress. Slim and elegant, though much shorter than my five foot eleven inches, her hair was precisely sprayed in place, her make-up perfect.

'Victoria, how nice of you to almost make it on time.' She proffered a cheek for a kiss and graciously accepted the champagne. 'What a pity my granddaughters were too busy to visit on New Year's Day.' The second barb in as many moments hit its mark as I followed her down the hallway and into the lounge. I'd suspected my daughters would be hungover on New Year's Day, and had bravely refused the invitation on their behalf.

Dad lounged on his favourite leather armchair, half-moon glasses on the end of his nose, strands of grey combed over his balding pate. He was reading *World Without End* by Ken Follett, a novel he'd failed to finish since my previous visit. He didn't look up, so I perched on the edge of a nearby overstuffed sofa. Mum disappeared into the kitchen and my palms grew clammy. Surreptitiously I rubbed them on my trousers as I calculated how many minutes I'd be expected to stay. The doorbell chimed and my mother's heels click-clacked back down the hall.

Slowly Dad placed the book on the mahogany side table, and removed his glasses. 'Victoria, good of you to join us. Where's your no-good husband?' He predicted my fluster, but I was well versed in his snide ways and had my lie prepared.

'Dubai. A last-minute thing.' The untruth slid easily off the tongue. The benefits of having a pilot for a husband; nonappearances easily explained.

'Humph,' was his reply and the silence grew long and sour, the overpowering scent of disappointment saturating the air between us. We were biding our time until my brother and his perfect family joined our happy band.

A small blond whirlwind ran into the room and launched itself at Dad, who'd opened his arms wide and embraced the hurricane with a laugh.

'Grandpa, Grandpa, Grandpa!' shouted the boy, my adored nephew Zander. The greatest success my younger brother Adam had achieved was to produce an heir to carry on the Harris name. The fact I practised medicine under my maiden name, and called my oldest child Alex after her grandfather, meant nothing once the golden boy had arrived. But that was an old gripe and one I couldn't rebuke Adam for, because he too had borne the brunt of our father's discontent until the revered moment his wife Natalie had delivered Zander.

Adam was tall and good-looking, and I loved my not-so-little brother. His wife Natalie I loved a lot less. She now believed herself to be the equivalent of Jane Seymour, having produced a sought-after male for the demanding head of the family. I assumed she was too vacuous to recall Jane's fate.

After I hugged my brother, Natalie and I air kissed, as she lavished praise on my mum's dress, hair and French manicure.

For me, a dismissive smirk. 'On your own again?'

'Yes, unfortunately,' I replied through gritted teeth.

Dripping with faux empathy, Natalie pouted, then delivered her stock 'Poor you Victoria, I couldn't bear it if Adam wasn't home every night. I'd miss him terribly and worry what he was getting up to on his own.' The same thing every bloody time. A cold shudder trailed up my spine as I wondered if Tom had made a pass at her at some point. It couldn't be absolutely ruled out, although he generally had never been interested in catty snobs.

We took our seats at the dining room table and I was sorry I was driving, as the inclination to drown my sorrows was intense. As Mum served coq au vin, I conversed genially and did what I had done my entire adult life. Diluted my aversion for my parents and sister-in-law with bland words and insincere smiles. Zander played games on an iPad, something neither of my girls had been allowed to do. It was unsurprising they resented spending time with their grandparents.

Lunch was a prolonged affair and my mind wandered to the past. Long ago I'd accepted I was a disappointment to my parents, a pale imitation of the dazzling offspring they'd anticipated. They discounted my career, family and accomplishments, and instead perceived me an abject failure.

My B in O-level French had resulted in a summer spent studying with a tutor, before I re-sat it the following year. My cousin had been taken in my place on our family holiday to Mexico and my grades never dropped again.

After my silver medal win in a major triathlon, Dad coerced me into running another five miles that night, in the pouring rain and along the city streets as punishment. Blistered heels and detached toenails served as a reminder to train harder.

Studying medicine hadn't warranted praise when I became a GP rather than the orthopaedic consultant he'd envisaged. It was one of the few things I'd held my ground on, and his eyes had bulged at my audacity. I'd driven home to Tom afterwards with his snarl ringing in my ears as tears dripped down my face. *'You couldn't achieve even that, could you! You've always been an embarrassment to me, Victoria.'* When I made the decision not to become partner in the practice due to family commitments, he'd sniffed dismissively.

Sitting in my parents' prosperous yet inhospitable house, I

wished I had the strength to stand up to them, to live a productive and independent life. Nevertheless, I again failed, as Tom and I had a tendency to live outside our means and relied on their one lavish gift. Money.

It was startling how two people so mean with their affection, should be generous with their cash. But their reasons were shallow and boasting to friends about me and Adam was one of the few pleasures we provided, although they rarely complimented us to our faces. My parents' one saving grace was they'd never beat us. Their bruises had been purely emotional. I didn't particularly like either of them, but remained too afraid of the consequences to sever our flimsy links.

After lunch I sipped my coffee on the same overfilled sofa in the sweltering lounge as the clock ticked down to four o'clock. Then I made my excuses, my throat thick with pressure, and awaited the command for my dismissal. Dad permitted me to leave thirty minutes later, with the brusque instruction to visit in two weeks with Tom and the girls. Meekly I agreed and discreetly once again thanked them both for their substantial monetary Christmas gift. I would be thanking them ad infinitum for the rest of their lives.

Free to leave, I fled to my car and started the engine. It purred reassuringly and a quick glance at the door confirmed my parents hadn't waited, but were already inside with the door shut. Their Christmas wreath of greenery and berries hung lopsided on a red velvet ribbon, wilted and curled in the bleak atmosphere. Duty done, I drove out of the driveway and indicated left. A few minutes later I pulled over to the kerb and examined my phone.

Worry drained from me. I read the messages which had been teasingly close throughout the afternoon, though resolutely out of bounds. My parents forbade mobiles to be answered when lunching with them. The exception was a life or death emergency, such as a rapid plunge in the stock market, or an unexpected four-ball at golf.

I replied to those which required a response, checked social media quickly and restarted the engine. When the city lights dimmed in the distance, I reached the country-bound carriageway and relief streamed through me, for I'd worried unnecessarily. Made a mountain out of a molehill. There was a chance I'd sleep well and wake revitalised. It had come to nothing.

As the road narrowed and twisted homewards, I drove the car down the country lanes. My mind bounced about as I anticipated a chatty meal with my daughters, while Tom and I papered over the fissures in our marriage.

Castlebrook was a welcome sight as I passed the crop of copper beeches and drove over the bridge. Unintentionally I slowed down to scour the footpaths and side roads, anticipating a glimpse of that one unwanted face. The village was quiet as everyone sheltered behind closed doors and drawn curtains. A solitary shadow appeared from the park, promptly joined by a bounding dog and I grinned at my jumpiness.

The car was at snail's pace when I reached the street. The streetlights scarcely brightened the darkness, and it appeared there was no one else about. Inevitably as I began to breathe a little easier, I saw them. Unmistakeable despite the gloom. Immediately my breathing became shallow.

It was far from over yet.

CHAPTER FOUR

On edge, I swung onto my driveway. Light peeped around the blinds on the ground floor, the upstairs windows in darkness. Motion sensors had kicked into action when I'd swung into the drive, and harsh light flooded the front of the house. Dazzled by the glare, I gripped the steering wheel and battled to stem my rocketing anxiety. The girls would be inside and I had to act as if nothing was wrong.

A few minutes passed and I composed myself before shakily walking indoors, where I called a faux cheery hello. Jackets were slung over the end of the banister, trainers lay discarded in the hall, right beside the cloakroom. Anxiety melded into resentment. I ached for order and tidiness, but suppressed my cross words, for my daughters rarely visited from their university digs.

True to form, Alex and Flora had adopted their usual sprawled positions on the sofas in the sitting room, intent on their phones, television blaring. Relieved they would ease the oppressive atmosphere between me and Tom, I gave both of them a quick hug. Hostilities would have to be suspended for a few hours.

Alex's pretty face was ashen, brunette hair limp and messily scraped into a long ponytail. The epitome of regret on New Year's Day following an exceptional New Year's Eve. Alternatively Flora's brown eyes were bright and alert, signifying she was hangover free. Or better at hiding it. They indifferently asked after their grandparents and I fabricated a wonderful afternoon, then requested they visit with us in two weeks' time.

'But, Mum,' Alex whinged, but I interrupted before she reached full flow as it was non-negotiable.

'I allowed you to miss today as it was a special night last night. You will attend in two weeks and I won't accept any excuses.' My tone was firm and rang with the echo of my mother's voice. 'I'm sorry, but they're very keen to see you; it's been a few weeks.' I lightened my tone, detesting a smidgen of Mum seeping through.

Alex's pale brown stare was defiant, jaw clenched. Flora quickly said she'd be happy to visit. Alex was my nonconformist child, Flora the wily one, cannily keeping her grandparents on side. To her, they represented pound signs, therefore she tolerated their tetchiness with good humour and awaited another handout.

We chatted about their night, when they disclosed nothing meaningful and I accepted their caginess. They were adults and I couldn't order them to tell me where they had been, or who they'd been with. Their attention soon drifted back to the TV and I headed into the kitchen, where Tom sat at the breakfast bar, intent on his phone.

In one smooth movement, he turned it over when he caught sight of me. Unblinking he exclaimed a jovial hello and questioned how lunch had been. He then informed me the pie was in the oven and potatoes were boiling. I almost snapped 'So what?' but couldn't bear his face to fall and a re-enactment of his poor-me portrayal. Instead I thanked him with the briefest smile.

'Why don't you watch TV with the girls and I'll take care of things in here?' I wanted him out of the way so I could have time on my own.

He agreed without argument and pecked me on the cheek. Fully clued in that his tight black T-shirt and Levis enhanced his gym-honed body, he meandered away.

Subdued laughter from the girls escaped the front room, in response to some comment from him. I aimed a dirty look in the general direction of the sitting room, for he'd pocketed his mobile as he left the room. Suddenly I was totally drained by the notion of him conducting whatever secretly, and had no energy to brood about it further. My limbs were heavy with his disloyalty and lies.

After a cursory check of the pie, I wearily clattered upstairs with my bag. It seemed to burn my hand, but I delayed examining my phone until I stripped out of my dutiful daughter outfit and dressed in a sweatshirt and jeans. Comfy slippers and my hair carelessly plaited completed my transition back to village mum. Finally I could study my mobile for the latest updates.

The unsettling episode from earlier scratched endlessly.

What should I do?

What *could* I do?

Constant observation and monitoring. From the break of dawn to the blackness of the night, there was no reprieve. Thoughts reeled and emotions whirled at the enormity of it all.

The heavy tread of a foot on the stairs warned me of Tom's presence, so I fled into the en suite and locked the door. There I blundered onto the lid of the toilet, where I received another alert.

Thoughtlessly I bit my thumbnail until the tip ripped off.

The throb was immediate as a spot of blood bubbled and I ran it under the tap. A streak of red circled the plughole as I made my decision.

I pressed the call button, and held the phone to my ear.

Afterwards, my angst had lessened as I'd hoped. Once I sorted myself out, I cautiously opened the door. No Tom, so I returned downstairs, set the table and mashed the potatoes. Cream and butter made them fluffy and smooth. Steamed broccoli for Vitamins C and K. A glass of Prosecco swiftly downed as a reward for surviving my parents' excruciating lunch. A second glass sipped more slowly.

Tom dandered through at six to offer help, but I simply asked him to see if the girls wanted a drink. A hair of the dog for Alex. A meaningful smile passed between us, words unnecessary as we recalled many similar days ourselves.

Possibly this is why I entertain his behaviour, I mused as he poured the drinks. *When you've been with someone this long, they instinctively understand you.*

He topped up my glass, handed it back to me and my animosity towards him thawed a little. Warm fingers brushed mine. 'I'm sorry for putting you through this.' The humbled, repentant husband.

And certainly he was sincere at that moment in time. I silently saluted him with my glass and he returned to the sitting room with the ghost of a smile playing about his lips.

Some people might suppose me ludicrous, staying with a womaniser, and a repeat offender.

But generally we made a good team. For he was my cover.

From my scathing parents, to whom divorce meant failure.

From unsolicited attention from other men.

From reality when it became untethered and too arduous.

We had been a couple for so many years, I didn't know how to exist without him and was too proud to split up. Therefore I appreciated him a little, that New Year's Day. The moon hung in the black velvet sky and frost shimmered on the grass. If I opened the back door, the brook would be babbling at the end of the garden. However, I didn't open the door nor stand in the garden to lift my head and admire the skies. Instead I flitted throughout the house to ensure the doors were bolted and the blinds closed tight, so not even a sliver of light was visible outside. Our family was safely locked away from prying scowls and loitering silhouettes.

Content, I lit candles and played soft music, drank Prosecco and ate dinner with my family. When my phone buzzed on the breakfast bar, I neglected it for a time. We chatted and after dinner played our traditional game of Monopoly at the kitchen table, complete with customary disagreements and fallings out. Tom held my hand at one point, and I endured it, pretending he wasn't untrustworthy and truly was the man he depicted to others. Our daughters laughed and squabbled, unquestioning we were still together, yet informed he'd cheated with my close friend Claire.

Reflecting on that, I released his hand and disregarded both my distressed words and urge to slap his face. For one night only I assumed the role of the magnanimous wife. As the good-natured sparring of my daughters and husband eddied around me, I rolled my last dice and admitted defeat. Then I kissed Flora's head, stealthily picked up my phone and carried it to the sofa in the conservatory, where I read multiple messages, obscured from sight.

One caused my mouth to dry.

Another text from Claire; begging, lonesome and rejected. For Will had left her when she'd confessed her sins and now her marriage was in ruins, her two daughters appalled by her behaviour. And I was torn in two, troubled by her desolation, but sickened by her actions. Stark words of misery laid bare her pain. Tom's loud guffaw broke my reverie. The embodiment of nonchalance as he teased Flora and topped up Alex's wine when he supposed I wasn't looking.

Undeniably the fault was fully his.

For a minute, the intensity of my dislike for my husband verged on hatred. A forceful, intense hatred which propelled so violently through my body it lodged in my throat. I glanced again at Claire's bereft pleading.

As harrowing as it was, I couldn't be seen to absolve her.

Tom was indispensable. Claire was dispensable.

The sinner was vital in his role as my protector. The sinned against had no role to play now.

My heart hardened as I finally acknowledged I had no choice but to accept Tom's apology. The road had come to a dead-end tonight, with no space for U-turns or alternatives. Ending our marriage was not an option. Claire's message was left unanswered, and my composure splintered a little.

I sighed heavily and walked over to my family. When I leaned forward to plant a kiss on Tom's neck, I allowed my hair to graze his skin in a way he found irresistible. A grip of his muscular shoulder as I murmured I was going to watch television. Hopeful eyes locked onto mine reflected his gratitude.

'We should watch some TV together.' He covered my hand with his and I dispassionately studied his fingers linked with mine, the fingers which had done unspeakable things to Claire, while I'd been blind to it all. For she'd described in minute detail exactly what and where it had occurred, this great deception. All in the name of revenge. A revenge she'd demanded years after the initial trauma, which had obsessed her.

Ultimately the only way I could maintain the impression of having won, was to remain with the pawn from her game. So I smiled through gritted teeth and lowered my lashes to mask my sadness. The four of us filed through to the front room, where we chuckled our way through reruns of *Father Ted* and *Derry Girls*.

Much later the girls disappeared into their bedrooms and Tom and I faced each other on the landing outside our bedroom. My decision had to be quick. It may hurt me, but was unavoidable. I reached for his hand, led him into our bedroom and softly closed the door.

As he pawed me later, my mind rambled free. He'd taken me for a fool, but I was no fool. Not about him. Later he slept the sleep of the blameless and I stared into the blackness. My mind careered chaotically, afraid this new year would bring nothing but heartache.

We'd reconnected physically, but emotionally we were further apart than we'd ever been.

CHAPTER FIVE

Alex and Flora stayed with us for a few days, until they returned to their student lives. The house was quiet when they left, but I consoled myself I wouldn't miss damp towels heaped on the bathroom floor, long hairs in the plughole nor half-drunk coffee cups staining the furniture. The coolness between me and Tom had defrosted for those hours, as we'd presented a united front.

Once the girls had left, I was impatient for him to resume flying and give me the small luxury of an empty house. No sullen gawping. No *What will we do today?* Incapable of refusing his requests for sex, dreading his hand creeping over to my thigh. This was how he demonstrated I was more alluring than Claire. How he proved she meant nothing, it was time I moved on and there was no point in prolonging his sentence. For it was noticeable by his intermittent stony expression, he presumed the whole sordid chapter should be forgiven and forgotten.

The night before he returned to work, the sheets cooled between us like his ardour. Back to me, his breathing slowed, but sleep remained infuriatingly elusive. The headlights of a passing car swept across the ceiling and my stomach tightened.

After the relative haven of the past few days, the hiatus was coming to an end.

I rolled away from my husband and the rhythmic sounds of his breathing helped settle my uneasiness.

Inhale. Exhale. Monotonous and mundane.

The sounds of our marriage.

Inhale. Exhale. Deceive. Repeat.

In time my last conscious thought was not of Tom, but a direct blue gaze and full black beard.

The next morning Tom dressed for work, self-important in his uniform. His case was packed, pilot bag on top. To make me laugh, he placed his cap at a jaunty angle, a tradition prior to every long-haul trip. My response was bitter and dry.

At the front door, I accepted his kiss on the lips as I shivered in the crisp morning air to see him off. It was a precaution so anyone snooping would see a dutiful wife and loving husband. Attentive for anything unusual, I browsed the street. A dark shadow. An unidentified car. Nothing. All was as it should be. Faint sunlight split the blanket of cloud, but the temperature would remain in single digits for the rest of the day.

The car revved before he reversed out of the drive with a final wave. Huddled in my fleecy dressing gown, I was deep in thought as the car disappeared. Peace descended on the street and I glanced at Annie and Matt's house, curtains pulled, both cars in the driveway. Kate and David's was a few doors down, its untidiness contrasting with the rest of the street. And at the corner, Laura's house. James no longer with us, she lived there alone most of the time unless her son Robbie or Sam stayed. I begrudged her nothing, for she'd withered through neglect with James, and bloomed under Sam's attention.

With a smile to myself I returned to the warmth, and locked the front door with a firm click. My joy was whooped quietly, as if afraid someone would hear and judge me. One day on my own and I'd numerous plans for it. There was no danger of Tom appearing unannounced beside me, or questioning what I was doing.

In the utility room I swopped my slippers for shoes and my dressing gown for a jacket before stepping outside to call for Keiko. The misty morning light threw squat shadows across the garden, bare branches of the mature trees extended heavenward. The brook separated us from the open fields, a fertile hunting ground for a young cat. Keiko appeared soundlessly at my ankles as I walked over the grass, which was wet with dew. She accompanied me indoors and I diligently locked the door before I discarded my outdoor shoes and clothes.

It was time to check social media and messages, so I lounged on the sofa in the conservatory with a cappuccino. Food could wait. Nervously I scanned the notifications, predicting the disagreeable, but miraculously found nothing problematic. Able now to relax, I devoured them fully.

Kate messaged the Book Club WhatsApp to invite us to her house on Friday night. Claire had subtly been removed from the WhatsApp group in a show of solidarity with me. Perversely I wished she'd remained, as I was a little fazed about her isolation. She lived in a huge house in the hills above the village, with no near neighbours, abandoned by her friends and immediate family.

Nevertheless I was powerless to help her, for it was essential I maintain the illusion I was the injured party. I'd spun my saga in such a way Annie and Kate were firmly on my side, but I suspected Laura was torn. Once I'd replied to say I'd love to come, I trawled again, afraid something could have been overlooked.

Satisfied my searches were complete and I'd missed nothing, I yawned with sudden tiredness. Probably it was the release after the past few days. I cast a critical eye around my open-plan kitchen. Nothing out of place. Immaculate. Spotless. The epitome of good taste and money. My parents had paid for the handmade units and granite worktops, Italian floor tiles and chrome accessories, but in exchange they demanded perfection, though they rarely visited. To them we lived in the wilds of the country, although the village was a short drive from Belfast city centre. Sarcastic comments were regularly made about wellington boots, flat caps and thick accents. Their perception of my life was as removed from the reality as their fiction of doting parents.

My gut clenched as I sat up. The briefest consideration of them disheartened me, and I wanted nothing to spoil my day. I forced myself to stamp out all thoughts of them and commanded the sound system to play upbeat music. Toast was washed down with cold coffee as I anticipated the long day ahead, ripe with possibilities.

First a shower, then a quick visit to my workplace, the Ballyrevy GP Practice. As it was Sunday, I wanted to sort a couple of things out while it was empty of chatter and inquisitive stares. Then an errand before returning home via a friend's house.

My internal voice nagged I should go for a run, or a swim, but I rejected it straight away. Long ago my father's bullying behaviour had destroyed my pleasure in exercise. In his opinion if it hadn't resulted in a gold medal, it was a futile waste of time and effort. I remembered the purest joy as I cut through the water, my stroke sure and strong or the wind on my face as I sped down a steep hill. Nostalgia and disappointment surged as I spurned my one true passion. Perhaps one day I'd overcome the mixed emotions and appreciate the benefit of running, cycling or swimming again. In their place I walked for miles and attended a yogalates class with Claire and Laura once a week at the local leisure centre. My heart missed a beat.

I used to attend the class with Claire and Laura. Before.

On autopilot, I put my cup in the dishwasher, before going upstairs to wash away my heartache. After my shower, I dressed in a grey sweater and jeans and knotted my hair at the base of my neck. Make-up free and in the muted morning light, I could pass for forty-five. Forty at a push in the right light. Fine lines ran from my nose to below my mouth, nasolabial folds or smile lines. I hated them, as they signified the compulsory smiles I wore at home, at work, with friends. Possibly it was time I succumbed to fillers or Botox.

As I walked out to the car, Kate appeared at the end of my driveway. A strong smell of garlic hit me full in the face as she greeted me. Kate's fondness for chewing raw garlic to ward off menopause was a source of much hilarity between us all, until she blew it into our faces.

'Hi,' she said brightly. 'I couldn't remember when Tom was heading off with work, but wondered if you'd like a coffee?' Bloodshot eyes regarded me thoughtfully, possibly anticipating I would sob about my lot in the middle of the street.

'Sorry, I'd love to, but I've got loads to do today. Would later in the week suit?' She was a wild swimming devotee and usually swam in the inclement Irish Sea each weekend, so it was unusual for her to miss it. Then I noted her pale face and wondered if she was hungover. I'd once quietly advised her she should consider medication other than the liquid variety along with the garlic and cold-water swimming, but she'd reacted so passionately, I'd never mentioned it again.

'That would be nice.' Her smile died. After a pause, she continued. 'This may be a strange question, but have you noticed anyone hanging about recently?'

In an instant, my armpits became damp. 'What do you mean?'

'Someone's been hanging about in the field behind the houses.' My head whipped round as I instinctively glanced at the back garden. The field ran directly behind both our houses and was easily accessible by the road.

I rubbed my temple. 'I haven't seen anyone. Are you sure it wasn't a dog walker now the farmer's moved the sheep?'

'Definitely not. They were there early this morning and I'm pretty sure someone was lurking a couple of days ago as well.'

'Did you get a good look at them? Was it a man or woman?' My questions were delivered in a volley as I tried to find out what exactly Kate thought she'd seen.

She wrinkled her nose. 'I don't know exactly, both times it was pretty dark so I couldn't be certain. David says I'm imagining it, but I'm sure there was someone wearing a long coat and bobble hat. The same person each time.'

It tied in with everything. Carefully I hid my emotions, played it down and promised I'd keep a close eye out for anything suspicious from now on. At last she left me with a small wave and a promise of coffee soon.

I slipped behind the wheel and replayed her words. Hopefully I'd been reassuring, there was nothing else I could do. My eyes roved around the street and I shuddered, though everything was as it should be. When I drove past the field a few moments later, a figure fleetingly emerged, but it had to be a trick of the light.

For there was no one there.

Was there?

CHAPTER SIX

As expected, the practice car park was empty that penetratingly cold Sunday morning. Like many of my colleagues, I'd occasionally make the most of weekends to get ahead of my workload, in anticipation of a frenetic Monday surgery. Today I was alone. The low whitewashed building was set back from the road, and its windows sightlessly watched me, not even a spark of movement within. I gasped when a blast of icy wind caught me off-guard as I hurried to the staff entrance.

Once I'd unlocked the door, I quickly punched in the numbers and the alarm's shrill beeping stopped. Quiet descended, the air still suddenly. CCTV would record throughout, but most of the cameras were dummies; only the ones at the external doors and in the nurse's treatment room worked. The cameras didn't cover the car park, and we kept no medication onsite. Needles were locked away, so break-ins were uncommon and it was more probable the pharmacy nearby would get vandalised.

My rubber-soled boots squeaked on the lino as I passed the row of consulting rooms. At the end of the corridor, I nipped into the office to the rear of reception. Five desks were pushed together, computer screens black, telephones soundless. Christmas cards from appreciative patients were incongruous against the clinical shelves and a dying poinsettia dropped petals onto a tabletop.

I crossed the room in a couple of strides, reached the pigeonholes and withdrew the heap of envelopes from my clogged one. My colleague's pigeonholes were similarly chock-a-block, mostly full of circulars and information from drug reps. Folded minutes from our last staff meeting caused the glimmer of a smile, because we'd also received them via email. So much for saving the trees. A single white envelope addressed in old-fashioned sloping handwriting, probably a belated Christmas card from an elderly patient. Everything would keep for tomorrow.

Then I retraced my steps down the corridor to my own consulting room and spent an hour catching up with communication from colleagues. This was the first year I'd had such a long festive break; usually we split Christmas leave evenly. However when I'd learned of Tom's extramarital activities, I'd spoken to Gloria, one of the partners, about the possibility of a few extra days off. Without spelling it out, I'd insinuated personal circumstances which needed extended leave. She'd accepted my request with no quibbling, just raised eyebrows and a query if I was all right.

The additional time off had resulted in a multitude of emails, but only one disturbed me. Worry drilled as I digested it and thought about how I should respond. I was completely at a loss. If I acknowledged it, things could spiral further out of my control. In due course, I chose to do nothing. Tomorrow I'd reconsider, when I'd be surrounded by people and the building would be a hive of activity, in contrast with the stupor of today.

I'd hoped to clear the backlog of emails and return to work

one step ahead, but now I'd spend tonight fretting, a bundle of nerves.

Foreboding crawled along my skin and I had a sudden compulsion to get outside, to hear the wind howl and feel its chilly draught on my face. I switched off my computer, snatched my bag and strode to the external door. A rumble of disquiet at the eeriness of the empty building, usually full of people. No sound but my own laboured breaths and squeaking soles. I punched in the alarm code and slammed the door. Head down, I scooted to the car and threw myself onto the driver's seat.

Concern coursed through me at the email's contents. Yet another attempt to disparage, to upset. I'd been intentionally misled again and it was demeaning. Threatening. I gripped the steering wheel until pain in my hands righted me. Slowly I loosened my hold, although the joints ached for long minutes after.

My fingers circled my mobile in my bag, and I glanced at it for the first time since I'd left home. Nothing. Not one message or alert. No missed calls or a friendly comment to boost me. It was such an uncommon occurrence, my head thudded with pent-up nervousness. Lack of communication was as disconcerting as excessive communication. It was as if someone was biding their time while they contrived their next move.

I exhaled slowly and massaged my temples, willing myself calm. More in control, I put the car into gear and drove towards the supermarket in the town centre. It had a large car park where I could weigh everything up, and I parked close to the shop to piggyback off their Wi-Fi. In Northern Ireland tills must remain closed until 1 pm on Sundays, and the clock on the dash indicted it was twelve thirty, which left time to kill. A day which had promised much was now tarnished.

Despondently I switched the radio on to Chill FM, and listened as Lewis Capaldi crooned about someone he loved. Not the best song for someone whose husband has cheated and betrayed them. Tears brimmed. For my lost friendship. For broken dreams and shattered trust. For the impossible circumstances I was trapped in. If you could lose weight solely by crying, I'd have lost a stone in the past few weeks without effort.

The seeds of a long-forgotten resolve took root and I wiped my face. I couldn't change the past, but I could influence the future with careful planning. Because I had time on my hands, I made a couple of calls, which tamed my uncertainties.

Much happier, my eyes drifted around the car park, which was now busy with early shoppers. There was nothing to worry about here. I could whizz around the shop, buy what was needed, then leave.

On the stroke of one, I got out of the car and briskly walked into the supermarket. I skipped the food, the clothes and the toiletries, added a couple of magazines and other items to my basket, and kept my head down in the off chance a patient spotted me.

Thankfully the self-serve tills were unoccupied, which left me free to scan my purchases without interruption and I made it back out to the car without bumping into anyone I knew. Before I started the engine, I debated whether to visit my friend as planned, for I recognised my agitation and it never made for good company. In the end, I preferred not to cancel as I'd been looking forward to it for several days.

Nervously I searched the cars and faces of the shoppers one last time. And there on the far side of the car park, a flash of red alerted me to them. Half hidden by a burly man with a crew cut, but distinctive when you're as fine-tuned as me. Their head was rotated away, as if to ignore my car, but I knew better.

Blood roared in my ears, and I dropped as low as possible into my seat. I tracked them until they disappeared from view into the entrance of the supermarket. My neck tingled. I didn't believe in coincidences. When I counted to twenty and they didn't reappear, I turned the key and exited the car park.

My jaw ached from grinding my teeth on the drive back to Castlebrook. Tension was presenting itself in physical form. Always alert, always anxious. Although exhausted, I drove towards my friend's house. When I left the busy town streets behind, I breathed a sigh of relief, but my mind danced about. Had they known where I was? And if so, how?

Castlebrook was a quiet haven, pavements deserted, roads empty. I passed the end of my street and parked in front of a red-bricked bungalow a couple of streets over. With a last glance in the mirror to establish my mascara hadn't smudged, I climbed out and walked up the path to the front door. A bedraggled Christmas wreath still hung from a cheap hook, and I yearned to take it down. Instead I rang the bell and stepped back to eye the vertical blinds in the adjacent room. There was movement behind them and within a minute, the door was answered by a tall, attractive man with a full black beard and bright blue eyes.

My jumpiness dissolved as I switched on my megawatt smile and said hello.

'Hi.' His face broke into a warm grin. 'Come on in.'

Light-heartedly I excused my early arrival as I stepped into the compact hallway, and followed him into the kitchen where he offered me coffee. Familiar with the layout, I took a seat on a wooden chair at the table and asked how he was.

'I'm all right thanks, looking forward to getting back to work tomorrow. What about you?'

'It'll be good to get back into some kind of routine.' I offered banalities and drank him in.

My friend Jake was an attractive man, though not quite as handsome as my husband, and fifteen years younger than me. I'd never had a platonic male friend before him, but our friendship was deep and fulfilling. From the first day we'd met, we bonded over our similar sense of humour, love of athletics and *Breaking Bad*. He made a mean Expresso Martini and from time to time when Tom was off doing whatever Tom did, I would visit Jake to binge-watch Walter White and sip a cocktail. It was quite some time since our last cocktail and crystal meth session.

With an almost physical hunger, I longed to once again have drinks with a man who was gorgeous, but out of bounds. Who'd seen beneath the surface of my shiny façade and liked what skulked there. He was one of my closest friends, and I detested when his attention was enticed elsewhere.

Although a good friend, I'd never confided in him about Tom's betrayal or my tribulations. The Book Club had learned my wretched secret only as a result of Claire's role. Ashamed, I'd begged Laura, Kate and Annie to keep it to themselves, and had no reason to doubt them.

'Do you want to come into the living room?' Jake's words broke into my trance and I nodded.

He handed me coffee in a chipped cup with a picture of a dachshund on it and offered me a biscuit, which I declined. Chatting away, I followed him into his snug front room. Such a masculine house, metal and leather, gadgets and remotes. No candles, flowers, nor knick-knacks. A distinctly male space, testosterone blatantly on display. A pair of framed photos on the mantelpiece were the solitary concession to a softer touch.

As ever, conversation flowed easily and he made me laugh, while Tom receded into the distance. I sat on Jake's slightly sagging two-seater sofa, opposite to where he reclined on a black leather gaming chair and put the past weeks to the back of my mind.

Instinct warned me not to relax too much, to keep track of

the time and too soon I had to leave, although he tried to cajole me into staying longer.

Fog had descended since I'd been at Jake's, dampening sound, blurring the village. The streetlights' dull glow barely cut through the haze as we said goodbye at the door, and I had a sudden desire to unburden myself to him. To reveal my heartbreak at home and worries for the future.

But I stamped it down, and without a backwards glance, walked to my car.

When I stopped at the junction of his street, a car passed me, the face unsmiling. Alarm compressed my chest.

Would I ever be free of them?

CHAPTER SEVEN

When I arrived home from Jake's, I pottered about, restless and unable to settle. The solitude I'd craved no longer promised freedom, but instead seemed like a punishment. I hankered after Tom's presence to keep dread at bay.

When I could bear it no longer, I decided to visit Laura after a walk. Her Mini had been parked in her driveway earlier, and it had been several days since we'd caught up. Dressed in my padded jacket, I pulled on my gloves and hat, knowing the freezing fog would chill me. Braving the cold was preferable to overthinking at home.

The enticing smell of turf hung in the wintry air and the fog swirled and shifted as I tramped along. No one was about. The street was still, and within minutes calm spread through me. From habit, I glanced around for anything out of the ordinary, but assured I was alone, tugged the hat low over my forehead.

As I strode along I contemplated each house in turn. Some in darkness, some with faint light seeping out. An engine revved nearby and predictably a dog barked forlornly. The quiet of the village worked its magic as I marched along the streets, and encountered no one except a group of teenagers sharing a sneaky cigarette at the rear of the park. They'd greeted me with sniggers and moved away quickly, fading into the murk, their laughs muffled.

I looped around the village streets and well over an hour passed before I reached Laura's. In spite of my warm clothes, my face was frozen and I was less inclined to see anyone. The urge to converse had vanished along with my misgivings, though I knew I should find out her opinion on Claire and Tom. We'd not had a proper chance to discuss it, and I was curious about her reaction. With a sigh, I plodded up her driveway and rang the doorbell before I could change my mind. While I waited for an answer, I studied the house across the street.

David and Kate's was so brightly illuminated it was probably visible from space. No curtains were drawn, so I could see David and his son Luke watching football on the giant TV screen in the front room. Momentarily uncomfortable, I felt like a voyeur into their private lives.

Fortunately Laura soon opened the door with a smile. 'Hi! Do you want to come in?' Typical Laura, always keen for company. Her normally pale face was flushed and she glowed in an emerald-green jersey dress, making my jeans and sweatshirt combo dowdy in comparison.

'Lovely thanks. Are you on your own?' The temperature of her house was a welcome in itself.

'Yes. Sam had to go into work at the hospice earlier, and Robbie's at his house in Belfast. Is Tom away with work at the minute?'

I peeled off my coat, deposited it on the wicker chair in the hall and followed her into the kitchen where she offered either coffee or Pinot Gris. As tempting as wine was, I chose coffee and sat at the table as she filled the kettle. With her back to me, she reached into a cupboard for mugs and asked how I was. I deflected the question back to her, which she appeared not to notice. When she offered biscuits, I refused, mindful of the extra pounds I'd comfort eaten over Christmas.

We went into her living room, where subdued lighting and soft furnishings created a cosy atmosphere. My attention was taken by two photos on the white shelves. The first, her and Robbie crouched together on a beach, taken when her son was young. Her red hair had been whipped by the wind and both of them pointed at something in the distance. The second, a new one, was of her and Sam standing together at Annie's charity dinner dance last October.

As she chittered happily, I recalled our surprise on the night, when she'd introduced her 'friend' to us all. Their chemistry had razed the idea of mere friendship almost instantly. I almost asked if she'd deliberately removed every trace of James, for there were no photos of him and it was as though he'd been erased in every way from her life. I wondered about their marriage. Happy and glorious? Or hopeless and doomed? She'd never complained about him when he was alive; she was unlikely to now he was dead.

Bitterly, I then recalled Claire and Tom's relationship had been thriving the night of the dinner dance and bile rose, which I swallowed with a gulp of too-hot coffee.

'How was your New Year?' I asked through sore lips.

Laura enthused for several minutes about a quaint cottage and a bracing walk on a windswept beach. Her contentment was palpable, at such odds with my own internal misery, I chewed my cheek to stop myself from blurting everything out.

She was not so self-absorbed she couldn't sense my unhappiness, and abruptly stopped talking, then lightly placed a hand on my forearm, and enquired if I was all right.

'No, I'm not all right.' The roar was exclusively in my head. Obviously I had to contain myself, to prevent the delicate walls surrounding my heart from crumbling.

I inspected my fingernails, suddenly keen to be honest with someone. 'No, not really.' It was barely above a whisper. Easy tears spilled, and I allowed them to stream unchecked down my face. 'It's a huge mess, isn't it?' The question was rhetorical, the answer obvious.

She pressed her lips together, nodded and waited to see if I'd say more. Her gaze was direct, as if she could see right through me. Heat began in my chest and crept up my neck at the memory of my past actions. I'd sugar-coated my convoluted history to Kate and Annie, but under Laura's perceptive stare, the truth was at risk of pouring out in an obscene deluge. Needing a kinder reaction, I sobbed more loudly. Tears always worked wonders. She allowed me to weep, handed me a box of tissues and finally my snuffles subsidised.

'Sorry,' I dabbed my face. 'Do you know the reason Claire did it?'

Laura nodded.

Face on fire, I replied, 'Revenge. Retribution. Call it what you want. Now our friendship group is destroyed, and I'm living with a cheat. Have you seen her? Is she okay?'

'Yes, I've seen her. No, she's not okay. Will's no longer living with her, and Eva and Poppy are furious with her. Did you know Robbie and Eva are in a relationship?' I shook my head, astonished two childhood friends had crossed the line. 'It seems she was a tower of strength after James died and their friendship developed into something deeper.' She smiled ruefully at the Claddagh ring she wore on her left hand. No wedding band. Scarlet nail polish.

I almost snorted my cynicism at twenty-two-year-olds

knowing anything about relationships. Then I reminded myself I'd met Tom when I was in my early twenties and thought I knew it all. How wrong I'd been.

'Are you looking out for Claire?'

'Yes, I am and I'll make sure she's not entirely alone.'

What remained unsaid twisted my stomach. She hadn't verbally condemned my conduct, but she hadn't condoned it either. Laura had climbed onto the fence and made herself comfy with a glass of Pinot Gris in one hand and a frothy coffee in the other.

Without thinking, I spluttered that forgiving Tom was harder than expected. No one else was wise to his previous affairs, or that Claire had purely been his latest conquest. Shame about his woeful secret was mine alone to bear. The words tumbled out of me with such speed, it was like someone else had spoken them.

Laura muttered something unintelligible. Then, 'I can't imagine how difficult it must've been to learn about their affair. Life isn't always easy, is it? Do you want to stay with him?' I was taken aback by her forthrightness, and silence filled the space between us.

Gradually it dawned on me. It was time to be honest, both with her and myself.

'Yes, I think so. But he seems to believe I should be over it by now and things should be back to normal. Whatever normal means.' Animosity leaked out. Normal with Tom meant doubt and uncertainty. Marriage provided only the camouflage of affection and security.

Tired of analysing my relationship and spent after finally voicing my emotions, I drained my coffee and made my excuses. I lifted my jacket on the way out and Laura gave me a quick hug at the door. Before I ventured into the cold night, she said something so wise it gave me pause for thought.

'Don't stay with him because you're petrified of change. Stay with him only if you love him and can forgive him. And if you can trust him not to stray again.' It appeared she was going to say more, but instead smiled and wished me goodnight.

I waited until she'd shut the door before I turned away. Keiko shot out from under a bush and wound herself around my legs as I reached my front door. Absent-mindedly I stroked her silky head as I filled her dish, and reran the conversation with my non-judgemental friend.

My mobile lay on the kitchen worktop where I'd left it, wanting nothing to interrupt my walk. The expected text from Alex hoping to get out of my parents' Sunday lunch. A plethora of messages on the Book Club WhatsApp about Kate's on Friday night. A single text from Tom.

Before I replied to them, I popped a ready-made lasagne into the oven and went into the sitting room. There I lit candles and commanded Alexa to play soothing music. Keiko leapt onto my lap and curled into a ball, warming my legs like a hot water bottle. As I stroked her, I reflected on Laura's words.

It was exquisite in its simplicity.

I was unsure if I still loved Tom, but equally was agonisingly afraid of the unknown. There was a slim chance he meant what he'd said and would change. Hypothetically we could move forward together. Visions of happy ever after crammed my head, until they were demolished by one irrefutable fact.

I didn't trust him.

Not one iota.

Trust had to be earned, it wasn't automatic. He'd taken a sledgehammer to mine, and now it lay strewn into dust around me.

Gently I moved Keiko to one side of the sofa, and went into the kitchen to extract the lasagne from the oven.

Becoming a singleton could offer some advantages. No tethers. No friendzone. Boundless possibilities.

But deep down, it wasn't an option. For some unfathomable reason, I would never leave Tom, no matter how bad his behaviour.

And if I was honest with myself, he knew it too.

CHAPTER EIGHT

The following morning was my first proper day back at work since the festive break. As I cleaned my teeth after a not-so-healthy breakfast of peanut butter on a toasted bagel, worry unfurled in anticipation of the day ahead. The holiday had been an interruption, before the tedium of reality resumed. A return to routine, slow and laborious. But with it, splinters of enjoyment, streaks of colour.

I spat out the toothpaste, rinsed my mouth and studied my reflection. In an effort to conceal my pallor, I'd massaged on a layer of Dove before bed, and the hint of colour plus abundant blusher suggested an invigorating start to the year. My patients and colleagues would be fooled by my impeccable exterior and professional demeanour. When I checked the time, I realised I was running late, and sped downstairs, attention already on the day ahead.

My colleague Gloria parked beside me in the surgery car park. We exchanged pleasantries as we walked inside together and she regaled me with a tale about her three boisterous children and a cracked coffee table. I smiled appropriately and reassured her that having a glass table hadn't been negligent with three children under eight.

The staff room hummed with conversation, new year's good wishes and gripes about thickened waistlines. My colleagues were a friendly bunch and as we drank instant coffee, commiserated with each other about another day on the treadmill of work. Most of the admin staff were already at their desks, awaiting a bombardment of phone calls come nine o'clock. Their tired smiles expected fraught patients and the occasional outspoken demand. Before we scattered into our consulting rooms, a few of us checked our pigeonholes.

I chatted with Gloria as we stood by the pigeonholes and recognised the white envelope I'd seen yesterday. Before I could sort through my pile, a pungent fragrance polluted the air and I wrinkled my nose in distaste. It emanated from Bronagh, one of the receptionists. Her blonde hair was newly bleached and cut into a sleek chin-length bob, which accentuated her fake tan. Although she wore the standard admin uniform of black blouse and trousers, she had one too many buttons open and the eye was subconsciously drawn to her cleavage by a strategically placed necklace. She had the physique of someone who spent many hours at the gym or hot yoga. A plum talon pointed at the wall clock as she made a witty remark about school starting, and we all duly laughed.

Three of us stood in a well behaved row to check our post, and rammed most of it into the recycling bin.

Then it happened.

A card was ripped from the inoffensive white envelope, but rather than Santa or snowmen on the front, there was a bunch of wishy-washy flowers, crowned with the words *With Deepest Sympathy*. A loud intake of breath.

Boldly handwritten inside in red pen:

Sorry to hear about your imminent bereavement

It was unsigned.

A short silence then a rising tide of voices at the nasty surprise on a Monday morning. The effect was immediate. Distress. Offence. Quiet anger at the person who would send such a spiteful thing.

If it had been an isolated event, it could've been dismissed as malicious but harmless. Combined with a bunch of dead flowers in early December, a broken car window and a spate of aggressive emails, it was too much to cope with.

My palms became sticky. Such a barefaced thing to do in front of so many. Thankfully my colleagues were a supportive team; kind words and offers of tea were made, along with attempts to downplay. The festive break had brought no respite from the deplorable goings on. We huddled together, neglectful of the time and patients already queueing outside the practice entrance.

Then Gloria voiced what many were no doubt wondering. Should the police be informed again? They'd been contacted after an email which warned of impending danger, and the other unsettling incidents had duly been reported as well.

'It's probably too late.' I couldn't disguise the tremor in my voice. 'Surely they couldn't brush for fingerprints or whatever it is they do. So many people would have touched it.' I glanced at the others for confirmation, but was met with shrugs and shakes of the head.

'Where's the postmark from?' asked Gloria, determined to do something. A blush brightened her thin face.

'Belfast,' I read aloud, knowing it meant little. The central sorting office dealt with thousands of letters and parcels a week.

A male voice broke through the hubbub. The practice manager. 'I heard what happened, can I see it?' Jake reached for the card, face tense. 'Are you okay?' A terse nod in reply. He read it, then turned it over, as if searching for a hidden message.

'What do you want to do?' His tone was light and he made no suggestions.

'Nothing. What's the point?'

'We can ring the police.' A statement rather than a question. Worry radiated from him.

'No, I want you to bin it. I don't want to have to look at it.'

I took a calming breath and forced myself to exhale slowly, then unballed my fists. It wouldn't do to reveal my apprehension in front of the other staff, they were upset enough. Jake may be young, but he had a firm manner and one by one they disappeared to answer ringing telephones or to their rooms. I hung back to see if he would say anything else, but he was engrossed in the card.

It was after nine now, and I needed to be in my consulting room, preparing for my first patient. When I reached it, I firmly shut the door, leaned against it and sighed. Jake would come to find me later. The adrenaline which had propelled through me was short-lived, and now I longed to go home rather than facing a busy day with multiple patients and varying ailments.

To be a good doctor required my full attention, up-to-date knowledge and the ability to put myself last. On that Monday morning, I wished I'd stayed in bed to eat crisps and watch daytime TV. Instead I had to put everything to one side and act as if nothing menacing had happened.

The memory of the email I'd read yesterday flashed through my mind. On the back of the card I'd just read, there was only one possible action, which I'd shirked from, but today would have no choice but to address. Self-pity, the most unattractive of traits, welled.

I flopped onto my chair. Beams of dusty sunlight streamed through the blinds as I rolled my shoulders. Our ancient computer system took an age to boot up and I listened for Jake's knock on the door as I waited. But the door remained shut and the phone resolutely silent. Presumably he would come and find me later, but for now I had to get to work. When the computer came to life, I opened the detested email, disregarded my hammering heart and forwarded my response.

The morning was busy with patients; an elderly man with a urinary tract infection, a baby with croup, a middle-aged woman with a chronic cough. There was no time to dwell on it, fretting was impossible when you had the worried well and the ill to care for.

By half twelve I was hungry and my throat was parched. After a fortnight of eating whenever I wanted, a return to fixed break times was a test. The waiting room was empty, the staff room crowded. Our treatment room nurses giggled hysterically over something and their laughter was contagious. The card and consequent alarm were temporarily forgotten.

There was a free armchair beside Gloria, and I lowered myself onto it to eat my ham and cheese sandwich. She chatted about her morning and I kept a surreptitious watch for Jake. Although disgruntled he hadn't sought me out earlier, I comforted myself his role within the practice kept him fully occupied.

Too soon the lunchbreak was at an end, and I was about to leave when he walked into the room. A smile and a request for everyone's attention. He didn't need to clap his hands, nor raise his voice, the room fell quiet anyway. I leaned against the wall, keys in hand and waited.

Bronagh was at his side, practically on top of him, and I bristled a little. She had the cat who got the cream smile in expectation of his announcement. Her lips were newly plumped with shiny lip gloss and the air around her buzzed with excitement. Although I was braced for what was coming, it was still a shock to hear the words.

'Everyone,' at once inclusive and yet detached, 'I'm sure you'll all want to join me in congratulating Bronagh on her appointment as admin manager of the practice. It's fair to say she excelled at interview and I, for one, am looking forward to working alongside her in her new role.' A soft chuckle, and polite, if reserved applause. A subdued ripple of *Well done.*

She flicked her hair, smirked and my sandwich got stuck in my gullet. Ever the consummate actress, I faked delight and made sure to congratulate her before I stomped back to my room. Somehow I stopped myself from slamming the door, and closed it as softly as possible. Shallow breathing filled the space and my palm ached from where I'd pressed my keys so hard they'd marked my flesh.

Mindlessly I massaged it with my thumb, walked over to my chair and peered out of the window. Small rivulets of rain ran down the outside of the pane. One merged with another, then another, until they pooled at the bottom of the frame.

It had been a discouraging day in many ways, but I could handle it.

I was expert at it now.

CHAPTER NINE

As I'd hoped, Jake made his way to my consulting room at the end of the afternoon. By then my emotions had stabilised enough for me to civilly discuss Bronagh's promotion and the morning's episode. My last patient had left, the blinds were closed and my neck ached from hunching over the desk. The sight of his face made me smile and forget my pains.

He sat on the plastic chair usually reserved for patients, and reclined back, hands behind his head. Long legs extended in front of him, crossed at the ankles. It was reassuring he came to me to talk things through after a difficult day and it alleviated my earlier disappointment.

'How do you feel about everything now?' Frank blue eyes searched for my answer.

'Fine,' I replied, almost honestly. 'What about you?'

He studied the ceiling before answering. 'That was pretty horrible to come into this morning and I know it bothered everyone.' His gaze settled back on me. 'Do you really think the police shouldn't be informed?'

'Perhaps. I don't know.'

We discussed it for a few more minutes, then he changed the subject. 'What's your opinion of Bronagh's promotion?'

I rubbed my temple. 'If she was the best person for the job, then good for her.' What I really meant was *She's a lazy bitch who's caused me no end of bother,* but it was spoken in the confines of my head. My smile was sweet. Men can be easily duped by a pretty face and an inflated chest, as I appreciated wholly too well. His next words were exactly as I'd forecast.

'There's been no talk about, well, favouritism has there?' He licked his lips and gave an embarrassed laugh.

'Not at all,' I lied smoothly. 'I haven't heard a thing.'

Predictably there'd been chatter about the promotion. Bronagh had been at the practice less than a year and many of the older women resented her. *Brash, brassy and brittle* was how one of my colleagues had described her in the quiet of the staff room. This was after she'd suggested five vape breaks before midday was excessive, and Bronagh had subsequently flown into a rage.

Now she was going to be in a position of authority, everyone worried the power would go to her head, leaving her ever more insufferable.

'Good.' Jake's hesitation endeared him further to me. 'I would hate to be accused of bias.'

My true opinion suppressed behind light-hearted words, I commented the appointment was a fair one. A split second, then I meaningfully stated Bronagh would have to prove she was up to the job.

He nodded without speaking, then straightened his tall frame. 'I'm sure she knows that.' With a tight smile he left me to continue with my patient notes.

After he shut the door, I stared unseeing at the computer, and worried I shouldn't have said anything negative. Then I argued with myself that I had to express my honest opinion or I'd have done us both a disservice. For I was livid with her promotion. She was touchy, arrogant and had always acted as if working on reception was beneath her. Which infuriated me, as receptionists are invaluable to the smooth running of a busy practice.

Sometimes things happen for a reason, and hopefully fortune wouldn't favour the bold this time. I put it aside, quickly finished my notes, switched off the computer and retrieved my phone from the drawer. The homepage was bright with unread alerts and I flicked through them. Most could wait until later, although I replied to Tom before I left.

When I arrived home, I closed all the blinds and switched on various lamps. Having instructed Alexa to play happy songs, I decided to treat myself to a takeaway. First though, I had to ring my husband. He'd suggested a time to call earlier, when he'd be free. Free of what, I wasn't sure.

When he flew with work, I rarely asked where he was going anymore. It could be New York, Cancun or Kuala Lumpur. It was irrelevant where he was physically, the bottom line was he wasn't at home and was with people other than me. The ideal screen for bad behaviour. I used to know exactly which route he was on, the name of the hotel he stayed in and the room number. Immaterial now. He could tell me anything and I wouldn't believe it. When trust is broken in a marriage, can it ever be regained? And yet ours limped on, scratched and battered.

From the sofa in the living room, I listened to the foreign ringtone. Seven rings and still not answered, although we'd agreed the time for me to call. Annoyance flared and I cursed him under my breath. Finally on the tenth ring, he responded with an indistinct hello. Music boomed, a horn beeped and voices gabbled. A woman's throaty laugh was hushed by a male voice telling her to be quiet. His long-suffering ball and chain was checking up on him.

'Sweetie, is that you?'

I gulped air, ignored the temptation to ask where he was, to allow the confusion over country versus actual location. Hotel bar? Or hotel room? His? Hers? My mind swirled, bitterness overcame discretion, and I lashed out. Of course it was me, who else would it be?

'Hang on, I can't hear you,' was his amused reply, as if I'd told a hilarious joke. When in fact, I was the hilarious joke.

A minute passed and then another. Whoever he was with wasn't leaving easily and I was about to hang up when he spoke clearly. 'Sorry, sweetie, we're in some dingy bar for Nicky's birthday.' Who was Nicky? I imagined a svelte twenty-something with a knockout figure and crush on my husband. 'Is everything okay at home?'

So much better for you being thousands of miles away. Bronagh got the promotion and there was a worrying card in the post.

'Same old, same old,' I retorted bluntly. He'd no idea of the hassle Bronagh caused. Nor did he know the card was the latest in a series of strange happenings. 'When are you back?' Had our conversation deteriorated to this extent? It was strikingly obvious I rarely talked to my husband about the things which daunted me.

'Thursday night. I'll be home late so you might not want to stay up.'

Before I could reply, the phone went dead and I didn't bother to ring back. He was alive, which was enough.

Keiko came meowing into the room, demanding food and I plodded into the utility room to feed her. Temptation to pour myself a drink superseded the vow to drink predominantly at weekends, and I helped myself to a glass of Prosecco. The bubbles fizzed on my tongue as I went online to order a Chinese takeaway. Sweet and sour pork. Special fried rice. Prawn crackers. Chicken satay. So much choice. Decisions, decisions. Once I ordered, I scrolled through my phone at the table. To make a bad day worse, one notification hissed venom. Tears stung, but before I got too worked up, my order arrived. I inhaled slowly, then answered the door with a smile, a gracious thanks and a £5 tip. The spotty teenaged delivery driver didn't even grunt his thanks, which stupidly hurt my already tattered feelings.

Once I'd eaten, everything took on a minutely less dreadful glow.

Tom was simply being Tom. I shouldn't let him get to me so much. I'd fallen for his looks, charm and temperament so why shouldn't anyone else?

Bronagh had unfairly been promoted, but now she'd have to prove her worth.

And the card? Minor in the grand scheme of things.

I drained my glass, stopped myself from having another, and dressed in my jacket, gloves and hat. Then I headed out into the cool of the night to find it had stopped raining and the air was fresh and clear. Thousands of stars twinkled innocently above me, the brook babbled nearby. From habit, my gaze swept the length of the street. All clear.

My feet carried me along a route I rarely followed, music loud through my Air Pods. As the beat thumped, life shifted behind windows, headlights dazzled and I disregarded everything except what I could hear and see. My breath was cold, matching my emotions. Before I made for home, I reached a decision about what I should do next.

Pleased with myself, I was eager to get organised. Tom would be back before I knew it and then the temperature would rise and silent accusations would recommence. Each moment had to count between now and then. Energetically I stripped off my outdoor clothes and took a seat at the breakfast bar with a notebook and pen. List-making was one of my favourite things, with a neat square beside each point, a goal scored when one was ticked off on completion. I jotted down everything I could think of, no matter how ridiculous or absurd. By eleven o'clock I was out of ideas and needed sleep, but not before I placed an order for the first item on my list. Then I buried my notebook at the back of a drawer Tom never opened.

A final check of my phone after I climbed into bed.

I bolted upright when I read a message from Kate.

> Hi girls, would you mind if Miranda from the end of the street came along to Book Club on Friday night? She's been asking me for ages and I thought the time was right!!!

The sudden rush of adrenaline at the sight of her name. Memories of a disturbance and raised voices. Threats and recriminations. I knew Miranda's reputation from way back, and the thought of her joining us was an immediate red flag.

Suddenly I was too hot and sweat rolled down my neck. I texted Laura privately.

> What on earth is Kate doing?! Miranda's not someone I'm comfortable spending time with

Patient confidentiality meant I couldn't reveal more; I had to hope she'd read between the lines. She messaged back in moments.

> Kate's lost the plot! Does she think she's going to replace Claire with Miranda?

My mind reeled as my hands were tied regarding her medical history. Also, Book Club was sacred. We were more than a book club, we were the best of friends, who told each other everything. Obviously that was essentially untrue, but the premise was correct. How could Kate be so insensitive to think someone who barely knew us could replace Claire? I pictured Miranda. Short and bony with a sharp nose and sharper tongue. From the little I knew of her she revelled in gossip, delighted in others' misfortune and would be my very last choice.

But I was too late. Annie had already replied:

I'm happy with that.

They must have planned this already. It was a two-pronged attack. If I disagreed now, it would seem petty and juvenile. But I couldn't bring myself to welcome her. It stuck in my craw. Claire, rejected and lonely, sprang to mind and I bit the inside of my cheek.

Miranda might come along on Friday night, but she would never be in my gang.

CHAPTER TEN

The busy week passed quickly, and I stayed late on Thursday to catch up on paperwork and make onward referrals. The highlight was when my online shopping had been delivered on Wednesday. It brightened an otherwise dull day.

When Tom shut the front door late on Thursday night, my form dipped. Sleep had evaded me before he arrived home, and remained determinedly out of reach. The harder you try, the more impossible it becomes. I was alert to every noise as he padded about downstairs; lights flicked on, tap running, calling for Keiko. Each footstep a soft tread on the stairs and then he blocked the doorway. A broad silhouette, his face in shadow.

'Are you awake, sweetie?' A sigh in the darkness.

Seconds to make a decision. My stomach jolted. 'Yes.'

The landing light was switched off and plunged the room into darkness. Small sounds as he undressed, my heartbeat loud as I waited for the inevitable. His body warm and reassuring as he joined me in bed, heavy and strong as I forgot my enmity. When he dozed off, I rolled towards him and lightly ran my fingers down the length of his spine. This dishonest, lying husband of mine who held my heart within his careless grasp, come what may.

The next morning I rose after nine as Friday was my day off. Tom slept on, spreadeagled in the bed. For a few minutes I could pretend I was fine. We were fine. I studied his face, relaxed in sleep, and it became crystal clear.

I would never leave him.

We were bound together forever. Through the good times and the bad. The hair-raising ups. The death defying downs.

Although it didn't mean I was going to make it easy for him.

I dressed in the en suite before going downstairs. In the kitchen, I reached into the very back of the drawer beside the sink, and withdrew my list. What should I tick off next? So many choices, but I'd choose an easy one. The shower started overhead. It wouldn't be long before Tom appeared.

Throughout our marriage, he'd developed a sneaky habit of grilling me about my credit card spending. It was wearisome to be checked up on, plus it took the enjoyment out of gift-giving when he'd already seen the bill. Therefore it made sense for me to have a private card where I could indulge my love of impulsive purchases without his knowledge. My prepaid debit card was a godsend, and I used it before slipping it into my purse.

Every spouse keeps secrets. It's the reward for tolerating morning breath and toenail clippings on the floor.

My secret was a debit card he knew nothing about.

His secret was sex with my friend.

Tit for tat.

I'd just settled onto a stool at the breakfast bar with my phone when Tom appeared behind me. He wrapped his arms around my waist and nuzzled my neck. The softest of kisses planted along my collarbone, as he trailed his hands up and down my sides before they swept over my breasts.

'What do you want to do today?' I leaned against him and stroked his biceps.

'How about a drive up the coast?' The weather was dry and bright, a contrast to the beginning of the week. 'We could go to Jennings for lunch.' He strolled over to the Nespresso machine, and helped himself to a strong black coffee, as my glower seared the back of his head.

Jennings was where we'd inadvertently had lunch with Claire and Will in the autumn. Unbeknown to me, she and Tom had been in the throes of their grand passion. Or at least I presumed it'd been a grand passion. I couldn't bear to think about it. Although Jennings was a fabulous seafood restaurant, it was forever tainted by that knowledge.

'How about we drive up to Portstewart and have lunch in Roberto's? They do a fantastic lobster ravioli and we haven't had Italian for ages.' I forced a level tone as he spun away to make toast. Pictures of hot, glistening bodies swarmed in my head, and I screwed my eyes tight against them.

'Great suggestion.' I opened them as he handed me coffee in my favourite mug, and managed a feeble smile of thanks.

He hummed as he buttered the toast, then slathered it with marmalade. Tall and muscly, his face tanned and rested, it became clear how much I loved him, despite his faults. Even his self-absorption and selfishness couldn't swamp it. It was time I showed him what he'd almost thrown away.

My phone pinged and I hauled my attention away from Tom. My latest purchase had been dispatched, although I would have to find the exact time to use it. Retail therapy had its place without doubt.

I walked over and circled his waist. His shower gel was minty, his cheek soft. My hands dropped to his butt and I kissed him with an intensity which caught him by surprise.

'I love you.' A husky undertone.

'I love you too.' The words were said without consideration and my heart healed a little as the cuts sealed over.

The chime of the bell broke the silence and I sighed heavily. Tom plonked himself down at the table and grinned as I went to answer it.

Kate. Tiny in an oversized padded jacket and pink woolly hat. Groaning to myself, I attempted a phoney smile and opened the door.

'Hi.' Forehead furrowed, her lips twitched in the approximation of a smile.

'Hi.' I kept the door half closed, unwilling to ask her in. She was tireless in her crusade to find out exactly how I was feeling, if I'd exonerated Tom and what we should do about Claire.

Her brows snapped together before she spoke. 'Um, Vicky. This may not be convenient, but I need to speak to you about the person who's been walking in the fields behind the houses.'

'Oh, right.' A moment. 'Do you want to come in?'

Before I got a chance to step out of the way, she darted past me and I shut the door with a loud bang. She'd already made her way into the kitchen. Tom's sullen 'hello' floated out to me.

Uninvited, she'd taken a seat at the breakfast bar and eyed my coffee longingly. There was no option but to offer her one, and she readily agreed as she took off her coat and hat. A girlish giggle for Tom's benefit as she requested a cappuccino. I had the sinking feeling this was going to be no short visit.

Once the coffee was despatched in front of her, Tom made his excuses. She watched him until he disappeared from view and softly asked how I was.

'Fine, we're fine.' I refused to admit anything else. Tetchily I changed the subject. 'You wanted to talk about the person you thought was in the field?'

Her face contorted at my refusal to discuss my marriage, but she rallied. 'There's no question about it, someone's been in the field. There was a torch moving from side to side on Wednesday night. It was late and the weather wasn't good, but David agreed with me. I was really quite worried, so yesterday morning I went to suss it out.' A long pause before she finally divulged the rest of the story. 'I'm so sorry, but the grass was flattened and it looked like someone had been standing there for ages.'

My fingers began to tingle. 'Standing where for ages?'

She swallowed and in a quiet voice said, 'Opposite your house. Your bedroom window to be precise.'

'You must be mistaken.' I rubbed my temple.

Stubbornly she insisted, 'I'm not. It's dug up because of the heavy rain. The track of flattened grass stops right behind your house. Exactly where the little wooden bridge is.'

The little wooden bridge Tom had built for the girls years ago so they could make a den at the edge of the field.

'So someone's been using the field to what? Watch my house?' My voice wobbled.

She bobbed her head up and down.

'But why?'

'I don't know.' She squinted at me. 'Has anything odd happened recently?'

The car window. The bouquet of dead flowers. The sympathy card. And of course the emails and messages.

'No, nothing out of the ordinary at all.' My lie was delivered like a pro. Kate wasn't to be trusted, and I didn't want to be the subject of more gossip so soon after Tom's affair.

'Well, David and I will be on the lookout for anyone hanging about. Especially when Tom's away with work. How is he, by the way?'

Straight back to the state of my marriage. I pinched my lips together in frustration. A frustration Kate failed to recognise.

I snapped, 'He's good. We're good. Sorting things out.

Please, don't worry. With time and space we can work through it.'

She patted my hand like you would a dog, and rose when Tom entered the room. His jaw was set and I wondered if he'd overheard her quizzing me. There was a frostiness about him normally reserved for our children when they misbehaved. She wittered merrily on to conceal her self-consciousness.

My temper was holding on by a thread as I showed her out. Before I shut the door, the dam broke.

'Kate, I don't want either Tom or Claire mentioned tonight at Book Club. Okay?'

She winced. 'Of course not. I won't say a thing.'

I should call her out for inviting Miranda, but simply didn't have the energy to cope with watery eyes and a quivering lip. Instead I contrived a smile and shut the door quietly, though I wanted to slam it so noisily Miranda would hear it at the bottom of the street.

Tom stood in the middle of the kitchen, hands on hips. He glowered so intently I began to laugh. Before long he joined in. Kate's words were suppressed along with my suffering as my husband enveloped me within his arms.

Today we'd go out for lunch and I'd pick the rest apart later.

CHAPTER ELEVEN

Lunch with Tom at Roberto's had been lovely, once I moved past my irritation with Kate. He'd driven me up the winding North Coast road with the writhing Irish Sea on one side, rolling Antrim Hills on the other. The weather was kind, and the hazy outline of the Scottish coast shimmered in the distance, while the rocky Ailsa Craig rose out of the sea. Sunlight sparkled on the water as we ate up the miles.

We sat at a window table in Roberto's and held hands like young lovers as he ran his foot up and down my calf. Decadent for a school day. The restaurant hummed with activity, the clatter of cutlery and chink of glasses. After lunch we'd strolled along the seaside path, past the Herring Pond and along the prom, where I'd insisted we eat ice cream in the shadow of the clifftop Convent.

The day had given me respite from my worries, but now they burrowed and bored as I got ready for Book Club. Hot water cascaded over me in the shower and I reflected on my friends while I lathered and soaped.

Book Club usually provided an opportunity to drink too much alcohol and catch up on each other's gossip. Laura had set it up about fifteen years ago and over time reading books had become secondary to our friendship. Books have the power to connect, even when you don't have much else in common. Ironically I had more in common with Claire than I'd ever expected.

This would be the first time we'd all be together since our night at the Mourne View Hotel in early December. All minus Claire. As I dried my hair, memories of that night surged along with the savage memory of her spite as she'd broadcast her deception a couple of weeks later in a different hotel. Shame singed my cheeks at the recollection. She'd done her worst and the fallout reverberated on. Head dizzy, I rested it on my hands until the world stopped revolving.

Once they'd learned of her subterfuge, Kate and Annie had united at my side, horrified by her deceit. Tonight I'd expected them to bolster my emotional support, but now Kate had invited Miranda, who was practically a stranger. The four of us hadn't yet had a proper chance to debrief in person. Annoyance jabbed and I wondered how the new addition would change the dynamic.

Before I left for Kate's I scrolled through Facebook and a comment below a post grabbed my attention. An Italian restaurant. A mouth-watering bowl of pasta. White wine so cold condensation coated the glass. Male hands loosely spread on the table.

Not having your usual Prosecco? It's not like you to mix your drinks.

Innocuous. However the poster 'Bea Goode' had a penchant for commenting on every photo. Their page was empty, the cover photo miles of golden sand, the profile picture Harley Quinn. I skimmed her other comments.

Have you painted your sitting room? I preferred the grey.

New dress? The black was nicer.

You were with another man yesterday. Keeping a secret?

Every recent post had a similar remark. A snide comment meant to undermine. The obvious answer was to block, but each time before, someone new had taken their place and the comments started again. It may have been days later, but before long a new follower meant a repeat of the pattern.

Potentially social media was the scourge so many believed.

But I, like so many others, was slightly addicted to it. Embarrassing for a woman my age, but when it worked, it worked well. It provided an opportunity to connect with distant friends and colleagues who worked abroad and more usefully, to keep an eye on my daughters and the aspects of their lives they hoped to hide. Plus I loved to share photos which showed off my gilded lifestyle. Like a teenager, I accepted every friend request, unless they were a patient or one of their relatives. The downside was the occasional unpleasant comment.

As I browsed, I had a piercing thought.

Previously I'd never worried about new followers or why they wanted to 'friend' me. Could one of Tom's ex-lovers be my Facebook friend? If so, why? To monitor our lives? Reluctant to let go of him completely?

I finished applying my make-up with a shaky hand, breath short. If I dwelt on it too long, it would tip me over the edge. I had to straighten my shoulders and bury it deep. There was no alternative.

Downstairs I popped my head around the door of the sitting room. Tom lolled full length on the sofa where he'd fallen asleep soon after we arrived home. His long legs hung over the end, mouth slack. My blood ran cold as I worried yet again about the shadowy women he'd slept with over the years.

But there was no time to brood as I had to leave, so rammed the phone into my bag and headed for the fridge to grab a bottle of Prosecco to take to Kate's. I shouted goodbye to Tom and stepped into the still night. The bite of freezing air was welcome on my overheated face.

Laura exited her house as I drew level with Kate's, and called a cheery hello, which I responded to with a smile and an equally cheery response. Sam's Ford Focus was parked in her driveway, meaning he was inside, but had no issue with her going to Book Club. She was lit from within, a woman in love. Discontent squeezed my chest despite my smile.

'Hi, how are you?' Her empathy was a far cry from Kate's meddlesome questioning earlier.

'All good. How are you? Though I don't need to ask, you're glowing!' My voice cracked and I cleared my throat.

She laughed, tucked her arm through mine and we walked down Kate's drive together. The living room curtains were open and Miranda gesticulated wildly on the sofa. Laura raised her eyebrows in a question and I shrugged my answer. Neither of us were impressed with our new member. It was going to be a long night.

David opened the door and invited us in. Tall and slim, his dark brown eyes flitted between us. A brief kiss on the cheek, a kind hello. I liked David because he had a heart of gold and the patience of a saint. He accepted the bottle of Prosecco with a smile and disappeared into the kitchen to pour us a glass. The hall was a mess, coats and shoes everywhere, the bottom stair piled high. As usual, it was in need of a good tidy. My mother's badgering criticism rang in my head.

Raised voices from the living room greeted us. Annie, Kate and Miranda were already in full flow. Miranda instantly jumped up from the sofa and I found myself enclosed in a tight embrace. Sour breath grazed my skin as she whispered, 'I hope you're okay,' in my ear. Unable to manage a civil reply, I brusquely stepped back and positioned myself as far from her as possible on an armchair by the window. Had Kate broken my confidence and told her about Tom's affair? I'd specifically asked her to keep it private and hurt crackled beneath my calm exterior.

'It's so lovely to be invited. Kate and I have been friends for ages, but I always thought Book Club was out of bounds.' A shrewd laugh. 'Although Kate says you don't really read books anymore, I brought one of my favourites, *The Affair* by N.A. Cooper.'

I choked when she said it, and hastily turned it into a cough. Miranda had the grace to blush, and Kate blustered past the flagrant faux pas. The two women nattered together, talking over Annie who tried to interject. Miranda's voice grated like a knife scraping a plate, until it made my ears bleed. There was no question about it. Kate had confided in her about Tom.

Unfortunately it was as though a tap had been turned on, and words gushed from her in a torrent. I caught Laura's eye and she covered her mouth with her hand to stop laughing out loud. Claire's absence had been filled, but with roughness and clamour, not laughter and fun. I missed her suddenly, puzzled why Kate had invited someone new so soon.

Fortunately David carried in our drinks, and interrupted Miranda's flow. I accepted my Prosecco with thanks and sipped it slowly. Hysterical laughter, jarring voices and raucous chatter. I rested back on the chair and contributed little. Kate and Miranda downed their glasses of wine in minutes and it became clear they'd one thing in common. An inability to hold their drink.

As I nursed my glass, I evaluated our newest addition.

She'd clearly gone to some effort to spruce up, though her heavy blusher gave the impression of a high temperature, and her roots needed touching up. It was more her behaviour I found disagreeable. Her overloud voice, unceasing giggles and habit of placing a proprietary hand on Kate's arm. Once she'd laid it on her thigh, which was positively bizarre. Laura spotted it too, caught my eye and winked. Miranda was trying too hard and perhaps I was too world-weary to accept a replacement for Claire. Or we were a tight-knit clique, though I'd never admit it.

The seconds ticked excruciatingly slowly to eleven o'clock. Eyes glazed and words became slurred. My mobile was in my bag at my feet and buzzed repeatedly. I yearned to sneak it into the bathroom, but was being closely scrutinised. By Miranda. Kate. Annie. Only Laura acted as though nothing was out of place.

When I could bear it no longer, I bent down both to hide my emotion and grasp my phone. To the top of my head, Kate's garbled voice asked about Tom and Claire. Quiet descended. Annie's eyes were round circles in a pale oval.

'I prefer not to talk about Tom.' My tone was ice, to match the hand which gripped my heart.

'You can tell us, we're all friends here.'

'And have your best interests at heart.' The words spewed from Miranda, their sharpness like vinegar poured over an open wound.

My throat closed and I quietly repeated the sentence. There would be no talk about my husband in front of an outsider. I looked at Miranda, who quickly hid her smirk with her hand, but not before I clocked it.

Kate bumbled on, regardless of my discomfiture. 'I saw Claire the other day. She looked awful. Her hair needed a wash and she was wearing an old pair of tracksuit bottoms. For a minute it seemed she was going to corner me, but then slunk away with her head down.'

'I can't believe she would betray your friendship.' Miranda swallowed another slug of her wine. 'It must be difficult for you when Tom is away with work so much, and Alex and Flora are at uni. If you ever want a coffee, I don't work now, so feel free to call any Friday you're off.' Miranda's beady eyes gleamed their delight.

Something about this woman was off. The knowledge of it chipped at my subconscious, but I was too uneasy about Claire to work it out.

Unable to bear it, I staggered to my feet. 'I'm not feeling well, I'm going home.' I no longer cared if I appeared rude, I needed to get away.

Kate's head shot up. 'I'm so sorry, Vicky. Please, please stay.'

Indignation flowed through my veins. These were supposed to be my friends, the girls I could tell anything to without judgement. Tonight they wanted me to bare my soul for their own amusement. The damage was done and if I didn't flee from the stuffy, untidy house I'd say something I later regretted. Laura rose too and calmly asked Kate for our coats. Annie was deep crimson, but sat on, clearly torn about what to do. Miranda's thirst for gossip was etched across her cheeks.

'I'm sorry, Kate, I don't want to ruin the night, but I must get home.' I lowered my voice, though it took every ounce of self-discipline I possessed. 'I know you didn't mean any harm, but I'm not going to discuss my marriage or Claire tonight.' *I told you earlier. I shouldn't have to ask,* ricocheted around my head.

Kate unsteadily led the way into the hall and rummaged about in the cloakroom for our coats. When she stumbled against the wall, my animosity dwindled. She really was very drunk. One by one she lifted jackets out and discarded them on the tiled floor. Laura's brows knitted together and she offered to help.

Kate refused and finally found our coats, which she flaunted like trophies. 'Stupid David hid them on me.' She giggled as she handed them over.

I zipped up my coat and thanked her for the evening. No doubt she wouldn't remember the disagreement or glacial atmosphere when she woke tomorrow. Although I was desperate to leave, she insisted on pulling me and Laura in for a hug. Disentangling ourselves with a forced laugh, we stepped into the cold night air.

'I can't believe Kate mentioned Claire and Tom, that was completely out of order. And I don't know about you, but I'm not going to Book Club again if Miranda's there.' Laura's tone was mutinous. 'She's a gossip and also has an unhealthy interest in you and your life.'

I balked at her perceptive words. A woman I spent no time with and had barely spoken to in several years, appeared intimately acquainted with my life, my family and my work.

The question was, why?

<h1 style="text-align:center">CHAPTER TWELVE</h1>

I was welcomed from Book Club by every downstairs light burning brightly, the blinds wide open. Our home was on display for anyone who happened to be passing. Or looking. Anger roiled as I unlocked the door. There was no sign of Tom and when I stepped into the sanctuary of my hallway, I was greeted with silence. Laura's perplexing words had circled on my short walk up the street. Miranda's behaviour and prurient interest in my life, worried me. I shut the blinds, switched off the lights and paced into the kitchen.

Here too the blinds were wide open which allowed anyone to peer in unhindered at me. My home. My life. The moon was suspended above the treeline and I focused on the bottom of our garden, jet black despite the moonlight. A shiver sidled up my back and I roughly closed the blinds, frustrated Tom had failed to do so.

Too het up to sleep, I went to get a drink of water. When I swivelled to reach for a glass, I spotted Tom's mobile, which glared balefully at me from the breakfast bar. I filled the glass with ice cold water from the fridge, sat on a high stool and placed the glass beside the phone.

Warily I prodded the mobile, expecting it to be switched off.

Instead it illuminated instantly and I withdrew my hand as if scorched. A smiling photo of me and the girls taken on Christmas morning greeted me. Plus notifications from someone called Ashley on Instagram. Dread pulsed. I'd been oblivious Tom had an Instagram account.

The phone was locked and I didn't know the passcode. I weighed up what to do, then swiped the screen to reveal snippets of three messages.

> I told Robin I'd be home

> We could book a room

> OK, I'll see what I can

Was he cheating again so soon after Claire? Were his earnest words of love and apology a bare-faced lie? Despair fluttered. Possibly this was the price for loving Tom. Always insecure. Never trusting.

Before my mind could descend further into the abyss, a door creaked and I swung round. Tom's face was creased with sleep, his hair tousled. He took one look at me, dashed over and grasped my chin between his hands.

'What on earth's wrong, sweetie?'

'Are you having an affair?' I sniffed pathetically.

He dropped his hands and his expression closed. 'Why are you asking me? Of course not.'

I pivoted round, snatched his phone and thrust it towards him. 'Who's Ashley?'

He spread his hands in front of him and answered quietly. 'Ashley's another pilot. And a bloke. Robin's his wife and we're planning a stag do for Euan.' I'd been introduced to Euan before, a naïve twenty-something with a rugby player's neck.

'Then why do it over Instagram? Why not text like anyone normal?'

'It's supposed to be a secret! Robin is a total pain who complains constantly about Ashley's job. He's afraid of upsetting her about something as trivial as this. Here,' he keyed in his passcode so rapidly I missed the numbers, and held out the mobile. 'Read them.' Tiredly he slouched onto the stool beside mine as I read the messages.

They really were organising a stag do and Ashley did have a nagging wife called Robin. Tom's face was tense and closed. My words got stuck in my throat and silently I handed it back to him.

'My passcode is our wedding anniversary, for when you want to check my messages again.' His tone was aggrieved.

'Okay,' was all I could summon before I buried my head in his chest. His familiar smell and strong arms surrounded me and I exhaled loudly.

I could either allow this to eat me up, or I could move on. Inch by inch. Mile by mile. When he led me upstairs by the hand, I repressed my swirling worries. It was the two of us, navigating our way through shattered dreams and injured pride.

Next morning dawned fine and sunny, though I slept late. Tom brought me breakfast to bed, then left me alone as he disappeared for a shower. I relaxed against the headboard and studied my phone. With the drama when I'd arrived home last night, I'd missed so much, but was relieved to find nothing out of the ordinary. No new emails. No unkind comments on Facebook. Not even a menacing text. I half expected a message of apology from Kate, but suspected she'd be nursing a hangover in bed.

Then I had a sudden thought; had Miranda been added to the Book Club WhatsApp? Nervously, I checked, but thankfully she hadn't been. Her thin lips and hooded eyes bellowed a warning, while her non-stop questions ruffled me. How did she know so much about me and my life? My instincts howled alarm, especially after Laura's observation, and I made a mental note. She was someone to be careful around.

As I drank my coffee, my thoughts rolled on. We lived at the end of the cul-de-sac where cars turned regularly. Deliveries. Neighbours. Visitors. When Tom left the blinds open on a dark night, it was like living in a goldfish bowl. I must remind him to close them as darkness fell, without explaining the importance. He was ignorant to what I was contending with, and it had to remain that way.

The shower stopped and I hopped out of bed, disinclined for a rerun of last night. I headed downstairs with my coffee mug, in my dressing gown and slippers. Streaky sunlight peeped around the edge of the curtains in the hall, and I yanked them open, keen for daylight. There was a bright splash of colour outside the front door and I did a double take.

Leaning against the door frame was a bouquet of flowers.

Pink, purple and yellow roses wrapped in cellophane, the ends concealed by a plain white plastic bag. My heart rate quickened as I scanned the drive and street from the safety of the hall. No one was about. No unfamiliar cars. No unwelcome faces partially concealed by a scarf.

Should I wait for Tom to come downstairs or go out and investigate now? He cleared his throat upstairs, I made a quick decision, prised open the door and lifted them cautiously. The door shut with a bang and I carried them into the kitchen. It was plainly time for a Ring doorbell, or CCTV, but I'd have to covertly discuss it with Tom.

Apprehensively I examined the flowers and inside the plastic bag. There was no card. Nothing to suggest who'd left them or why. A thorn sliced my finger and I dropped them into the sink with a yelp of pain. My finger throbbed as I ran it under the tap, and pressed firmly to staunch droplets of blood. I should have left them for Tom. Whoever had deposited them would see they'd been brought indoors. Although no one was obviously hanging around, they could be hidden, studying our house.

I moved over to the table and sat heavily on a chair, my injured finger wrapped in damp kitchen roll. Tom found me there a few minutes later.

'What's up?' He was disinterested until he spotted the flowers. 'Where did these come from?' His eyebrows lifted.

'They were on the doorstep. I noticed them when I opened the curtains.'

'Who left them?'

I answered as neutrally as possible. 'There was no card so I don't know.'

'Weird. Do you want another coffee?' Tom put them out of his mind and popped a pod into the Nespresso machine. Clicking and whirring filled the kitchen and I raised my voice to be heard.

'I should bin them.'

'It seems a shame. There's probably a simple explanation for them.'

Tom mooched out of the kitchen towards the sitting room, and the sound of the television filled the silence. I stared at the bouquet for a few moments, and tried to work out who would have left them. Despite Tom's casual response, I was unnerved. Then a thunderbolt. What if they were for Tom and not me as I automatically assumed?

Repulsed, I unlocked the back door and stuffed them into the wheelie bin. Fatigue washed over me at my complicated life. It was peace I craved, not malicious communication and unwanted gifts.

My thoughts moseyed on. Could they be a peace offering from someone at Book Club after last night? I gathered up my bag from the hall table, and slowly climbed the stairs. In the bedroom I composed a message for the Book Club WhatsApp.

> Strange question, but does anyone know anything about flowers left on my doorstep this morning?

I sat on side of the bed and studied my phone while I absent-mindedly rubbed my sore finger.

Laura is typing…

Kate is typing…

Annie is typing…

My patience was wearing thin. One by one the replies came. *No. No. No.* The question answered, I waited to see if anyone would be brave enough to mention the elephant in the room.

Miranda's bizarre behaviour and how out of place she'd been.

No one did and my exasperation rose. I gnawed a fingernail and questioned if I should begin the conversation. The longer I left it, the less confident I became. Ultimately it would be better discussed face to face, for a text can't convey tone and can be misconstrued. Before I raised the subject, I should talk it through with someone. If I was too rash it could have unforeseen repercussions.

I stabbed the numbers into my phone and made a call. Afterwards I was much calmer, my nerves reduced.

My calm didn't last. I checked my mobile as I dried off after the shower.

One message was all it took and I was as ill at ease as I'd ever been.

CHAPTER THIRTEEN

Book Club was forgotten by the time Sunday arrived along with a bitter wind and splatter of rain. It was time for lunch with my parents. Tom dressed for the occasion in a slim-fitting shirt and chinos, and had polished his shoes, experienced in how exacting his father-in-law was about such things.

Flora had taken the train from her university on the North Coast to stay in Alex's student digs in Belfast overnight. I should've laid down the law and instructed them not to party too hard, but I'd been preoccupied and forgotten. Foolishly I expected them to act responsibly, then remembered too late they still needed to be badgered occasionally.

When they exited Alex's house, puffy eyes and wan faces gave the game away. My fury rained over their heads, fuelled by trepidation about my parents' reaction. Tom placed a warning hand on my thigh and tightly informed the girls to 'buck up'.

Rebellious glares drilled into the back of my head on the short drive from the Holylands, where Alex lived. Hangovers and my parents. A match made in hell.

Initially Tom was affable and complimented Mum, then

asked Dad how his golf swing was. The girls behaved beautifully and praised the food, though I quashed a smile when Flora became a greener shade of pale.

Things deteriorated when my mother asked Tom how Dubai had been at New Year. From bathing the room in a warm glow, he grew monosyllabic. I'd forgotten to tell him about my lie on New Year's Day, and he tripped straight into the quagmire with his newly shined shoes. Mum had jerked upright, Dad's cutting retort could have shattered glass. The atmosphere hadn't improved when Flora scampered from the dining room to the downstairs toilet to be sick.

Sooner than expected, we were coldly excused and when the front door slammed behind us, I relaxed.

"Thank feck that's over,' Alex announced dramatically, and I didn't have the heart to reprimand her language. The oversight had been mine and I'd have to own it.

The silence in the car was heavy on the drive down to Alex's house as Tom studiously focused on the road. He manoeuvred into a space on the street a few doors down from Alex's, and I climbed out of the car to give my daughters a hug. They begged not to have to visit their grandparents again 'for a long time', and I promised to make excuses for them. When they turned on their heels, I watched their retreating backs forlornly. My parents possessed the unique skill of making me feel like an incompetent mother.

'I take it you'll be written out of the will now?' Tom asked with a wry smile when I got back into the passenger seat.

I grimaced in return. 'As of this moment, I don't care. I'm sorry to have dropped you in it with them.' My hand found his and the earth stopped rocking. We'd been playacting for my parents and the girls, but could release a sigh of relief now we were on our own.

The following day, I drove to work through torrential rain. Chitchat and gossip greeted me and I prepared myself for the onslaught of patients. Almost everyone had disappeared to their rooms by nine o'clock, but I'd spilled coffee on my blouse and ineffectually rubbed at it with a damp cloth in the staff room.

Before I made it the length of my consulting room, the buzz of voices in reception captured my attention. Bronagh's strident tones cut through the racket and my curiosity was piqued. A burly delivery man with a shaved head systematically unloaded cardboard boxes from a trolley onto the floor by the reception desk and pointedly snubbed Bronagh's raised voice.

Her gaze landed gratefully on me.

'What's going on?' I was imperious and hoped my unfriendly tone would stop him in his tracks. No such luck, he never glanced my way.

Jinty the receptionist waved an invoice under my nose. 'Envelopes. Ten thousand of them!' Panic was evident in her panting exclamation and wide eyes. Normally unflappable, her cheeks flamed red.

The delivery man continued to stack the boxes on top of each other, creating a precarious tower.

'Please stop. Who ordered them?' It was as though he was deaf or I hadn't spoken, as he continued to ignore me.

'All it says is Ballyrevy GP Practice.' Jinty's gaze shot over to Bronagh, who cowered by the desk as alarm rolled off her in waves. I didn't need to ask: it was clear the error was hers.

The delivery driver finally reached the bottom of the trolley and straightened with a groan. His trousers had slipped down to reveal the waistband of his boxers and he hauled them up with one hand. Fluorescent lights reflected off his bald head, which shone with exertion.

'That's them unloaded.' He held out a clipboard.

I switched on the charm. 'I'm very sorry, but there's been a mistake.' I reached for the clipboard so I could read the invoice. It should be easy to rectify. 'Someone must have ordered the wrong number and not spotted it before payment.' The finger was pointed at clearly at Bronagh, the new admin manager, although her name wasn't on the invoice. I handed the clipboard back without signing.

'Please reload the trolley and take them back.'

The delivery driver folded his arms across his beer belly. 'Are you serious? It's taken me ages to unload them all.'

What I wanted to say was, *If you'd listened to me in the first place this wouldn't have happened.* But there are many ways to skin a cat and I opted for the soft touch. My first patient was already in the waiting room, fully engrossed in the unfolding charade. Several other patients queued to check in, attention fixed on us. The predicament needed to be defused as quickly as possible and for once Bronagh was speechless. She chewed on a talon, face mottled and tight. Fake tan had caked around her fingers and her palm was a tell-tale orange.

'I'm sorry to inconvenience you, but there's clearly been a mistake with the order. If we give you a hand to reload them, could you please return them.' I almost batted my eyelashes, and at last his lips lifted in the briefest smile.

He sighed. 'Okay. But don't you be lifting them, you might damage yourself.'

'Well, you'll get it done far faster than us as you're so much stronger.' I tinkled a laugh and thought, *Men can be so gullible sometimes.* All it takes is a bit of flattery and a pretty face.

Noting the time and rapidly filling waiting room, I indicated to Bronagh we should move into the back room. Her heels tapped after me, which grated on my already thin nerves. She was like a deflated balloon, all the bluster gone.

We reached the privacy of the staff room. 'I'm really sorry.' She was chastened, a far cry from her usual overconfident self. 'I must've ordered the wrong number last week. There was a delivery for me when I was doing the ordering and I got side-tracked. When I went back to the order, I didn't check the price or quantity. It was a very strange delivery of extra-large gym kit—'

Her eyes glistened brilliantly, as though begging me to sympathise with her incompetence. Our budget was tight enough, mistakes like this could be costly.

Summoning my patience, I cut in. 'Mistakes happen, Bronagh, but you must be more careful in future, especially as you have responsibility for ordering admin supplies now. Let's hope there's no problem with the return and no damage done. If not...' my voice tailed off. I'd leave her to jump to her own conclusions.

Jake was elsewhere for training; he could sort it when he returned to work tomorrow.

'Thanks for your help. I've got to organise staff meetings and training now, so if you hadn't stepped in, I'd be even more pushed for time.'

I had no interest in what her job entailed, but nodded politely and left her to it. My patient accompanied me down the corridor to my consulting room and I switched into Doctor Harris mode. She was a sweet elderly woman with arthritic knees and accepted my apology for the delay with good grace.

It wasn't until the end of morning surgery I was able to give the shambles with Bronagh some thought. Like many of the staff, I had reservations about her ability to do the new job. It was busy with many more responsibilities than she'd had before. Unfortunately as I wasn't partner, I'd had no say in her appointment. It had been a *fait accompli* when I'd been informed.

Irritated again, I watched the rain, which bounced off the ground and lashed the panes. Puddles dotted the car park, impossible to avoid completely. A woman struggled past with a multicoloured umbrella, which blew inside out as she reached her car. Another miserable January day.

My stomach grumbled as I checked my phone.

On the home page was one message.

> Is everyone free for coffee at the Village Café on Friday? I've got a half day in work, so could make it by one. There's a few things we need to chat about and I know you can't make Friday night Vicky.

Laura had bitten the bullet and was going to discuss the contentious issue of Miranda with Book Club. They were going into Belfast for a meal on Friday night, but I'd declined as I had other plans.

Grimly I answered to say it suited me. I wanted Miranda out of Book Club before she ingratiated herself any further and was glad Laura was onside.

One by one the girls answered and we arranged a time. No one proposed inviting Miranda, which was a relief, as I'd been half expecting Kate to suggest it.

Towards the end of afternoon surgery a patient failed to attend, which gave me a few minutes to myself. My throat was dry and I returned to the staff room to make a cup of coffee. Jinty and another member of the admin staff clustered together by the kettle. Groaning inwardly, I fixed a smile in place and said hello. Startled, they swung around. They hadn't heard me enter.

'Is everything all right?'

Jinty scowled. 'Oh, everything's great.'

I cocked an eyebrow and waited. They exchanged a look and an almost imperceptible nod of encouragement.

Jinty launched in. 'Bronagh's made another mistake. She's now in charge of scheduling meetings and she's booked a staff meeting for next Friday afternoon. Half the staff don't work Fridays.' Friday was a terrible day for a staff meeting, Bronagh should've known better.

I rubbed my temple before speaking. 'It's easily sorted. Frustrating yes, lethal no.' I forced a warm smile while Jinty pouted. She'd been vociferous in her criticism of Bronagh's promotion already. Two mistakes in one day would antagonise the staff further.

Coffee forgotten, I walked back to my room and opened the staff intranet on my computer. As a GP I could change and add to the practice diary, unlike most other staff. I fidgeted with my earring as I ruminated what to do. Should I change the day of the meeting or discuss it with Bronagh first? I'd been involved in the morning debacle, I didn't want to be associated with this one too. After a while, I emailed the staff's issues to Jake. As practice manager, he'd had a role in her promotion, now he could oversee the resultant problems. Rather than express annoyance with the day's events, my email was light-hearted and kind. I reinforced the issues raised were not mine, but those of nameless, general staff and pointed no fingers.

It was still raining when I left work and hurried to my car. The continual mizzle meant there were few people around. Streetlights and car lights cut through the gloom, and tyres sprayed lying water high across the footpaths. I sat for a while, lost in my thoughts. Figures shifted indoors. Shadows loomed in the dark. I made a phone call which went unanswered and irritation trickled through me. I made another call. And another.

I'd assumed Tom would be home, but he was answering

neither the house phone nor his mobile. He could be anywhere, with anyone. I switched on the engine, decision made.

The who, the what and the why would drive me crazy.

I had more insistent anxieties. My husband and his wayward behaviour would have to wait.

CHAPTER FOURTEEN

Tom had another long-haul trip early on Wednesday, and left with a kiss before dawn. The pillow curved from his head and I extended a hand to find it cold beneath my fingers. Although early I was wide awake and reflected on his behaviour over the past few days. His mobile had not-so-subtly lain on the countertop, or on the bedside table, where I could examine it if the notion took me. Doubtless he believed such over-the-top transparency would placate me, but it multiplied my suspicions. I'd made a point of not handling it and carefully kept my distance, as though I fully trusted him.

But the knowledge he'd made an Instagram account behind my back needled.

The excuse he used it to message Ashley about the stag weekend was a poor one. Who was to say he hadn't made another, or how long he'd had the account for. The girls had once shown me how straightforward it was to have more than one Instagram account. Or Facebook. Or X. He could have multiple accounts and I'd be none the wiser.

Later in the shower, I mulled over the Book Club coffee on Friday. Kate had never apologised for dragging up the subject of

Claire and Tom last week, which was unusual. She was never normally so remiss, always petrified of causing offence. Laura had messaged to ensure we'd be singing from the same hymn sheet when we met for coffee. Neither of us wanted Miranda at Book Club. It was too soon after Claire. I was too susceptible and needed friends who could be trusted, not someone with a desire for me to dish the dirt on my husband's betrayal.

I was the cheated wife who deserved sympathy, not spiteful interfering.

After work on Wednesday, I trekked as usual around the village. The fresh air and quiet streets helped soothe me after hectic days in work. When I wore a hat, scarf and dark jacket, I was anonymous. Even the keenest of eyes would've been hard pressed to recognise me in the dark, and the knowledge was invigorating.

The pavements were glassy with rain, the wind bracing on Thursday evening. Nevertheless, I couldn't wait to get outside and ambled along the village streets. Lights shone from some houses, leaving them on full show, which baffled me. Perhaps my own experience had forever changed me from carefree to careful. Other people's lives played out under a bright glare and they were unbothered by who observed it.

I wanted to stop with Jake, so my walk took me up his street. The day after the envelope and staff meeting fiascos, his usual good-natured expression had darkened when Jinty pounced first thing, eager to fill him in on Bronagh's slip-ups. I'd lurked nearby, ready to intervene if needed, but he dismissed us with the gentle instruction he would deal with it. A glance thrown in my direction and a tight smile was the closest he'd come to sharing his opinion with me. For the first time, a sliver of disappointment pierced me. I'd wrongly assumed he'd be rattled and want to discuss it with me.

It had languished between us all week, as I futilely waited

for him to seek me out. Miffed, I'd been short with him once or twice, which didn't seem to faze him. By Thursday evening I was ready to make amends and smooth over any bad feeling. When I reached his bungalow, it was in darkness and there was no car in the driveway. Fuming he wasn't there, my phone buzzed in my pocket as I exited his street.

When I read it, I instantly turned for home, my walk cut short as I sped along the rain lashed streets.

Kate was confident the mystery person was in the field behind my house again. I needed to return home as soon as possible. Head down against the wind, I passed first Miranda's, then Laura's, Kate's and finally reached my front door. My eyes had patrolled incessantly, but there was no one around. No one I could see anyway.

With the door locked, I texted Kate back. My response was measured and at odds with the turmoil in my head. Once I'd removed my outer layers, I made myself a coffee, then headed upstairs to run a bath. My trousers were soaking, my legs numb with the cold.

Before I sank under the bubbles, I made a phone call, which helped settle me. From the depths of my bath, I reran everything again. Working through it helped to straighten out the chaotic jumble in my head.

I'd clarify everything with Jake soon; there was no need to brood about it.

Kate was unreliable, easily excited and prone to exaggeration.

My doors were locked, the blinds tightly closed.

Although my phone glowed with notifications, I avoided them.

My thoughts ebbed and flowed as I gradually warmed up and my to-do list lured. So many items still to tick off, so much fun to be had.

Relaxed now, I dried off, dressed in my pyjamas and dressing gown then checked my mobile. It was time I took charge again.

In the kitchen, I rifled into the back of the drawer, retrieved my list and carried it into the sitting room. There I lit a couple of candles and made myself comfortable on the sofa, with a throw over my legs. Keiko slept on the armchair nearby and her purrs made me smile. The list was creased and well thumbed, but I added another couple of items which I'd come up with when walking. Anticipation fizzed at seeing it in black and white. There was one glaringly obvious online purchase I could make, which would take a bit of time to sort, but was perfect for the task at hand.

Which reminded me, it wasn't long until Tom's birthday and I'd need to buy an appropriate present. A reminder of our recommitment to each other. Something showy and expensive to silence questions and vicious tongues. I'd rack my brains for the ideal gift in the next few days.

My laptop was on the coffee table, where I'd left it last night. I became engrossed and before I knew it, it was after eleven. Once my order was placed I sighed contentedly. Another item ticked off. My earlier aggravation was forgotten, subdued by the thrill of achievement.

Tired but not ready to sleep, I swiped through social media. I shouldn't check, it did nothing but upset and throw me off balance. But I did anyway.

Despite the risks and the almost inescapable heartache.

Foolish. Always foolish.

On Instagram the cursor hovered over search and before I could change my mind, I typed in Tom's username and clicked on his profile. When he'd been home, I'd boldly not given in and examined it. Now he was a continent away, I could wallow with no risk of being caught.

He had nearly fifty followers and in turn followed forty back. Fifty people who had access to his life when he'd hidden it from me. At some point I'd pitifully click on each and every profile to see who he followed and to agonise over them.

There were half a dozen photos he'd posted over the past year, the last one a couple of weeks before Christmas.

An outdoor jacuzzi with two pairs of flip-flops discarded by the steps.

A far-flung beach spanning miles, turquoise sea lapping the shore.

Skyscrapers unforgiving against an azure sky.

Colourful dishes of tantalising food.

Tense, I clicked on the first photo, the tropical beach. Ten likes and a single comment.

'Looks amazing, I can see myself sunbathing in a bikini there!'

The username was 'C_Wood.' It meant nothing to me.

Next photo. A square white plate on an oak table. Same commenter.

Sushi's my favourite, you've put me in the mood.

Quickly I checked them all. C_Wood had commented on every photo.

My stomach heaved as I clicked on their profile. An arty shot of Napoleon's nose, the basalt rock face which towers over Belfast, a loan figure near the edge faced Belfast Lough. Their account was private, which gave no indication who they were, except for the suggestion they were Northern Irish.

My loving, unreliable husband lied compulsively and strayed persistently. My mind trundled down the rabbit hole of self-reproach and doubt. Once I had finished with his Instagram page, Facebook became my focus.

His profile photo was an old one, taken years ago on a family holiday to Portugal. In it he peered out to sea, shades on top of his head, chin propped on his hand. His face was tanned and unlined, and my heart flipped. It was almost unfair how handsome he was. The cover photo was four pairs of sun kissed bare feet in a circle, golden sand beneath. It was the four of us, taken when the girls were young teenagers.

The hurt was exquisite, like a burn from standing too close to a flame.

Could I ever trust him again? Inundated with despair, I closed the laptop with a soft thud. Over and over he'd betrayed me. Time and time again I took him back. Was I a masochist? Did I deserve his contempt?

Was this retribution for past sins?

I rose so fast, I became light-headed and the room swayed. That specific path was the route to madness and I couldn't go there. Not now, not ever.

On unsteady legs, I returned to the kitchen and hid my list at the back of the drawer. My earlier optimism had abated. The mysterious C_Wood weaved around my psyche. I was certain it was a woman, by the sugary comments. Was it an old lover? An admirer? In the past or hideously current?

I caught sight of my reflection in the window. Sallow complexion and bruised eyes observed me. The insecurity beneath the veneer was oozing out. I forced a brilliant smile, mouth contorted. The grin faded. My gloss was dulling.

Carefully I made certain everywhere was spotless before I climbed the stairs with leaden feet. My body desired sleep, but my mind whirred into overdrive.

Without cleaning my teeth I crawled under the duvet, lugged it up to my chin and flicked off the light. Darkness fell, Keiko jumped on the bed and stretched out alongside my legs.

Her weight was a consolation as the knot in my stomach unkinked.

My reservations about Tom lessened. The ties which bound him to me were tatty and torn, but tough.

Contrition for past deeds was crushed deep into the crevices of my mind.

My present situation shifted and shimmered in the shadows.

Tomorrow I'd move forward and confront whatever it brought.

CHAPTER FIFTEEN

The rain stopped overnight and a cool breeze chased the clouds eastwards. When I opened the blinds I was greeted by pale sunlight and a clear blue sky. Contentment bubbled as I stretched and yawned. It bubbled until I checked my phone, when it was replaced with a raging fire.

Kate wanted to invite Miranda for coffee.

I slammed my palm onto the dressing table with such force it ached. Miranda's sly meddling chafed and Kate's suggestion doused my good humour. Without hesitation, I typed.

> I need to see you girls on your own today.
> Don't dare invite her.

Fortunately I read it before sending. Too brash. My teeth were bared and I rarely dropped my guard, so deleted the last part of the message. If Miranda did appear, I'd manufacture tears and leave. There was more to this get-together than simple coffee with friends. It was an opportunity to unravel what Kate thought she'd seen last night. I had an inkling of who she suspected, and wanted her to confirm or deny it. With careful questioning, I could tease it from her.

I planned to walk to the café, but social media side-tracked me. When I glanced at the clock, it was late and I'd have to drive. Repeated scrolling through Tom's Insta and Facebook hadn't resulted in anything new, so I had to pull myself together and set it aside.

The café car park was half full and I recognised my friends' cars. I raised my chin to the sun and inhaled the earthy fragrance of the ground after the rain. Green fields rolled away from the village, and in the distance the Antrim Hills were lush and grassy. I was more at home in the quiet village than I'd ever been in the city centre.

The others were already seated at our usual table by the window and I noted the fifth chair hadn't been removed. Claire's absence was disguised under a heap of coats. Steaming mugs of coffee and a variety of scones littered the table, though I'd no appetite, and opted for a flat white.

Laura was mid-story about Sam's dog Nigel stealing a sausage, and an enrapt Annie tucked a shiny chestnut curl behind her ear. Kate's pallid complexion was poorly concealed by heavy foundation. Her eyes wandered restlessly, never settling for long on one person. Uncertainty was engraved between her brows. There was no sign of Miranda, but part of me expected her to emerge like the genie from the bottle.

'Hi, girls.' I smiled warmly at my friends. 'How are you all?'

Lukewarm replies and vague nods. Laura's nerves were obvious as her fingertips drummed on the tabletop.

'All fine, thanks.' Laura cleared her throat, but delayed speaking as the waitress set my coffee down. 'It's time we had a wee chat about Book Club.' She launched straight in with no preamble. 'Kate, I'm sure you meant well inviting Miranda, but to be honest, I found it a bit strange and hard going.'

The usually timid Laura had grabbed the bull by the horns and was wrestling it single-handedly. I hid my surprise and waited for her to continue. Annie blushed, and Kate's bottom lip wobbled. Laura's eyebrows rose, as if daring her to interrupt. A cold gust from an open window brushed my skin as I mutely appraised my friends. Laura was rosy cheeked, Annie hugged herself and Kate's chin shot up.

Laura continued when no one spoke. 'Look, Vicky needs the support from people who've known her for years, not someone we don't know very well.' Kate opened her mouth to answer, but Laura held her hand up and she shut it again. Her tone was kind. 'We know Book Club means more than it says on the tin. We're friends, confidantes, and we as a group have to muddle our way through this situation. We need time to process and come to terms with it. Unfortunately the time isn't right for a new member, any new member,' she was careful to stress it wasn't just Miranda, 'to join us.'

She flopped back against the seat and sipped her coffee. Her set jaw dared anyone to contradict.

'I'm sorry if I offended anyone.' Kate's lip had stopped wobbling and there was a surprising frost in her tone. 'Miranda's a good friend of mine and has wanted to come along for ages. This seemed like a good time to invite her. It's going to be both embarrassing and difficult for me to un-invite her.'

I cursed under my breath to stop myself from snarling she should have discussed it properly before announcing it as a done deal.

Laura calmly jumped straight in. 'You didn't offend anyone, Kate, but I personally think for now it's best we keep Book Club to the four of us. Perhaps in time, we can reconsider.'

My snort of delight quickly became a cough. I liked this new Laura, the one with fire in her belly. For too long she'd been a shadow of herself, but without James's overbearing presence, she revealed hidden depths.

Kate replied it would be hard to let Miranda down and I clenched my teeth. Who cared? She'd rammed her way onto a front row seat to watch my life combust.

'Maybe she could come along in a couple of months?' For some reason, Kate wouldn't drop it. She was like a dog with the proverbial bone.

'Perhaps.' Laura was noncommittal.

Annie nodded in agreement, and I expressed my gratitude for their support and apologised to Kate for my oversensitivity. The conversation I'd dreaded had been sorted with barely a bang. I squeezed Kate's hand and readied myself. It was time to discuss the person behind the house. Then a sudden movement outside distracted me.

Blonde hair and stooped shoulders. A dejected green stare. My heart thumped unpleasantly.

Claire.

Dressed head to toe in black apart from a red handbag, she was frail and in danger of being blown over in the wind. Snapshots swarmed of that awful day at the Averie Hotel in December, when she'd exposed her affair with Tom and my life had spectacularly detonated. Annie too had spotted her, and comically halted mid-sentence, hand mid-gesture.

Claire froze on the other side of the window, misery carved into her face. She should've been with us, drinking coffee and gossiping. Instead she was outside both the café and Book Club, an impenetrable wall divided her from us.

Blood rushed to my head, and my mug clunked onto the table.

Kate's head swung around and she bayed furiously. 'She better not come in here.'

'She's not. Please stop staring.' Laura's tone again invited no disagreement and I threw her a grateful glance.

Claire had moved away and was now out of sight. The silence between us was prickly and loud. Everyone waited for my reaction.

'Thanks, that wasn't pleasant.' I allowed a slight hesitation in my voice and a single tear rolled down my face, which I slowly wiped away.

My unknowing, trusting friends comforted me. As if Claire would cause me harm. A stone of shame sat heavy in my stomach. Laura said little, but stared intently at her silver Claddagh ring. I narrowed my eyes, uncertain whose side she was on. Claires? Mine? Both?

Then Kate spoke. 'Vicky, this brings me on nicely to the "unknown person" behind your house.' She drew air quotes with her fingers, and I almost laughed at her. Luckily the laugh got stuck, I observed her solemnly and leaned towards her. A deliberate pause. 'I'm almost certain it's Claire.'

'What's Claire? What unknown person behind the house?' Annie demanded.

Kate animatedly filled them in about the person walking in the field, and how she was convinced they were spying on my house. She rounded it off by announcing firmly, 'And the fact she was outside the café today when we're all here proves she's watching Vicky.'

Kate was in her element. Laura's sceptical expression didn't change until I admitted there was indeed a flattened patch of grass directly opposite my bedroom window. Kate's triumphant smile lit up her whole face and I raised my palms in defeat.

'I've not seen anyone hanging around and especially not Claire.' Annie folded her arms in front of her.

'I don't mean to be funny, but your house doesn't back onto

that field, does it? Yours overlooks the neighbouring one, with no direct access to the road.' Annie couldn't argue with Kate about that point. 'Also I'm pretty certain they were wearing a green bobble hat like Claire's.'

Annie and Kate sparred good-naturedly, Laura said little and I listened without contributing.

Claire. Not Claire. A stranger. A harmless dog walker. Round and round in circles.

'We're considering a Ring doorbell,' I finally commented. 'And external cameras as well.'

My friends nodded and I stopped myself from saying more. The seed had been sown; Claire was far from finished with either my husband or me. I worked to disperse her image which had taken up residence in the forefront of my mind.

Any coolness between us melted as we finished our coffees. We'd been friends for years, so no disagreements smouldered for long. Outside in the car park, we had a group hug before we went our separate ways.

'Are you sure you can't make tonight? We can easily change the booking,' Laura asked and I shook my head, with vague mutterings about other plans. 'Yogalates then on Tuesday evening?'

I murmured an indistinguishable reply and again shook my head. 'No, me neither.' Her face contorted sadly.

My stride was sure when I left them with a wave, knowing they'd discuss me later when they went out for dinner. I got into the car and watched them leave, until the car park was deserted again. I sighed with sudden fatigue, haunted by Claire's angst-ridden expression.

To divert myself, I checked my phone. It was bright with notifications and I spent a few minutes doggedly reading them all. Suddenly I sensed eyes on me and my head shot up.

Nothing moved. There wasn't a sound. No one was there, but my cheeks burned.

I longed for a day without worries, or trials. A clear sky and a free mind.

But as was increasingly usual, the day brought its own darkness.

CHAPTER SIXTEEN

Before I'd joined the Book Club for coffee, I'd messaged Jake to suggest I visit him later. That was the vague plan I'd alluded to with Laura. The Book Club knew he was a friend from work, but weren't party to how close we really were. My need to discuss everything with him outweighed my hurt at his distance over the past few days, and the invitation from the girls to go out for a meal. I wanted to glean his true opinion on the issues with Bronagh earlier in the week.

He still hadn't replied by the time I reached home, and I clutched my phone at the breakfast bar. The sloshing of the dishwasher couldn't mask the booming of the Book Club discussion about Claire, and resulted in a headache I couldn't shift. The sight of Claire gazing sadly at the four of us had tugged at my heartstrings.

Still waiting on Jake's reply, I carried the laptop into the sitting room and settled on the sofa. Outside the wind wailed, and a pall of pewter cloud rolled in to hide the sun and snatch the daylight. Within minutes rain pattered on the window, but I made myself cosy by switching on a floor lamp and tucking the woollen throw around my legs. Although I was tempted to light the wood burner, I decided there was little point as I'd hopefully spend the evening at Jake's. Soft music played and my misgivings about Claire drained from me as I indulged in retail therapy.

Jake's reply illuminated my mobile while I scoured the internet on the laptop.

> Sorry, busy this evening but could have a quick coffee after work.

My heart sank. I'd assumed we'd spend time together and order a takeaway like so often before. A dull ache in my jaw cautioned I was grinding my teeth again. Enraged, I massaged my sore face and mulled over his message.

The detachment between us pinched and burned. A lick of doubt. Was he annoyed with me? Had I inadvertently insulted him? I replayed the week. Could his coolness be related to Bronagh's errors?

To me, her behaviour had been unprofessional, but I hoped my poker face had hidden my honest feelings. On Tuesday Jinty had confided a quiet rebuke from Jake had been given when Bronagh complained the mix-up about the staff meeting had been someone else's fault. I wondered how long the practice tinderbox could survive without igniting completely.

My reply took me several minutes to compose. Coffee at a café near the practice would have to do. I checked the time to find there was two hours until we could meet.

First Claire, now this.

A noisy rapping on the front door broke into my musing. I peeped through the wooden slats and although distorted by the rain, I recognised the red anorak.

Miranda.

Impulsively I ducked down on the sofa and hoped she'd

disappear if the door wasn't opened. But she was persistent and rang the bell as well as knocking. Too late I remembered my car was in the driveway, and she was sure to hammer on the door and ring the bell until I answered.

Furious with her, I flung back the throw and strode to the door. Her face lit up when she saw me, and I opened the door just wide enough to see her clearly.

'Hi, Vicky. I saw you drive past my house earlier and knew you were in.' Her hood was up which accentuated her bony features.

I blinked and fought to keep my face straight, unwilling to show how shaken her comment had made me. When I didn't respond immediately, she held out a grubby plastic bag. It would be churlish of me not to accept it, or to invite her in, so I opened the door a few inches wider. Despite the lack of invitation, she stepped past me so swiftly the damp of her coat assailed my nostrils.

'Come in then,' I snapped, unable to hide my annoyance.

She ignored my surliness and grinned as she lowered her hood and ran a hand through her lank hair. Her eyes flicked up and down the hallway, past and around me. She rocked on her feet as she absorbed my home. My safe space.

'I brought a few books I thought you'd like.' Again she proffered the bag, which I now accepted with a vague smile and feeble thanks. Without looking inside, I set it on the hall table. 'There's some mint Aero traybakes from the bakery in there as well. Kate said they're your favourite.' No doubt she was anticipating the offer of coffee along with gossip about my marriage and ruined friendship.

I hid my frustration, switched on my gloomy face and said, 'Thanks so much, Miranda. Unfortunately I have a headache, otherwise I'd offer you coffee.' I moved decisively towards the front door, turned a blind eye to the anger which blazed across her face, and turned the handle. When I glanced back, she remained rooted to the spot, fixated on my sitting room.

'I wanted to ask you something.' It was as though I hadn't spoken or opened the door. An icy blast chilled me and I suppressed my groan of impatience. Not wanting to close the door and thus by implication, keep her indoors, I pushed it over a fraction. She turned from my sitting room and spoke in an undertone. 'Kate told me she thinks Claire's been walking in the field behind your houses. As you know, I'm on the other side of the street, so don't have a clear view. However I don't work and am home a lot. Would you like me to watch out for her? I could come up here and check she's not sneaking around when you're out.'

Alarm swept over me and I gaped at her. If I agreed, Miranda could legitimately call at any time and say I'd given her my blessing. A suspicion as to her reason floated into my mind, but it was slippery and indistinct, gone before I could seize it.

'Thanks for the offer, but as I explained to Kate, I doubt Claire would be prowling around. There's no need for you to worry.' I'd remembered in the nick of time not to mention our earlier coffee.

Her smile vanished as her fake geniality evaporated. 'Fine.' It was spat out. 'I'm in a good position to help a friend out, but don't worry, I know when I'm not wanted.' Too late she recognised her error, the mask dropped back into place and she gave a humourless laugh. 'I'm sorry. You're probably right. I like to help my friends when I can.'

The casual use of the word *friend* caused me to shudder. Once Miranda took hold she was rampant and suffocating. I hid my antipathy, smiled blandly and opened the door again. This time she took the hint and left with a couple of taps on my hand. The imprint of her sticky fingers stuck to me, and I went directly into the kitchen to wash my hands.

As I soaped, discomfort itched my skin. It was both her overfamiliarity and her interfering. Desperation to be my friend seeped from her like a bad smell. On my way back to the living room, I spotted the plastic bag. Sighing, I peeked in. Three books and a squashed box of traybakes. Gingerly I reached for the first book.

Men are from Mars, Women are from Venus. I tossed my head in annoyance and withdrew the next one.

Why has Nobody Told Me this Before by Dr Julie Smith. A self-help book which I flipped through. Miranda had annotated the margins.

I huffed out my anger. Overfamiliar indeed.

Lastly a novel. *The Paper Palace* by Miranda Cowley Heller. About an affair and a lost love. I slammed it down with such force, the table vibrated. Bitch. I removed the traybakes and carried them to the sofa. Mint Aero traybakes from our local bakery were indeed my favourite, and I devoured one in moments. As I munched, an idea formed, which cheered me up considerably.

I had time to relax with more online shopping before meeting Jake. There was something special I had in mind, but it might be difficult to source.

An hour later, everything was good. My order had been placed and there'd been nothing worrying on Instagram or Facebook. I was about to delve into X, when my phone vibrated.

Is it OK if Bronagh comes for coffee?

An angry retort formed, then slipped away. No one could accuse me of rashness, nor loss of control. My true response had to be whitewashed beneath the polished exterior I was at pains to portray.

I deliberated before replying. The sole explanation for Jake inviting Bronagh was to discuss the week, as I was his friend and presumably they needed some guidance. Eventually I lied it was no problem and I'd see them both later.

A little happier, I went to change my clothes. Make-up and a carefully curated shell were my barrier. Upstairs I applied more make-up, then changed into a more flattering top. It had a low V-neck which required a necklace, so I rummaged in my jewellery box and selected a gold calla lily pendant. Unfortunately the clasp was minute and I struggled to close it as my nails were too long. I leaned forward to see better in the mirror over the dressing table and finally fastened it. Once secured, I was about to turn away, when I caught sight of a charging lead plugged into a socket behind the dressing table.

Obscured from the room unless you leaned right over.

Intrigued, I reached down as far as I could, but it was too low and all I felt was wall. I dropped onto my hunkers, crawled under the dressing table and scrabbled around on my hands and knees until my hand finally closed around the plug. Despite wriggling it around, it was firmly stuck in the socket with no room for manoeuvre. Frustrated but not defeated, my fingers trailed along the lead until they encountered something firm and solid. Panting by now, I worked at it until a corner was visible and I yanked more forcefully.

A sleek black iPad toppled out from its hiding place.

Bemused, I picked it up. I'd never seen it before and dread constricted my lungs before I opened it.

It must be Tom's.

I summoned my nerve and flipped open the cover.

And there it was.

His clandestine device with all his dirty secrets laid bare before me.

CHAPTER SEVENTEEN

Marriage is complex. Full of nooks and crannies. Disappointments and delights. Some like mine, would never be boring or humdrum. Neither would it be secure and steadfast.

The drive from the village to Ballyrevy to meet Jake and Bronagh helped clear my head. Allowed me come to terms with my discovery.

Tom's not-so-secret iPad would give me access to his plans and allow me to stay one step ahead of him. Rather than crumble under the knowledge, I'd use it to my advantage and he'd be none the wiser. I could secretly inspect his messages and emails, Instagram, Facebook and DMs, along with his photos. I smiled in satisfaction as I drove into the car park beside the coffee shop. Instead of worrying about him straying and imagining all sorts, I'd be able to check up on him any time I wanted.

Which made the GPS trackers I'd recently purchased redundant.

Maybe though I should err on the side of caution and slip one into his gym bag anyway. Or sew it into the lining of his jacket. The trickiest issue was he could wear a different jacket or leave his gym kit at home. If he were a woman he'd mostly use the same handbag. Which was why I'd bought two trackers. My initial idea had been to hide one in the glove compartment of his car, but so far it remained an idea, rather than an action. For I was afraid he would locate it, or it would beep and alert him.

I'd made use of the many lonely hours on my own to study how to turn iPhone tracking notifications off. My plan was to adjust the settings the next time I got my hands on his mobile. There'd been nothing especially incriminating on the iPad since Christmas, just some earlier overt messages between him and Claire, which he'd archived but not deleted. I'd sagged with relief there were no obscene photos, for my face had flamed when I recalled how Claire had texted me photos and a video as proof of his affair. Despite his declarations, a year was a long time to cheat with someone, indisputably there must have been genuine emotion involved.

The car park was poorly lit and as I reversed into an empty space close to the coffee shop, I spotted Jake across the street. His outline was out-of-focus in the murk, but I'd recognise his tall, broad frame anywhere. A quick glance in the mirror, I applied some lipstick and exited the car. Something moved in the periphery of my vision. Was it a bush or a person hidden in the shadows? The streetlights were muted, the boundaries of the car park jagged, and I peered into the shade until my eyes ached. It was only a bush.

The heels of my boots broke the silence as I walked towards the coffee shop. I longed for summer, with short nights and balmy, sunny evenings. Winter's frost and dank skies depleted my energy. A burst of noise and light greeted me when I opened the café door. Jake had his back to me at a table near the faux fire and was so intent on his phone he didn't see me arrive. No sign yet of Bronagh, so we'd have time to chat before she interrupted.

I placed a hand on his shoulder and admired his firm muscles as he swivelled round. His hair was newly trimmed and I stopped myself from trailing my fingers through his short back and sides. Which was strange, as he seldom induced such desires. Uncovering Tom's latest subterfuge must have triggered the unfamiliar reaction.

'Hi.' His smile was wide and I took a vacant seat on the far side of the table from him.

'Hi,' I beamed back and skimmed the room, but recognised no faces. 'How are you?'

'Good.' He placed his phone on the table. 'Do you want to go ahead and order, or wait until Bronagh comes? She had to go to the supermarket, but won't be long.'

She could take as long as she wanted, but I smiled and we ordered coffee.

'Sorry I don't have much time, I'm meeting some mates later.' He really was young. *Mates.*

'No problem. It's good to catch up. How's work been today?' Not exactly subtle, but Bronagh's arrival would limit our intimacy.

Jake steepled his hands together. 'Uncomfortable if I'm honest. There's been a few issues this week and I get the impression staff are antsy.'

I nodded and carefully kept my face blank, although I was eager for him to continue.

He paused momentarily before saying, 'Bronagh's struggling a bit with her new role and so much has gone wrong already. Is there any chatter about it?'

He valued my opinion and it warmed my heart. I'd rehearsed my response to such a question over the past days, expecting him to ask. For Jake trusted me completely. When he had work problems, he ran them past me. Gradually, I'd become his confidante.

Slowly and with apparent reluctance, I said softly, 'Yes, I'm afraid there's been some chitchat. You know what they're like. The envelopes. The staff meeting. Was there anything else?'

He studied his coffee and took a sip before speaking. 'Money's gone missing from petty cash.'

'Bronagh can't be blamed for that,' I fired back.

'It's money paid by a patient for a private letter. Although we've been slowly changing the system to bank transfers, some of the old-school patients have been vocal in their objections, and insist on paying cash or by cheque.'

It was something he'd tried unsuccessfully to change. Most GP practices had already stopped cash payments, but our partners were disinclined to make bank transfers the sole method, and used the argument some patients could struggle with the technology. There was already some awkwardness at having to charge a fee for such letters.

Jake continued. 'Bronagh took the cash yesterday and swears she locked it away. But Jinty discovered it was missing from the safe this morning.'

Biding my time before replying, I swallowed a mouthful of coffee. 'Everyone knows where the key is kept. Anyone could have taken the money.'

He nodded. 'I know, and you know, but the finger of blame is being pointed firmly at Bronagh and she's upset.'

A flurry of activity at the entrance broke through our chat and I glanced up. Bronagh. I raised my hand in a wave to warn Jake and his head pivoted around. A quick smile accompanied by a blush. Poor Jake. He was caught between a rock and a hard place.

'Sorry I'm late.' She arrived in a flash of colour and cold air, unwrapped her long red scarf and heaved the chair beside Jake's out from under the table. The feet scraped on the tiles and I flinched. Seemingly oblivious, she sat down and waved the waitress over. She gripped her vape, which appeared to be surgically attached to her hand when out of work. Her tone irked me and I gave her a hard smile.

'I'd forgotten to collect my new EpiPen from the pharmacy, and then I had to buy some wine. I'm going to see mates later.' That word again. It made me feel ninety, not fifty. 'I'm starving. Do either of you want anything? What do muffins do you have?' she asked the waitress when Jake and I shook our heads.

The waitress suggested she go up to the counter and see for herself, and she flicked her hair, tutted and sauntered up to the counter, hips swinging. Jake excused himself to use the bathroom and I watched her crossly. She gesticulated and pointed at the display as her loud voice rang around the coffee shop proclaiming the importance of knowing exactly what ingredients were in each muffin.

A commotion beside our table diverted me. Bronagh's scarf trailed across the floor and had looped around the wheels of a pram. I rose to help the frazzled mum disentangle it and as I straightened up, saw Bronagh's expensive handbag had got caught in the chair leg.

It took me a couple of minutes to sort it all out, as Bronagh finally selected her muffin and marched back to the table. Embarrassment grew as she eyed her bag, which I still nursed on my knee.

An uncomfortable laugh as I handed it over to her. 'Sorry, your scarf got snarled in a pram's wheels and your lovely bag got caught in the chair leg. I was worried it would get damaged.'

'Thanks.' Dismissively she set it on the floor again. 'The waitress was useless. She had to ask someone else the ingredients of the muffins and took ages to find out if any of them contained peanuts. I'm highly allergic, you know.'

As she lectured us about it ten times every day, there was no chance I was ignorant. Thankfully Jake reappeared and the conversation continued in fits and starts. There was no real reason for Bronagh to have been invited, and my tolerance plummeted.

She blowed about her new job and neatly sidestepped my question about how she was getting on. There was no mention of the missing money, but instead she blethered on about responsibility and I nodded in response. Jake was quiet and I wondered if he was sorry he'd included her. Perhaps he thought with her new role, she'd appreciate being asked.

When she began a monologue about booking a holiday to Tenerife, I stopped listening and devised an excuse to leave. Then Jake glanced at me and cleared his throat. Bronagh dithered and they exchanged a look I couldn't decipher. Uncharacteristically nervous, she toyed with her vape.

'Actually there was a reason Bronagh wanted to come along today.' She blushed, which was a first, I'd supposed her incapable of it. 'Something else has happened which only we know about. An email was sent to both of us, with a compromising photo attached.' He reddened as he plucked at the cuff of his shirt.

'What do you mean, a compromising photo?' I kept my tone low.

Bronagh reached into her bag and withdrew a mobile. It was a new Samsung Galaxy Flip, ostentatious and flashy like its owner. 'Do you want to see?' she asked with a grimace.

'I'd rather not.'

Her eyes were downcast. 'I'd prefer not to have to describe it.'

'Okay, let me see.' I held out my hand.

Her nose wrinkled as she handed it over.

I stared at the photo. 'Who sent this? Who else was it sent to? Who would do this?' The questions shot from me and I involuntarily rubbed my temple.

Jake was gentle. 'Me and Bronagh were the sole recipients. When I replied to the email, it bounced back as the email address doesn't exist. Obviously it's not a photo we'd want either colleagues or patients to see. Unfortunately they threatened to forward it to other practice staff. We wanted to chat it through with you privately.' He was a good friend and I was touched by his consideration.

Bronagh sighed, muffin forgotten. I laced my fingers together on the table and collected my thoughts, though my heart pounded and head throbbed. They sat across from me and listened intently. Jake nodded once or twice, and Bronagh remained uncommonly silent.

'Should the police be informed?' Bronagh was pale under her fake tan.

'Perhaps. I don't know. What do you think?'

We talked it over, back and forward, until the coffee cooled and we were the last ones in the coffee shop.

Once we had a plan of action, I needed air. To get away from the confines of the room. We said our goodbyes and I crossed the car park to the seclusion of my car. Strangely my eyes didn't roam and my mind didn't career madly around. I was intent and focused.

Things had stepped up a gear.

CHAPTER EIGHTEEN

With the engine running and the heater chugging warm air over me, I sat alone in the car. Goosebumps sprinkled my skin as damp fingers crept up my spine. Across the car park Jake and Bronagh walked along the footpath, heads together. She petite and blonde. Him tall and dark. I tracked them until they rounded a corner and disappeared from sight.

The mortifying photo on Bronagh's phone seared my eyelids. It looked to have been taken after excessive alcohol had been drunk. Huddled in the car, I recalled a frigid December evening in Belfast. The practice Christmas night out at the city centre Laganside Hotel. Sequins, sparkles and stilettos. Turkey and ham. Copious bottles of bubbly and the lights down low as the DJ began to play.

It was the week after I'd learned of Tom's affair. My heart was broken, my pride shredded. I shouldn't have gone, but had to maintain the pretence my life was picture-perfect. To conceal the defects beneath layers of lies. I'd wanted to wound Tom in the way he'd taken a knife and plunged it into me.

The music had slowed and one by one my colleagues had waved goodbye. And still I stayed to flirt with a man half my age at the bar, consolation for my splintered heart. Sadness oozed from me as strangers revelled nearby.

The explicit image taunted me. A drunken kiss on the neck, the man's face hidden. Barely concealed inner thighs caressed by a large hand, the dress short and tight. Mouth parted, gaze unfocused, facing the camera.

A horn honked and disrupted my recollections. The car was now too warm and heat spread across my face. I opened the window to gasp fresh air, put the car into gear and drove off, mind racing.

The email had been creepy, there was no question of it. Possibly the police would be informed. A sense of impending doom crashed over me and my palms became slick on the steering wheel. My throat jammed at the injustice of it all.

Rather than go straight home, I took a detour in an attempt to cure my anxiety. The evening lay before me; empty, lonely. Tom would be back tomorrow and we would recommence our dance of betrayal. Oddly my quiet house held no appeal as my mobile illuminated with alert after alert. I should make the most of my obligation-free time. No children to mind. No husband to consider. I now wished I hadn't refused the meal out with the girls, but I'd presumed I would be busy with Jake.

I should think of this night on my own as a bonus, not a calamity.

Unexpectedly ravenous, I slunk into the nearest chippy and treated myself to fish and chips. The smell of vinegar was tantalising as I devoured the greasy takeaway in the car. It would linger for days, a reminder of my temporary loss of control. It was indulgent. Irresponsible. Around me the town was waking up from its early evening stupor. A nightlife I'd forgotten existed emerged from side streets and along pavements.

The light drizzle ignored, teenagers tottered in stilettos, and skirts barely covered their buttocks. Fresh-faced boys with fake IDs bought alcohol to take to 'pres' at a friend's house. Sad-faced forty-somethings fell out of a sports bar. Vibrant and noisy, this world materialised every Friday night, when I was shielded in my suburban home amongst velvet furnishings and Jo Malone candles. Secluded in my car, I stayed out much later than expected, and enjoyed watching the town buzz around me.

The mundanity of my life was blisteringly apparent as a young couple threaded their way through the crowd. Hands entwined, passion brightened their faces. That life was the one I used to live, before middle age and an unfaithful husband sapped me. When parenting and responsibilities had engrained their stories across my face.

Most of the time I relished my life.

On nights like this, regrets multiplied.

Miserably I drove away from my sheltered parking space and along the jet-black lanes. My silent home greeted me, no garish lights, no vivacious voices. I'd been so preoccupied, I'd forgotten to phone Tom, and he in turn hadn't rung me. My daughters sent a cursory text once in a while, and unforeseen longing for company floored me.

Before I closed the curtains at the front door, I glanced outside. Standing under the lamp post outside Annie's house, was a solitary figure. Too far away to see their face. Too indistinct to reveal if it was a man or woman. Bundled up in winter clothes, they were squat and bulky. I was afraid to blink as they walked down the far side of the street, until hidden from view.

I almost dashed outside after them, but it was too dark and too risky. Instead I trudged upstairs and Keiko's amber eyes regarded me from the bed, reflecting the landing light. Her purrs broke the silence when I stroked her soft head. She was naturally nocturnal, but the rain was relentless and my bed lonesome. I allowed her to stay in my room and her rhythmic purrs soothed my rattled nerves.

Next morning, I slept late and when I woke the email was foremost in my mind. Keiko had jumped off the bed in the early hours and I was alone. Automatically I reached for my phone and retrieved it from where it had charged overnight on the bedside table. A rash of notifications, which I hungrily scrolled through.

One curt message from Tom. His flight was delayed and he'd be later home than expected.

Claire had drunk texted again; pleading, begging, desolate. I deleted it and wondered again if I should block her. Yet again, I found I couldn't. A jolt of remorse before I moved on.

Comments on Instagram which caused my stomach to knot.

An alert to notify me my latest purchase had been dispatched.

The long day stretched out before me. Impetuously I opted to drive into Belfast to fill the meaningless hours ahead. Guilty about our disastrous lunch at my parents', I messaged Alex to suggest we meet. Two grey ticks showed it had been delivered, no blue ticks to let me know it had been read.

My daughters' lives were fulfilled and busy. Flora was at university on the North Coast and worked part time in a popular hotel. Alex led a hedonistic student life before the reality of a full-time job. An unexpected poignancy pricked me. They didn't need me anymore. No one needed me.

I wished my relationship with my mother was better.

I yearned for a happy marriage.

Last night I'd been enticed by a more exciting life. This morning, I wanted to submerge myself under the bedclothes, eat chocolate and watch television, but I must rise, paste on a smile and tackle my demons. *Lounging about in bed is a self-indulgence for the lazy and boring.* Mum's words resonated from decades ago. Contemplating her for even the briefest moment eroded any happiness or pride I had. Over the years I'd learned to compartmentalise my life.

Daughter meant failure.

Mum brought joy.

Doctor equalled satisfaction.

Wife. There were many words I associated with *wife.* Inadequate. Lacking. Second best. Failure. That word again, which ripped and stung and tore strips off me.

Furious with my maudlin ruminating, I threw back the duvet and leapt out of bed. I'd have breakfast then go into the city. Rather than a lonesome, drab day, I'd immerse myself in things I enjoyed.

My positivity lasted until after my shower and while I dressed. As dried my hair at the dressing table, the recollection of Tom's iPad poked and prodded. It was too tempting to ignore. I found myself on my knees again and hauled it from its hiding place.

Although I searched methodically, there was nothing new. No unread messages. No incriminating photos. His DMs were old ones. Satisfied my reservations were unfounded, I stuck it back into its hidey-hole, and headed downstairs.

Over breakfast, I browsed social media. Laura had posted a photo from the evening before on Facebook. The night had gone ahead without me, as if I was irrelevant. Three laughing faces, busy restaurant in the background. Plates loaded with delicious food, chic décor and smart clothes.

Laura, grinning as she raised a glass of wine.

Kate, face scrunched up.

Annie, curls bouncing and head thrown back as she laughed at something unknown.

While I'd kept out of sight in the shadows, my friends had spent time together. Despondency lugged me down. I'd chosen poorly. My life had shrunk to such an extent, I actively missed out on so much. It was time I focused on the good and forgot the bad. Put my problems to one side and fully participate in life again.

Then a question popped into my head. *Who'd taken the photo?*

I recoiled when I noticed the fourth plate of food and a glass of red wine. Had they invited Miranda?

Surely not. I thumped out a private message to Laura and anxiously chewed my nail. Three rolling dots then the response pinged.

> Miranda was there. Unbelievably Kate invited her and only told me ten minutes before the taxi arrived!

I was gratified she ended the text with a furious face emoji. Laura did like a good emoji and I laughed. Feeling much less regretful I'd missed out, and by default skipped Miranda, I asked how she'd been.

> Total nightmare. Can't hold her drink and encouraged Kate to drink too much. She was downright paralytic at the end of the night. Going to have to speak to Kate about her.

We texted back and forward for a while, and I felt so much better for it.

It was time I dragged myself from my navel gazing and re-entered real life.

Then my phone pinged with an alert and all good intentions flew out the window.

CHAPTER NINETEEN

After the rain, the air was crisp, and I inhaled deeply. Low lying cloud veiled the tops of the Antrim Hills and my attention flicked to the bottom of the back garden. Bare trees and open fields beyond. No insubstantial shadows nor unwanted stares. The grass was wet and water dripped from the conservatory roof onto the paving slabs below. I wrapped my padded coat around me and set off on foot. There was something I needed to do before my excursion into Belfast.

The street was deserted except for two young boys who zipped past on bikes and whooped loudly. Annie's windows were blank, Matt's car missing from the drive. He was probably rowing with his club on the Lagan. I walked down the path towards Kate's house. Although it was early, I wanted to make a point. Tired of procrastinating about Miranda, I was going to call her behaviour out. Nicely. In a passive-aggressive manner which brooked no argument.

With a glance at Laura's silent house, I turned onto Kate and David's driveway and squeezed past Kate's car. It had been abandoned at an angle beside the neglected flower bed. There was a huge indentation on the passenger door, along with several gouges. Possibly her son Luke had driven into something as he'd recently passed his driving test. The driveway was empty where David's car was usually parked.

The downstairs curtains were tightly closed, and there was no sign of life. Nevertheless I rang the bell. No answer. I pressed again. Eventually Kate's youngest daughter Sophie glared at me through the glass. I raised my eyebrows and eyeballed her expectantly. Rather than open the door, she bolted away and a muffled shout reached me.

Good manners cost nothing, but Kate always labelled her the problem child.

Several minutes passed and irritation grew as I swithered between standing with my finger on the bell and leaving. When no one reappeared, I had no choice but to walk away. I was certain Kate was home, but for some reason refused to come to the door. I'd have to send her a message instead, although tone could always be mistaken in a text.

The walk home calmed me, as I assured myself she was sleeping off her bender and it had been foolish to call so early in the day. I reapplied my lipstick in the mirror, lifted my bag from the table and set off. A quick glance confirmed the curtains in Miranda's house were still closed. Meanly I hoped she had a thumping headache and queasy stomach.

On my drive into the city, I ruminated about Miranda. Although my inherent dislike of her was a tad irrational, she set my teeth on edge. Kate had let it slip she'd been estranged from her adult daughter for several years, though she didn't know the reason. Otherwise, Miranda was divorced, didn't work and had a tendency to overstep boundaries. I couldn't quite put my finger on what annoyed me.

Envy? Definitely. I could spot it a mile off.

Dishonesty? Likely.

That she was a gossipmonger was undeniable.

Green fields were replaced by houses and businesses as I drove alongside Belfast Lough. High above the road to my right was Napoleon's Nose, shrouded by wispy fog. Miranda was forgotten, replaced by the cryptic Insta commentator *C_Wood*. I'd have to carefully explore Tom's iPad to learn more about them.

As usual the West Link was snarled with traffic, stop-start, with tooting horns and red lights. At last I exited onto the mobbed city roads which required my full concentration, with their many one-way streets and congestion. Here rows of red-bricked student houses sat cheek to jowl with slick apartments rented by young professionals. Coffee shops, boutiques and high-end jewellery shops nestled beside charity shops and takeaways.

Cars were parked in every available space, nose to tail, an inch between bumpers. Wheelie bins clogged the pavements, interspersed with toppling piles of rubbish. Broken gates and chipped paint, discarded beer bottles and overgrown gardens. Fast food wrappers drifted in the gentle breeze. Up and down I drove, losing patience, until I found a space and reverse parked haphazardly. I sat on, glad to have parked but in no hurry to leave the warmth of the car.

Soft eighties rock thrummed from the radio as I visualised Miranda again. She'd tried to barge her way into our group, although unwelcome. We'd not exactly been friendly, but she was brazenly unperturbed. I acknowledged that possibly I was too inflexible to accept a newcomer.

A volley of noise erupted as the door of a nearby house opened and a group of people spilled out. Miranda was forgotten as I hunched lower on the seat. My car was out of place amongst the scratched and dented, and I wanted to draw no attention to it.

Head down, I checked my phone, but there was still no

response from Alex to my offer of lunch. It struck me how ridiculous I'd been driving to within a few streets of her student digs, but in my loneliness, it had seemed like a good idea. If she replied I could legitimately claim to have been window-shopping the new season's fashions in *Oliver Bonas* or *Please Don't Tell* rather than somewhat sadly hoping for a catch-up.

Meantime the group had walked in the opposite direction from my car and made their way along the pavement. Once they were out of sight, I exited into the pong of exhaust fumes, overflowing bins and spilt beer. Certain the car was safely locked, I made my way onto the lively Lisburn Road.

My attention was taken by a window display and I temporarily forgot Alex's lack of reply and my cares. Instead I absorbed the silks and the pleather, and treated myself to a new burgundy crossbody bag. My phone bleeped in my pocket and as I stepped out into the sunlight, I read the message.

Alex would love to meet me.

My heart lifted for I was inordinately pleased. After Sunday lunch with my parents I'd agonised she was still mad and was avoiding me. Happily I suggested brunch in one of her favourite cafés in an hour's time, which allowed me plenty of time to shop and her to get out of bed.

I was captivated by the jewellery section in *Oliver Bonas* when I detected someone hovering nearby. An insipid middle-aged blonde openly inspected me. She wore a battered wax jacket and black Doc Martens. Nondescript apart from the challenge in her pale blue scowl. Her boots squeaked as she marched over and my hackles rose, though I didn't recognise her. An elusive memory of those eyes and the tight sneer. She'd invaded my personal space, but I couldn't step back without knocking into a cabinet. Her snarl was unashamed, pupils dilated.

'Well, well, well, if it isn't Doctor Harris.' The moment she spoke, my skin tingled at the abrasive, cruel voice. 'We missed you at the school reunion. Such a shame you couldn't make it. Or were you too important to make it?' Her head tilted to the side as the words slithered out.

Elodie Brooks. A blast from my past.

She'd been the leader of the pack. The queen bee, who I'd feared and admired in equal measure. Nausea swilled in my gut. It had been years since I'd seen her as I'd steered clear of any contact since our time at university. Memories of our school days glittered and blurred my vision. I blinked them away, drew myself up to my full height and coolly appraised this deceptively bland personification of poison.

Her lizard smile widened and years of loathing spewed out. She'd never forgiven me for moving on at Queens University. Medical students had naturally garnered respect and her payback had been vicious.

I had seconds to react. If I showed weakness, she'd launch herself for the jugular. Bullies generally backed down when confronted head-on. I plumbed the depths of my courage and fixed a haughty smile. My tone was caustic. 'Elodie. I didn't recognise you. I see you get your blonde from a bottle these days. Are those the same DMs you wore as a teenager?'

The smile wavered before she recovered.

'I'd recognise you anywhere. The same conceited know-it-all with a few more wrinkles and lines.'

'Well, we're fifty now. Wrinkles are to be welcomed except in our clothes.' I copied the slow inspection she'd subjected me to a few minutes ago and regained my composure. She wouldn't needle me further.

'Anyway, it's been delightful, but I'm meeting my daughter for brunch. On your own, are you?'

Before she could answer, I mustered my dignity and aimed for the exit. My leg banged against a table but I kept going, keen to put space between her and me. Head down, I tore away from the shop and our chequered history.

How could she have this effect still? Blindly I sped up the street, each step putting distance between us. Lost in the past, I almost missed the café where I was due to meet Alex. With quaking hands I wrenched open the door and scurried as far from the entrance as possible. A table was free at the very back, and I lowered myself onto the banquette seat. I set my bags on the floor and laced my fingers together to stop them shaking.

My emotions charged around until I got them under control. It was incredible how a confrontation with her could distress me. As they settled, I glanced around the café. It was long and narrow, with an adjacent room. Busy and popular with both students and shoppers, I was lucky a table had been free. Laughter and chatter from a group in the next room filtered through. An older couple sipped coffee and read the papers in silence. A young mum spoon-fed a toddler in a highchair and stared at her mobile.

A normal, unremarkable Saturday morning for those who'd not been goaded by the school bully. Claire sprang to mind and I shuddered. Would I ever recover from her deception? Did she feel she'd evened the score? Or was there more doom and gloom ahead?

The appearance of Alex saved me from falling into the pit of self-loathing. She barrelled through the door in a flaming ball of brilliance, though she was pale. Her presence cheered me, I hugged her tightly and savoured both her youth and her perfume.

When I went up to the counter to order lunch, I sensed a pair of eyes on me, but when I swung round, no one was looking in my direction. Everyone was absorbed by their phones or in conversation.

I returned to Alex and quickly forgot all about it.

CHAPTER TWENTY

I remained keyed up after my run-in with Elodie and on the drive home from the city it replayed again and again. Now I was courageous and brave, but then had been very different. She reminded me of a time long ago when I'd been desperate to fit in, to be included in the popular gang. Even at the expense of others, I'd been prepared to do whatever was needed. Remorse pricked me. I usually kept my mind firmly away from those years and my abysmal behaviour.

She'd knocked the wind out of my sails, and when I reached Kate's house, I'd no heart to confront her. It would keep for another day. When I opened my own front door Keiko rubbed against my ankles before shooting outside. A night indoors and she was ready to prowl in the fields. I switched on the coffee machine, shrugged off my coat and unpackaged my new handbag.

It was a beauty with multiple pockets and zipped compartments. The ultimate everyday bag. Meticulously I transferred everything into it from my old one, then glanced at my phone. One missed call from Tom. I played his voicemail, as I prepared the coffee. He'd be home around seven, would bring a takeaway and was looking forward to seeing me. He missed me.

My breath caught, for his voicemails were usually practical and short. Was it a sign of a guilt? I tore upstairs with my coffee, grabbed his iPad and systematically scrolled through it, confident there would be something incriminating. A photo. A message. An email.

But there was nothing suspicious at all.

My pulse raced as though I'd run ten miles. I hunkered back. The situation was driving me crazy. The iPad slipped onto the carpet as I buried my head in my hands. How was I ever going to move past this?

Could I ever truly move past it?

The doorbell chimed and I jumped. Too deep in misery to see anyone, I would've ignored it, but it rang again. Someone was persistent and wouldn't leave until I'd answered it. Defeated, I thrust the iPad carelessly back into its hiding place, swiped my face and checked myself in the mirror. Mascara had left faint trails of black and I rubbed them with a wet finger. The bell rang once more, so I trudged downstairs.

Kate had her back to the door, hands in pockets, pink woolly hat hiding her black hair.

I opened the door and she swung around.

'Hi.' Her voice was raspy, as though she'd smoked fifty a day for thirty years. She cleared her throat and tried again. 'Sorry I missed you this morning, Sophie only told me a wee while ago you'd called.'

'Come in,' I waved her in out of the cold, and offered coffee. She nodded in reply. Kate was usually ebullient, now she was strikingly subdued. A spark of disquiet as this was out of character. Silently she followed at my heels into the kitchen.

'Is everything okay?' I reached for a mug as she whipped off her hat and ran a hand through her hair.

A grimace. 'No, not really.' She unzipped her coat. 'I need some advice.' It was dropped onto the table along with her hat.

Coffee made, I handed her the mug and suggested we move into the sitting room.

'Would you mind if we sat at the back of the house?' She jerked her head towards the conservatory.

'Of course, not a problem.' Now I was apprehensive, for she was a pale shadow of herself.

She flagged onto one end of the sofa and I took the armchair. The sky outside was a thunderous grey, so I flicked on a floor lamp. It cast a shadow over Kate and drained her completely of colour. She licked her lips before speaking.

'I've had a terrible row with David and he hasn't come home. He's furious with me and I don't know where he's at. He's not answering my calls or texts. The kids are really angry and blame me.' It flooded out in noise and bluster, like a dam bursting. Snot bubbled and tears streamed down her cheeks.

Stunned by her admission, I offered the box of tissues from the side table. She sniffed and blew her nose, eyes wet and shoulders bowed. I switched into GP mode, familiar with encouraging the deepest, darkest fears from frightened patients.

'Do you want to tell me what happened? If you don't feel up to it, then you don't have to.'

'He says I'm drinking too much and he's worried about me.' The words were muffled, spoken to her chest. The hankie was back at her nose as she snuffled unhappily.

My training kicked in, so I waited, certain there was more.

A lengthy pause before she continued, 'He doesn't like Miranda and says she's a bad influence. That she's always hanging around the house with a bottle of wine in her hand. The last straw was when he got up this morning and she was asleep on the sofa in the living room.'

'The sofa in your living room?' I was dumbstruck. 'Why didn't she go home when you got back last night?'

'I wanted her to, but she insisted on coming in when the taxi dropped us off. Laura and Annie probably assumed she'd walked down to her own house, but she was determined. Then we finished a bottle of white I'd opened before we went out. She fell asleep and it was easier to leave her. I thought I'd be up in time to get her out before anyone woke this morning, but I slept in.' Her voice petered out.

'What happened this morning?' I stamped down on my anger towards Miranda.

'David found her and came storming upstairs. He made me go down and wake her. She was livid, I could tell by her face. When she left she slammed the door and then all hell broke loose. David shouted at me, took his keys and drove off.'

There was more to it than a simple argument; this had been the behaviour of a man at the end of his tether. I wasn't sure what Kate expected of me, but I had to voice my uneasiness about Miranda, especially now.

'I'm sure David will come home when he calms down, but this isn't like him. What he said about Miranda, well, I can see how he'd be annoyed if she's in your house a lot.' I frowned and abruptly changed the subject. 'Are you concerned about how much alcohol you're drinking?'

She rubbed her nose with the tissue. 'Not really. David's concerned about how much alcohol I'm drinking, but that's because he rarely touches the stuff. He thinks most people are raging alcoholics.'

'When one spouse doesn't drink much, it can seem like nagging if they comment or complain.' I had to tread carefully and kept my voice conciliatory. 'However, you know it's because he's worried about you. If you do want to reduce how much you're drinking, I can recommend several resources which could help.'

The change in her was immediate and unmistakeable. Her expression shut down and she pursed her lips. White knuckles grasped the mug. I was afraid she'd up and leave, so helplessly changed tack. Miranda and her dubious influence on my friend had to be addressed, and I dived in. 'You and Miranda seem to have become very good friends very fast.'

She sniffed and nodded. I scrabbled around for a harmless remark.

'It's great you've friends outside Book Club, but the rest of us don't feel ready to replace Claire. With anyone, not specifically Miranda.'

'Miranda was determined I invite her to the Book Club at my house. I tried to say it was too soon after the Claire business, but she insisted there was no time like the present.'

This wrong-footed me, for I'd presumed it had been at Kate's invitation. 'Why was she so keen to join?'

Kate drank her coffee before she replied. 'I don't know. Though she's always asking about you all, how you are, what you're up to. Especially...' her voice died away.

'Especially?' I prompted when the silence became painful.

'Especially you and Tom.'

The hairs on the back of my neck stood up. 'Especially me and Tom? Why?'

'She admires you and asks where you buy your clothes or what your favourite restaurant is. Where you go on holiday.' She gave a short laugh. 'It's flattering actually, she never asks me where I buy my clothes.'

It was emphatically *not* flattering, it was disturbing. My nerve endings jangled a warning.

'I'd rather you don't invite her along to Book Club again.' My tone was firm. It was the tone I adopted when the girls behaved badly or Tom pushed me too far. 'I'm sure she means no harm, but I'm not in the right place for it at the minute. Tom and I are still finding our way after Claire.' I dropped my voice and added a quiver. 'And, Kate, you need to sort things out with David. If he's not happy about Miranda being in your house so often, you need to tell her to stay away. Fighting with David is a bad sign.'

She nodded as if she was listening and absorbing what I was saying, but her light had dimmed and I got the impression she was agreeing because it was the easy option.

When she left, a strong gust buffeted me as I stared into the street. Tom had cut the hedge back in early winter, and now I could see directly across to my neighbour's house. If I stretched far enough, I could make out the light from Miranda's upstairs room. Which meant she could see mine.

I hightailed it inside and banged the door. Kate's words swam around my head.

If I hadn't been so preoccupied and encouraged her to be more forthcoming.

If I'd been less selfish.

Would it have changed anything?

Tom arrived home from his work trip in a jovial mood and bearing gifts. A Chinese takeaway, Prosecco and a bottle of Daisy by Marc Jacobs. I smiled my thanks, and my brain hummed with questions and doubts. Why would he bring a present? Was it an olive branch? An expression of remorse?

It was exhausting always second-guessing his motives.

After we finished the Prosecco and ate the takeaway, he made love to me with a passion which did little to ease my distrust. Typically he rolled away afterwards and fell asleep quickly, while I remained awake for hours. The blinds were open a crack and I stared at his back in the moonlight. The defined muscles. The inch of tan line on the nape of his neck. Was there a graze beneath his shoulder blade? A long, slim red line made by a nail? Or something entirely coincidental?

When sleep came, I dreamt I was in the Belfast Gardens surrounded by a baying mob of teenagers. I jolted awake, skin damp. Tom's side of the bed was empty, the sheets cold and rumpled. The smell of bacon frying filled the house. Full-on repentance mode from Tom this weekend.

He was so very predictable. Gifts. Sex. Making breakfast

and bringing it to bed on a tray with a frothy coffee. Odds on he would suggest a walk by the ocean this afternoon.

My head was fuzzy through lack of sleep, but I propped myself against the headboard and reached for my phone. Footsteps on the stairs alerted me to him and I set it on the bedside table before I got a chance to examine it fully.

'Morning, sweetie. I've toasted you pancakes with bacon and maple syrup and made a frothy coffee.' He beamed as he set the tray on my lap and I muttered my thanks.

So far, as expected.

'We could go for a walk on Ballydunn beach later. It looks like a nice day.'

Full house! Bingo!

'Great idea, you're so caring.' He pecked me on the lips and disappeared into the en suite to shower, self-righteous smile in place.

As I chewed a piece of bacon, I was certain dirty dishes would be scattered around the worktops and fat from the frying pan would have japped everywhere. On the rare occasions Tom prepared food, he used multiple dishes, most utensils and then left me with the washing up.

But it was the thought which counted, and when I'd cleared my plate, contentment stirred. I headed downstairs to clean up long before Tom reappeared in the bedroom. He'd been right, the sky was a clear blue as far as the eye could see and although dew tipped the grass, it was a promising day for a walk.

Laura loved walking by the ocean and I missed her company. Although short notice, I texted to see if she and Sam would like to join us. As I waited for her answer, I made another coffee. Tom silently appeared at the kitchen door, which startled me. A tight T-shirt, bare feet in sliders and face tanned from his recent trip implied summer rather than midwinter.

'Oh, you surprised me!' I laughed at his serious face. 'What's up? You look very solemn.'

'Nothing. I just wondered where you were.' His expression clouded. 'You should shower if we're going for a walk.' I was flummoxed by his monotone. What could have happened between bringing me breakfast to bed and now?

'Yes, I'll go now. By the way, I texted Laura to see if she and Sam wanted to join us. Was that okay?' He nodded, but didn't answer and strode over to the coffee machine. I slid my phone into the pocket of my dressing gown and sipped my coffee. Back to me, his hands splayed on the counter.

Inexplicably nervous at his rigid stance, I walked over, circled his waist and asked what was wrong. I stroked his stomach until he relaxed against me and gripped my hands with his.

'Do you trust me?'

'Yes,' my voice said.

No, my mind squealed. *How could I?*

'We can't move forward if you don't trust me.'

'I'm trying, Tom, I'm really trying.'

He swung around and wrapped me in a tight hug without speaking, until my phone vibrated in my pocket and he loosened his hold. Then he cupped my chin and raised it, eyes boring into mine. 'I'm sorry for what I did. I'll never hurt you again, you have to believe me.'

'I know.' I kissed him full on the lips in the impression of normality, before I went upstairs, head crammed with blame and objections. But I couldn't face another row, more pleading apologies and tepid reassurances.

Naked, I stepped under the pounding water and wondered what had triggered his sudden change in mood. As I washed my hair, I mulled over our many secrets and how our marriage survived by the finest of threads.

Laura had replied when I got out of the shower.

> Sam and I would love to go for a walk and then something to eat at Jennings?

There was no way I'd have lunch in Jennings, but I'd persuade them to go somewhere else. After I replied, I called down to Tom to let him know they'd join us. His voice floated up to me and as I dried my hair, I pondered Laura's situation. She'd been widowed last September when James had a fatal heart attack after a bike ride. Rather than break down under the loss, she'd seized life with both hands and thrown caution to the wind.

Her resilience was admirable and I envied her a little. She hadn't succumbed to her grief, but had risen each morning and kept her suffering private. When she was with the Book Club she'd never wallowed or complained. Mortification flooded me.

Her husband was dead and she was thriving.

My husband was alive and well, and I was drowning in my own sea of misery.

'We're nearly out of milk,' he called up the stairs, 'so I'll nip to the village shop. Do we need anything else?'

I shouted we also needed bread. Unexciting, everyday married life which unquestionably conflicted with his exhilarating, unencumbered spells abroad with work.

The front door shut with a bang and I stared at my reflection in the dressing table mirror. Sad, shadowed eyes. Pallid skin. I clapped my cheeks gently to coax some colour and nibbled my lips. Marginally better.

Earlier I'd been able to ignore my mobile, but now it drew me to it, like a magnet. I sat on the edge of the bed and meticulously thumbed through it.

Kate thanked me for listening yesterday. No update on

whether David had come home, but it was safe to assume he had, though I imagined cross words had been exchanged.

Alex promised she'd visit soon, thanked me for lunch and I beamed to myself. Whatever grudge she'd harboured, had been forgiven. It reminded me to text Flora, as it'd been several days since she'd been in contact.

Up to date with everything, I dressed quickly, the lure of the iPad irresistible. I'd have a quick gander before Tom arrived home. A glance outside established he'd not driven up and I'd missed the growl of the engine, so I kneeled in the usual place and reached behind the dressing table.

But all I felt was the wall; no lead, no iPad.

I stretched a bit further and tracked the skirting board with my hand. Still nothing. Strange, for I didn't think I'd pushed it too far the last time. Frustratingly I couldn't feel the plug, so rose with a soft groan as my knees complained, and bent over the dressing table to check the socket.

It was empty.

I gasped aloud and wriggled back under the dressing table.

No plug. No lead. No iPad.

Tom must've moved it, there was no other explanation.

Had he rumbled me? Or maybe I hadn't tucked it back in the right place. Then I remembered Kate had rung the bell the last time I'd inspected it, and I'd carelessly pushed it into place before answering the door.

Rather than meticulously ensuring it was exactly as Tom had left it, I'd roughly shoved it behind the dressing table, and therefore part of it must have stuck out from the hiding place. My gut twisted.

If he guessed I'd found it, it would explain his offhand manner in the kitchen earlier. And now he'd hidden it somewhere else.

Futile sobs built and I slapped my hand hard on the dressing table.

My one method of checking up on my husband's messages had been ripped from me. I'd have to strip search this room when he next went on a work trip to locate its new hiding place.

Meanwhile I still had the GPS tracker, which would allow me to know where he was going – if not his communications. Minimally happier, it was apparent the time had come to use it. I'd hide it in the glovebox of his car when we drove up the coast later.

Really he gave me no option but to monitor him.

He'd made his choices and now had to accept the consequences.

No matter how harsh or bitter they may be.

CHAPTER TWENTY-TWO

I'd only met Sam a couple of times and was unsure how to describe him. 'Friend' was Laura's preference, so I opted for that, though their chemistry was potent and it was plain they were friends with benefits. She hadn't been around much, many nights when I walked past her house, it was empty with black windows, no glint of movement inside. Although Kate liked to stress it was 'too soon after James,' or Sam was nothing but a rebound relationship, I disagreed with her.

When she'd first introduced him to us last autumn, he seemed friendly and kind and Laura now exuded happiness. It was time to learn more about him, to form an objective opinion on whether he was good enough for my friend. We arranged to meet them at the beach car park in Ballydunn, a seaside village about an hour's drive from Castlebrook.

The sun was low in the sky as we zoomed up the coastal route and sunglasses shielded my eyes from the glare. As the car ate up the miles, Tom admitted he was a little uncomfortable about Sam, as he'd been good friends with James. My opinion was that he should know better than to throw stones at someone else's choices, and I was glad the glasses hid my real expression.

The discussion fizzled out and the radio filled the resulting silence.

We sped along the same snaking road we'd driven recently. Today slow-moving campervans trundled in a convoy in the opposite direction, no doubt aiming for Glenarm Harbour. Motorbikes whizzed past us, taking the racing line, risking blind bends. I rested my hand on Tom's thigh, his muscles firm and strong under my fingers.

'I've never walked on Ballydunn beach. What made you suggest it?' I ducked slightly to get a better view of the towering hills above us. Sheep peppered the landscape along with gorse and picturesque ruins. The question was innocent with no ulterior motive.

'I've heard good things about it.' The rough edge to his voice caused me to swivel around. His attention was firmly on the road, but a blush warmed his complexion.

'Have you been before?' I retracted my hand and asked as lightly as I could.

'Once a long time ago.' Abrupt to the point of rudeness, which made me imagine all sorts.

Silence descended and hung heavy between us for the remainder of the drive. My head was full of questions, but I bit my tongue to prevent them exploding out. Tom concentrated on the road ahead, and didn't speak or try to ease the now sulky atmosphere.

The village was an ancient settlement with one street lined by boxy whitewashed houses, a village store and thatched pub, The Stile and Donkey. Puffs of white smoke belched from the chimney and the smell of turf pervaded the air. Tom swung into the empty car park and killed the engine. Sand had blown over the low seawall and splattered the tarmac during a recent storm. I removed my sunglasses to soak it in.

A long golden beach curved around the bay and seaweed

sprinkled the sand as waves broke angrily on the shore. Seagulls dive-bombed the lone picnic table and to our right a lighthouse kept watch over a sheltered harbour. In the distance, the horizon was too indistinct to see Scotland, though on a clear day the Paps of Jura could be seen from the North Coast.

Thankfully Sam's beat-up Ford Focus drew alongside us within a few minutes, and I bottled-up my cynicism. There was no real reason to suspect Tom, but his manner was stilted and awkward, and my radar hissed a warning. This village and beach walk had not been as routine as he'd led me to believe.

Before we exited the car, he rested his hand on mine.

An audible sigh. 'Someone in work mentioned this was a lovely place for a walk and the pub did great scampi, which is your favourite. That was the reason I suggested a walk here, there was no hidden agenda. I promise.' Pale brown eyes regarded me intently as his eyelid flickered. Another lie.

I studied his large, tanned hand, plastic smile in place. 'It was a good idea. Thank you.' He visibly relaxed and waved over to Laura. When he opened the door a blast of wind caught it and he gasped theatrically. I adopted my brightest façade, then stepped out into the biting air.

Sam's chocolate Lab Nigel bounded out of the boot, tail wagging. He nosed over to me and nudged my hand, expecting treats. I giggled as he padded away when none materialised. The wind whistled and I was glad of my gloves and hat. It was almost the end of January and storms sweeping in from the west were commonplace.

As we set off towards the harbour, I invented a misplaced phone, and asked Tom for the car keys.

Smoothly I explained, 'I'd forget my head if it wasn't screwed on,' and walked back to the car. I eyed the three of them as they continued along the coastal path and opened the glove compartment. It was disappointingly bare, and contained only the handbook, a packet of wipes and a pair of leather gloves. If Tom rummaged around in there, he'd find the GPS tracker in no time. I didn't have long before questions were asked about my delay.

Eventually I dropped it into the passenger back seat pocket, and hoped he never delved in there. I remembered to lift my mobile from where I'd purposefully pushed it down the side of my seat, slammed the car door and jogged to catch them up.

Nigel gambolled far ahead and Laura tucked her arm companionably through mine. Tom and Sam walked together, discussing that great leveller of men, sport. Fishing boats bobbed about in the harbour as ripples chased across the water's surface.

'How's things?' The standard Northern Irish greeting.

'Good, what about you?' Laura tugged her fleecy hat over her ears.

'Great, never better.' She tilted her head and I frowned sadly. 'I'm okay. Not great, but okay.' Worried Tom would overhear, I changed the subject with the subtlety of a brick. 'How was the meal out with Miranda?'

As expected Laura took the bait, and launched into a full-on mini tirade, which continued all the way to the lighthouse and back to the beach. She grinned at herself. 'Sorry, she wound me up big time.'

I thought about not sharing how she'd slept on Kate's sofa, but couldn't stop myself and spilled the beans. Laura bit her lip at the news, as I also blabbed about Kate and David's row. It was done from a place of care, not gossip, though guilt panged at the broken confidence.

The sand was soft as we made our way towards a quaint stone cottage set back from the beach. Light glowed from one of the rooms and the garden ran down to a white picket fence, which bordered the beach. A fabulous location for a short break. Ominous rainclouds obstructed the sun just as we reached a cluster of black rocks at the end of the bay, and we turned back as the first spots of rain fell.

Nigel had calmed and trotted alongside Laura. Tom and Sam slowed to allow us to catch up and Sam reached for Laura's hand. Sparks flew and his smile was for her alone. A twinge of envy at their undisguised bliss in each other's company. Meanwhile Tom walked a couple feet from me, hands in pockets, head turned towards the cottage. A muscle twitched in his cheek and I doubted the beach recommendation had come from a colleague. The lie eddied precariously between us.

The rain quickly became a downpour and we dashed towards The Stile and Donkey. Breathless from the exertion, the rain stung like needles by the time we reached the shelter of the porch. We hurried inside and the waitress showed us to a table beside the fire, where peat burned in the hearth and smoke lazily drifted up the chimney. A worn-out Nigel made himself at home and curled up at Sam's feet, eyelids dropping. I glanced around the bar at the open beams and whitewashed walls, which were festooned with old memorabilia. Multiple donkeys glared forlornly out of grainy photos.

Tom gallantly offered to drive home, so Laura and I ordered a bottle of Pinot Gris, the men alcohol-free Guinness. Conversation never faltered and I realised early on how much I liked Sam. Intelligent eyes studied me from behind round glasses, as he spoke about the rewards and challenges of working in a hospice. We traded medic black humour and I was gratified when he got my jokes, which usually went straight over Tom's head.

One thing caused prickles of discomfort. Laura mentioned her son Robbie was in Scotland with his girlfriend Eva, Claire's daughter. As soon as she said it, she blushed and shifted her weight apprehensively from side to side.

Intentionally casual, I replied how nice, and moved the

conversation on. Tom stared at the fire, but I was impervious to his embarrassment. He deserved to be. The second glass of wine I'd consumed with my scampi and chunky chips had blurred my boundaries, and I was seduced by a third.

'You're a bad influence, Laura.' I grinned as we ordered two large glasses and toasted each other. With the orange glow from the fire, wine and hum of conversation around us, I realised how much I'd missed this. Friendship and laughter, meals out with friends. For the past few weeks I'd been insular and distracted. Claire's big reveal before Christmas and accompanying disruption had left me unanchored.

Sudden weariness swept through me and I fervently wished it was over, or at least the end was in sight. And yet, I had no say about the future. Rather than relax me further, the third glass of wine soured my stomach and I declined another. It was time to go home, shut the door and lock out the world.

The elements outside the pub were ferocious in their intensity. Rain was like stair rods and wind pummelled as soon as we stepped out of the protection of the pub porch. Its howl was matched by the roaring of the waves as they boomed on the shore.

I pulled on my hat and gloves and we made for the car park, but had to wait before crossing the street. A white convertible hurtled towards us, splashing through puddles, headlights on full. Tom jerked me back from the kerb before it reached us, to avoid the spray.

It drew level, and as it passed, a haggard face regarded us through the windscreen.

My stomach soured further.

Claire was the driver.

CHAPTER TWENTY-THREE

If Tom had recognised Claire in the speeding car through Ballydunn, he kept it to himself. On the drive home, he wordlessly concentrated on the road, and it festered between us. My erratic pulse finally settled into its usual rhythm once we reached the outskirts of Castlebrook. When he pulled into our driveway, I could contain myself no longer. Rain beat on the roof of the car and reduced the din in my head. Before we could exit the car, my pain spilled over.

'It was Claire who drove past us in Ballydunn.' The tremor in my voice was genuine.

'Aye, I know.' It was quiet, reserved.

'Why was she there?'

'I don't know.' His face was white. 'Honestly, I don't.'

'Every time you say honestly, you're telling a lie.' I spat it out and he shook his head in denial.

'I haven't spoken to her, or contacted her since the night at the Averie Hotel. I can't make you believe me, but it's true.'

'I'm tired of this. Sick of it. Each time I feel we're approaching semi-normal, something sets us back to square one.' The shrillness hurt my ears.

His voice rose. 'I'm sick and tired of it too. Sick of you watching me like a hawk. Tired of the revulsion in your face when you look at me. If you can't forgive me, maybe it's time I moved out.'

Sorrow bubbled so fast, it left me woozy. The very idea of life apart from Tom was overwhelming. Despite my agony, despite his cheating. So I did what I did best. I cried. I was adept at it, having honed my skill over the years. First I willed my eyes to well, allowed the tears to pool and roll dramatically down my cheeks. I didn't wipe them away, but focused on my trembling lower lip and dejected sobs.

It always worked. On Tom. My friends. My colleagues.

My parents were immune to it, therefore I'd stopped faking it in front of them years ago.

I could tell from the repetitive clenching and unclenching of his fists, Tom was fighting to resist my weeping, but was softening. One last throw of the dice.

'I'm sorry, Tom.' A soft moan. 'I don't know why I say these things. Of course I believe she hounded you, but it was still a shock to see her in Ballydunn the very day we were there.' The minute I spoke, I realised there were only two possible explanations.

She was familiar with the village and it was simple bad luck she was there at the same time as us.

The alternative was more sinister. She was following us.

I coughed several times to dislodge the obstacle in my throat. If I allowed myself to wonder why she was familiar with the village, it opened a huge can of worms. Such as, why was Tom familiar with it too? The memory of the secluded cottage on the shoreline burned my eyelids. This was not the time to untangle it further, it would keep for another time. When I was alone and could consider it sensibly.

'It was a shock for me too. Could she have been following

us?' The one thing I was afraid of. Then he laughed, as if it was a game and so absurd to be impossible. I too forced a laugh and his fingers unwrapped from the steering wheel. 'Come on, we'll have to run or we'll get soaked.'

Before he could pull the handle, I cupped his cheek and held it tight. Myriad emotions wrestled, but the most fundamental was sadness.

'I love you. This *thing* you had with Claire was one of the worst things I've had to contend with. But I made my choice, tough as it was. I don't want you to leave, but you must understand I can't forget it as easily as you.' I was rarely this honest with him. 'Sometimes I'm going to get annoyed, sometimes angry. You have to accept it.'

Now the tears were very real, no performance required. Lured by the luxury of honesty, I almost admitted I'd found his iPad, had resorted to using a tracker to keep tabs on him and was embroiled in something I could see no way out of, which kept me awake at night and wired during the day. A problem shared is a problem halved after all.

Then wisdom took hold and I said nothing. He leaned over and rested his forehead against mine. The hammering of the rain combined with the sound of our breathing, and the earth temporarily steadied.

'I can't keep apologising for my mistake.' The heady smell of his aftershave swathed me. 'I understand why you doubt me, but I was simply a fool who fell for her story. She used me, deliberately and maliciously used me for her own reasons and I was the eejit who should have said no, but gave in.' He fell back against the seat and for the first time, distress was written over his face.

I couldn't allow myself to dwell on it, so kissed him with more emotion than I had in weeks. Hands linked around his neck, I held him close for a few moments. When at last we pulled apart, the rain had eased.

'Shall we make a run for it?'

We sprinted for the front door and splodges of rain soaked my hair as Tom fumbled with the lock, but I didn't care. I'd moved on to a new phase of 'coping with my husband sleeping with my friend.' Now I'd hit rock-bottom, I could begin to crawl towards daylight.

Finally the door opened and he ushered me into the dry. We shook ourselves like dogs and deposited our coats in the hall cupboard. It was dusk and soon the streetlights would come on.

Tom called from the kitchen to ask if I wanted coffee or Prosecco.

'Coffee, please.' I'd had more than enough alcohol for one day. I sat on the bottom stair to remove my boots and with a groan, untied the laces and removed the first one. Outside a blaze of red caught my attention as it streaked from the side of the house towards the street.

There was no mistaking what it was.

Miranda.

My jaw dropped as she scrambled out of the drive and crossed the street without a backwards glance. Undoubtedly she assumed she'd sneaked away unobserved.

She must have been loitering in my back garden. How long had she been there? And more importantly, why had she been there?

I'd refused her suggestion of 'keeping an eye out' for Claire, so she couldn't use it as an excuse. Also Claire had been in Ballydunn, so nowhere near the village. I wondered what reason Miranda would've dreamt up if she'd been caught red-handed. Annoyance nipped at her poking around my garden when I was out.

Furious, I pulled off my other boot, hauled myself into

standing and strode into the kitchen. Tom scrolled through his phone at the breakfast bar. A frothy coffee sat nearby and he smiled when he heard me.

'That's for you, sweetie.' Then a frown. 'What's up?'

I paced over to him. 'You know Miranda, who lives in the last house on the left?' A nod. 'Well, Kate invited her to Book Club and I don't like her at all. She's crafty and has been hanging round, trying to wheedle herself in. Seems to think there's a vacancy and she's the right person to fill it.' I didn't want to highlight his indiscretion was the root of it all. 'She's just snuck out of our driveway, which means she was in our back garden when we were out.'

'But why?' Tom's brow wrinkled.

'I don't know and I'd taken my boot off so couldn't chase her.' I sighed heavily. 'We need to get a Ring doorbell and maybe CCTV.'

'Isn't that a bit over the top? There might be a good explanation for her being around the back. Have you checked? Maybe she left something?'

Surprisingly his calm answer had the opposite effect. I exploded over the frothy coffee and wiped Tom's sceptical expression from his face with a few well-chosen words.

'For feck sake there is absolutely no reason she should've been at the back of our house. We talked in the car for ages, she must have watched us, bided her time and waited till we were indoors before she raced out the front.'

'Okay.' He held his hands up. 'You're right. There's no plausible excuse. Do you want to check outside or do you want me to?' Relief coursed through me. He believed me. There was something distinctly odd about Miranda.

'Will you, please.'

I remained in the kitchen as he unlocked the back door and the outside light automatically illuminated the garden, suppressing the dark. He wandered down to the bottom of the lawn, where he faded into the shadows for a few minutes, then reappeared empty-handed. When he reached the patio, he directed a shake of the head at me, then squinted and bent down until the very top of his head was visible.

When he straightened up, he held a dirty plastic bag.

CHAPTER TWENTY-FOUR

Tom reluctantly carried the plastic bag indoors as if contaminated, carefully placed it on the floor of the conservatory and nudged it with his shoe. His face reflected my sentiment, bafflement mixed with aversion.

'Go on, open it,' I demanded finally, as curiosity battled with distaste.

He winced but agreed. 'Okay.'

Unenthusiastically he bent down, and with two fingers opened the bag and gaped in.

'It's some sort of tin. Should I take the lid off?' I nodded, intrigued. He reached in and withdrew a round lid. Laughter rang around the room.

'What's so funny?'

'You need to see for yourself.' He stepped away from the bag to give me space to look inside.

A bashed home-made cake decorated with slices of mint Aero.

At the side of the tin, a white envelope was visible, smeared with sticky chocolate icing. Horrified, yet perversely fascinated,

I extracted it from the bag and ripped it open. The card was flimsy and cheap, with a bunch of wishy-washy flowers on the front. Inside a few words were scrawled in vaguely familiar writing.

Sorry you missed our great night out in Belfast!
Hopefully you'll join us next time
Love,
Miranda xx

Tom was convulsed with laughter, and I too began to giggle. She was over-the-top and a bit dull, but from the safety of my kitchen and with Tom beside me, I was baffled by her, not afraid. If she got the slightest inkling of inclusion, we'd never get rid of her.

But it didn't make her dangerous.

'I'm not going to eat the cake, it could be laced with laxatives or something equally as unappealing.' I declared once my giggles had subsided.

'There's no way your new friend would be that vile, is there?'

'She's not my friend,' I growled and carried the bag outside, where I thrust both the cake and card into the wheelie bin. A creeping sense of uneasiness caused me to glance over my shoulder. I listened intently, but all I could hear was the distant rumble of traffic on the village bypass and the gurgling of the brook. The exterior light blinked off, leaving me in darkness. A flutter of discomfort as I returned indoors and shut the blinds, though it was barely half past four. A turn of the key and whatever, or whoever, was securely bolted out.

Tom disappeared to watch sport on the television in the sitting room, and I settled on the sofa in the conservatory with my coffee. I pinged a quick WhatsApp to Laura about Miranda's cake and the slightly unnerving card. She replied with a shocked emoji, then followed with a text.

> She's trying to buy your friendship. Run for the hills 😬

She'd summed it up in a nutshell. There was nothing especially menacing and I was well versed in sorry overtures of friendship. Most of them I ignored, having been deeply scarred by damaging relationships as a teenager. The Book Club had been enough for me. Five friends who shared everything. Even husbands as I'd learned to my cost.

Unwilling to sink into despair, I put negativity aside and surfed through social media. Relieved there was nothing worrisome, I checked Tom hadn't silently reappeared over my shoulder and opened the GPS tracker app on my phone. Sure enough, it showed Tom's car in our driveway. A tiny fizz of pleasure.

Then I remembered the missing iPad. Tom must've worked out I'd unearthed it, and secreted it in a different hiding place. I tapped my fingers together as I wondered where it could be concealed. In reality it could be anywhere in the house. Or the garage. Or his work. I'd have to hunt for it when he was next out.

Before that, I needed to access the settings on his mobile, to switch off tracking notifications. Energetically, I jumped up so fast I spilled my coffee. I cursed, patted my jeans with a damp towel and combed the kitchen.

No mobile.

Potentially Tom could have it with him in the sitting room and was at this very moment furtively messaging someone.

Heart in my mouth, I tiptoed to the door of the sitting room and quietly opened it. He was sprawled on the sofa and dozed in front of rugby on the TV. No sign of the phone in his hand or lying beside him. There was no way I could sidle over and explore his pockets without waking him.

Then it struck me. His coat pocket. There was a slim chance he'd slipped it in there, as I hadn't noticed it in the car or since we'd arrived home. As quietly as possible, I crept out to the cloakroom under the stairs and groped about in his pockets.

My fingers circled his phone in the inside pocket of his coat, and I jubilantly carried into the kitchen. There I leaned against the worktops, with a clear view to the sitting room door. If he woke and came to find me, I'd pop it into a drawer. Breath shallow, I entered his passcode and read his latest texts and emails.

Everything was as it should be.

Astonishingly, I was mildly disappointed. I'd expected something, anything, to be out of place. To verify he hadn't really changed, but was still the cheater he'd always been. Who told a lie with the same sincerity he told the truth. Swiftly I turned off tracking notifications and returned the phone to his coat pocket, not in the least guilty at my actions.

Really it was his fault. Broken trust and injured feelings had led to this situation. Irrespective of what he said or I'd asserted earlier, he shouldn't expect me to move on so quickly. Trust had to be earned. There was a long way to go before he earned mine back.

I lifted my handbag from the hook in the cloakroom, and slowly climbed the stairs, preoccupied. When I reached our bedroom, my spirits nosedived. There were so many hiding places for an iPad, and no way of searching when Tom could interrupt me at any moment.

It wasn't fair.

So I did what I always did when anxiety swelled, I made a phone call. Except this time, there was no answer, and it left me tetchier than ever. I rang Flora next, but it went to voicemail. Everyone was off having fun while I floundered in gloom.

Determined not to give in to the doldrums and with Tom sleeping, I changed into jeggings and a warmer jumper. I'd go for a walk around the village. Wrapped up within my hat and scarf, I'd be nondescript and even Miranda wouldn't recognise me. Suddenly I needed fresh air, the atmosphere in the house dense. Despite our walk on the beach earlier, I was too restless to settle.

Tomorrow I'd be back in work, confined to my desk for hours and at the mercy of patients and colleagues. A memory of the photo that had been sent to Jake and Bronagh blurred my vision. Downstairs I stuck my head around the sitting room door. Tom was awake and stared at his phone although rugby still played on the television.

'I'm going out for a walk.' My tone was light.

'Another walk?' He grinned at me, virtue personified.

'Yes, I feel cooped up in here.'

He thankfully didn't suggest accompanying me. If he came with me, he'd insist we rehash things again. In the utility room, I opted for my long padded jacket and deliberated which hat to wear. Once selected, I pulled on my boots and closed the door with a thud.

The rain had stopped and I gulped the cold air, as though starved of oxygen. I squinted up at the star-strewn sky, exhaled slowly and headed down the street. When I reached Miranda's house, there was no sign of life and a spasm of unexpected sympathy at her barren existence gripped me.

As hoped, calm surged through me as I walked the pavements in the semi-darkness and luxuriated in the silence.

On the still streets, no one could disturb me. An hour passed and my load lifted. It was then I could face returning home to Tom and his misplaced hurt.

But rather than turn onto my street, I continued along the country-bound road. There was no footpath here, just a narrow, grassy verge. I kept walking till I came to the gate of the field which ran behind our houses. This was where Kate thought she'd seen someone. Someone being Claire. I rested against it and strained to see into the field, knowing it was pointless, but unable to stop myself. If someone was lurking, they'd be camouflaged among the shadows, hidden in the shade. Even now observing me.

Mentally and physically I gave myself a shake. Kate was wrong. With a sigh, I turned for home. As soon as I set foot on my street it was as though a switch had been flipped. My senses tingled and I scanned around.

No one was about, but it didn't mean I was alone.

The exterior lights burnt brightly at Miranda's, which accentuated the overgrown garden and grimy paintwork. As usual her rusty car was parked in the same spot on the driveway, condensation on the windows. The curtains in the front room were slightly open, though I couldn't clearly see inside. Nerves thrummed and I jumped as a loud bang broke the hush. I swung around. Nothing stirred, nothing moved.

I scurried on with my head down as the sound of maniacal laughter harassed me, though rationally it was a figment of my imagination. The possibility I was losing my mind was real in that moment. Out of breath and with my pulse galloping, I reached the safety of my own garden, where I flattened myself against the sidewall to recover. Tom mustn't see my alarm.

He knew nothing about what haunted me or spurred me on.

It was my secret. One I had to keep at all costs, or my cosy life would be upended.

Once I was back in control, I moved from the dark into the light of my home.

Tomorrow would bring its own dilemmas and rewards.

Until then, I'd lie beside my untrustworthy, duplicitous husband and pretend everything was good.

CHAPTER TWENTY-FIVE

The persistent beeping of the alarm clock ripped me from a pleasant dream on Monday morning. Pale slivers of dawn peeped around the blinds as I reached over to silence it: 7am in the middle of winter held none of the promise of a brilliant summer day.

I sluggishly eased myself out of the warm bed and reached for my slippers. Tom snored with his back to me, as far from me as possible without actually falling out. This was a standby week, which meant he may be home or could have a short notice flight. He loved these weeks, when he had the house to himself and all manner of time on his hands. I was less enamoured, especially as I wanted him elsewhere so I could comb the place for his iPad.

I'd dressed in the half-light and quietly snuck downstairs, conscious I was running late. My bed had been too inviting, the air too chill and I'd dawdled under the duvet. Breakfast would be on-the-go, with coffee in my takeaway cup and a speedy slice of toast. I raised the blinds in the kitchen to fuzzy light. A thin layer of ice coated the world, making paths and roads slippery, increasing the chance of falls.

The front door shut with a soft thunk, and I nervously slid my way across the drive to the car. Although the air was freezing and dry, it was a welcome respite from the rain. Once safely seated, I turned the heating on full blast. Hatred for the ice mingled with nerves about the day. A strange sense of foreboding uncoiled, though there was no particular reason and I put it down to a combination of the peculiar morning light and treacherous conditions.

Shunning the ungritted country roads, I took the main route into Ballyrevy. A van had already mounted the pavement outside the village school, and was now abandoned with the hazards flashing. Fifteen long minutes later I pulled into the deserted surgery car park. I was later than usual, but had still arrived before most of my colleagues. Many of them lived rurally, meaning icy roads and late arrivals.

The surgery was warm and I gladly unwrapped my many layers in the staff room. Jinty was on her own, brimming with gossip about the weekend. She launched into a long-winded tale about her dog and I nodded along with one eye on the time. Ten minutes later we were joined by Bronagh, whose gloss was a little less shiny. Lipstick had bled into the fine lines around her lips and there was a white stain on her blouse, suspiciously like toothpaste.

'Morning.' A dry mutter.

'Morning.' My cheery reply appeared to fall on deaf ears. Jinty disappeared out to reception with an undisguised sneer.

Bronagh's glare at the back of her head was penetrating and I was glad not to be on the receiving end of it. When we were alone, her shoulders relaxed and she cracked a smile.

'Is everything all right?' I finished my coffee, not wanting to prolong our one-to-one time.

'Not really.' With a quick bow of the head Jinty's direction, she charged on. 'She's been criticising me again, although she thinks I don't know it's her. All the weird things that happened last week, I'm sure she's behind them.'

Before I answered, I swallowed the last of my coffee and wondered how I could feel dog-tired so early on a Monday morning. My tolerance for petty bitching was at an all-time low. 'What makes you say that?'

'Isn't it odd how much has gone wrong for me in a short space of time? Someone has it out for me and she's jealous of my promotion,' Bronagh grumbled.

A moment's silence as I pondered how to reply.

Honestly. *Everyone agrees your promotion was undeserved, not just Jinty.*

A half-truth. *You're not great at your job.*

A blatant lie which dodged the matter entirely. *Everyone makes mistakes, be kind to yourself.*

Obviously I opted for the lie.

'Thanks. I really appreciate your support.'

I smiled pleasantly and stood, excuse that I needed to check the post before my first patient already on my lips. At her next words though, I faltered. 'By the way, were you in Café Musgrave on the Lisburn Road on Saturday?' She nibbled on a talon and I noticed she'd removed the worst of her fake tan disaster from her fingers.

Tense, I worked to keep my voice indifferent. 'Yes, I met my daughter Alex there for a catch-up. How did you know?'

A blasé shrug. 'I thought it was you. I was with friends and would've said hello, but you were engrossed in conversation.'

'What a coincidence.' My tone was intentionally glib, to hide my agitation at being spotted. 'You should have come over to meet Alex.' I turned my back and washed the mug, as my breath got trapped in my lungs.

'Next time I will. Were you all right after our coffee on

Friday? About the email and the photo I mean.' She flipped from cocky to tentative in a heartbeat.

'Yes, though it was quite upsetting. Were you okay?'

A nod as she sucked her lower lip between her lip. When she spoke, her teeth were stained pink and I could have warned her, yet remained silent. 'It was a nasty surprise. I can't understand how anyone could do something so intrusive.' She expelled a loud breath.

'I know, I can't understand it either.' Unwilling to discuss it further, I said, 'You have lipstick on your teeth.' I squeezed her hand in a show of solidarity, knowing I would scrub mine clean at the sink in my room. 'I'd better go, it's almost nine, and half the staff still aren't here. It's going to be a busy morning.'

She turned to the mirror and I fled down the corridor to my room. There I soaped my hands, keen to wash the sickly smell of her perfume down the plughole. Once dried, I sank onto my chair and booted up the computer. The room smelled musty and I flung open the window to guzzle clean air.

As I waited to get online, I replayed the conversation with Bronagh. Something had jarred when she'd asked about the Lisburn Road on Saturday morning, She'd seen me and yet hadn't come to speak to me, or acknowledge me. The hairs on my arms stood up. She'd been cagey, then deflected attention to the photo.

A gentle knock at the door hauled me from my brooding. Jake opened it when I barked 'enter.' He smiled and I unthinkingly beamed back. His beard was neatly trimmed and he was unusually formal in a shirt and tie.

I swivelled around in my chair. 'Going somewhere posh today?' Usually he wore chinos and an open-necked shirt.

'I'm meeting my solicitor later.' His blush made me long to stroke a cool hand along his cheek. 'I wanted to catch up after our chat on Friday.'

'I hope you didn't lose any sleep over it.' Why was he seeing a solicitor?

He shook his head and ran a finger under his collar. Before he spoke, he cleared his throat. 'I've been wondering about everything that's happened over the past few weeks. I'm still of the opinion the police should be involved again.'

My stomach lurched violently. 'I'm not so sure. They weren't much help before and there's no way of knowing who's doing it. Everything is untraceable.'

He leaned against the door, hands in pockets, legs crossed at the ankles. 'Here's the thing. I know the emails and so on are untraceable, but there must be a way to track down who's sent the unwanted gifts. Then there's the comments on social media and the crank calls. I can't believe nothing can be traced.' Exasperation made his voice firm.

A few days before Christmas, I'd stayed late and he'd found me alone in the staff room. He'd taken one look at my face and I'd no choice but to show him an offensive comment on Facebook. Since then, the comments had continued on a regular basis.

Mechanically I rubbed my temple before speaking. 'If you're sure it's the right thing, then go ahead and speak to them. Is that why you're going to the solicitor?'

He grinned and I relaxed. It'd been a stupid question which he took with good grace. 'No, I'm going to see the solicitor about the house. Long story.' He made a show of looking at his watch and moved away with a smile. 'I'll see you later.'

His words hung in the room and my face ached from my obligatory smile. The repeated suggestion of informing the police made me faintly nauseous. I leaned forward, elbows propped up on the table as his words resounded around my mind. Another uncomfortable thought hammered and banged.

In some ways, Jake knew me better than my husband. He

cared how I was, whereas Tom cared first and foremost about himself. Unquestionably it was the wrong way of things.

A reliable husband's role was solace and security.

A friend shouldn't replace that.

And yet Jake looked after me better than any other person.

Than the Book Club. My family. My husband.

Jake was conscious of what was happening and guilt pricked me. Tom had no idea what I was coping with because I concealed everything from him.

Jake was purely a friend and I'd never wanted more from him. Our relationship had never crossed the line, nor would it. However I valued it as much as my marriage. In the same way I'd do anything, no matter how demeaning, to protect my marriage, I was prepared to do anything to protect my friendship with Jake.

I rarely corrected him when he was wrong, nor complained when he cancelled or put others before me. But to assume I didn't bruise when he let me down or fret when he failed me, was to assume incorrectly.

Nothing and no one would stain or corrupt my friendship with Jake.

Although they might try.

CHAPTER TWENTY-SIX

Monday morning sped past with no issues. Some patients cancelled, giving me unexpected free time to catch up with paperwork. Others had requested a phone call, and by lunchtime, I was less uptight and more on top of things. I'd been so flustered before I left home, I'd forgotten to bring my packed lunch with me. Irrespective of the icy footpaths, I'd have to venture to the corner shop to buy a sandwich.

Angry and hungry, or as Flora would say, *hangry*, I reached the front office to find Jinty had been on reception on her own all morning. Her colleague had phoned in to say she wouldn't make it in until the afternoon, and Bronagh had been 'too busy' to help. The words spat and sizzled as she slammed folders into the filing cabinet. The atmosphere between them deteriorated daily, and I'd no idea how to improve it. A lopsided stack of post was piled high on the desk below the pigeonholes, and Jinty pointedly raised her eyebrows at me, as if daring me to comment.

'Would you like me to sort this for you?' My growling stomach would have to wait.

Her face broke into wreaths of smiles and I bit down on my

grouchiness. Helping a colleague went a long way to a peaceful workplace. Bronagh strutted in as I was feeding the letters into the pigeonholes, but rather than offering help, she perched on the edge of a desk and launched into a speech about her hectic morning. Hostility flared from Jinty in such strong flames, I expected Bronagh to combust.

Soon though I'd reached the bottom of the pile and there was one package left. I inspected the company logo on the box, but it was one the surgery hadn't used before. The cardboard was ripped open with little consideration.

'What on earth this is?'

Jinty, Bronagh and I crowded around, hunger and animosity temporarily forgotten.

Out fell a calendar, with a sepia photo of Ballyrevy town hall on the front. A frown before opening it. Page after page of arty monochrome photos, some taken up close, many snapped from a distance. No people. All local places.

There was nothing to suggest when they'd been taken, or who'd been behind the camera.

The last page rang alarm bells, the intention to frighten explicit.

A photo of two cars parked outside Ballyrevy GP Practice.

Mine and Bronagh's. The parking spaces alongside were empty and there was no one around.

The calendar clattered onto the table and was followed by silence, broken by the ticking of the wall clock.

The photos were all places I'd been to recently.

Bronagh bit a long, plum nail as she watched me, face flaming. Jinty lifted the cardboard package, and groped about inside it. She withdrew an invoice, but there was no note and nothing to indicate who'd sent it.

Bronagh said throatily, 'This is so bizarre. Why have they done this?'

Unable to speak, I shrugged helplessly.

Jinty intervened. 'I'm going to ring the company and see who placed the order.'

She marched from the office, leaving Bronagh and me on our own. She toppled onto a chair and I swayed on my feet, before reaching out for the calendar. It was poor quality with cheap, shiny pages and I flicked through it slowly. Castlebrook Park. An empty street I knew to be Jake's. The pharmacy next to the practice. The coffee shop where we'd had coffee on Friday afternoon. The pages swam and I dropped it onto the desk.

Jinty bustled into back into the office, face matching her neat pink scarf. 'They refused to tell me much, except the order was placed by a B.R. Logan and the delivery address was here. No personal message from the seller or for the recipient, which they said isn't out of the ordinary.'

'There's no Logan working here.' Full marks for stating the obvious Bronagh. There was a B.R. though.

Bronagh Reeve.

I kept that knowledge to myself and dropped onto a hardbacked chair. The three of us looked at each other.

Ridges were etched on Jinty's face and her eyes flitted between us. 'What do you want to do?' Asked quietly.

A forced smile. 'What can I do? Like everything else that's been happening, it's weird, but too ambiguous to do anything about. It's simply a calendar of local places. Except for the one of the practice and our cars, there's nothing overly intimidating about it.'

My feet tapped on the floor until Bronagh pointedly stared at them. With an effort, I stopped.

'Jake needs to know.'

We nodded in unison. Another issue to lay at Jake's door. The three of us smiled grimly at each other until I offered to nip out to the corner shop and buy chocolate for everyone. A squeak of delight from Jinty and a wan smile of agreement from Bronagh.

I pulled on my coat and shuffled across the car park and down the street, greedily inhaling the air which was invigorating after the sickly scent of Bronagh's perfume in the confined office. Fortunately the footpaths had been gritted, and reduced the chance of falling. The morning played on a loop.

Each day now brought its own trials. At home. At work. There was never a reprieve from it.

When I reached the corner shop, it was a relief to step into the warmth. The soft prattle of voices greeted me, the weather and slippery paths the main topic of conversation. I selected prepacked sandwiches for myself and a chocolate cake for the team, then went up to the till. The bell tinkled at the entrance, but I didn't turn around. The assistant scanned the items and mumbled the total. Metal studded her ears, nose and eyebrow and she scratched a patch of eczema on her chin. Flakes of skin floated downwards and I removed my purchases before they were sprinkled with them. My already fragile stomach soured.

Outside the shop I bowed my head against the wind and tramped back towards the surgery. Jake would by now know about the calendar, and may even at this very minute be on the phone to the police to report more strange goings on at the local GP Practice. I entered through the staff door, and followed the hubbub of voices. Anyone who was in work had congregated in the staff room, and I set the cake on the counter. Smiles and thanks replaced troubled expressions. There was no sign of the calendar and Jinty whispered that Jake had removed it.

'What's he going to do about it?'

'He's going to consider it.' Which was code for *He didn't tell me*.

I'd tactfully raise the subject with him later. Bronagh inched up beside me and loudly announced she'd need to read the ingredients of the cake to ensure it didn't contain nuts and I clenched my teeth together. I'd already checked the ingredients and knew there were none, but she was understandably fastidious about it.

With lunch over I returned to my consulting room in an irritable frame of mind. There'd been no sign of Jake, so I still didn't know what he was going to do about the calendar. Nor had he enquired how I was feeling, which rankled. He'd let me down. Although loath to admit it to myself, this was increasingly common. It never crossed my mind that I expected too much from my friend, when he had other responsibilities and duties.

Grumpily I opened my patient list to see who was scheduled next.

I grimaced at the screen.

My day was going from bad to worse.

It was Miranda.

She wasn't my patient! Why had she inveigled her way onto my list? How had she done it? Before I called her through, I rang Jinty to find out. The phone rang again and again, and I was about to slam it down when she answered.

'What's Miranda Stevenson doing on my list?'

'Sorry, Vicky, she was insistent. Said she wouldn't see any other doctor.'

'She's not my patient,' I snapped, then massaged the back of my neck. It wasn't Jinty's fault. Patients didn't always see the doctor they were registered with. 'I'm sorry. She's a neighbour and I've seen her a couple of times socially so it would be unethical to treat her.'

'What would you like me to do?' Jinty was chastened and I hated myself for making her feel bad.

'It's okay. I'll call her through and explain it to her myself after I've familiarised myself with her notes. If she complains about a delay, tell her I've been unavoidably detained. And don't worry, I know she can be persistent.'

Remarkably I managed to refrain from bashing the phone down. Furious, I accessed Miranda's notes and gasped aloud when her frequent consultations and medications filled the screen. Although I'd known of her distant medical history, it was her more recent issues that unnerved me. I was so riveted that when a bird hit the window with an almighty blow, I uttered a loud yelp. My head shot up with such force, I jerked my neck.

Was it a bad omen?

In a cold sweat, I closed the computer and called her in.

CHAPTER TWENTY-SEVEN

I had a few moments to gather my nerve before Miranda reached my consulting room. Beads of sweat dotted my hairline as I wondered about the reason for her appointment, and I dabbed them with a tissue. She made me jittery, but I'd have to hide it.

Half a dozen raps on the door and I worked to keep my voice strong.

'Come in.'

Slowly the door opened and her head appeared, accompanied by a titter. 'Doctor Harris, so good of you to see me.' In she traipsed and sagged into the plastic chair at the end of my desk. She unzipped her red anorak and placed a worn navy handbag on the floor by her feet.

She smirked, her eyes sparkled with excitement and I feigned a polite smile. Indolently she crossed her legs and rested her hands in her lap. Forcing a confidence I didn't feel, I adopted my most professional manner; calm, clear and concise.

'I'm afraid you've had a wasted trip. Unfortunately, as we've occasionally seen each other socially, it would be unethical of me to treat you.'

Two vertical lines appeared between her brows. 'So you're saying because we're friends, you can't be my doctor.'

Her words enflamed, but the memory of her medical history made me guarded. As neutrally as possible, I replied, 'Rather than cancel your appointment completely, my colleague Doctor Corrie has a free slot in fifteen minutes, so you could see her then.'

'But it's you I came to see.' The smirk was gone, replaced by a curled lip. 'You never thanked me for the cake, which was very disappointing. I spent a lot of time on it and had to get the bus into Ballyrevy to get Aero bars as the village shop had sold out.'

My blood pressure rose. 'That was remiss of me and I apologise. Thank you for the cake.' Deciding attack was the best option, I repeated, 'Again, I'm sorry I can't treat you, but rules are rules.'

She rested back in the chair, uncrossed her legs and continued as if I hadn't spoken. 'It's Kate I wanted to see you about. I'm worried about her.'

My temper boiled and I held on to it with difficulty. 'This is my place of work, I can't discuss Kate now. I'm sure you appreciate the practice is very busy.'

'Actually, it's not. I overheard your receptionist say there's a number of cancellations today because of the ice.' The smirk was back. It was clear she wasn't going to leave till she was ready, regardless of what I said.

'Please, I'm at work. I can't chitchat about Kate here. I'm sorry, but this is neither the time nor the place.' How many times had I now apologised?

'I understand completely.' In one quick movement she stretched over the desk until her fingertips almost touched mine. 'I could come to your house later.' Rancid breath wafted over and instinctively I leaned away.

My gut had warned me about her, and now she handed me

a spade to dig my own hole. 'I'm afraid Tom is home this week and we like to do things together in the evening. Maybe another time.'

'I'm sure Tom wouldn't mind a friend calling to discuss her worries about Kate.'

'Why don't I pop over to yours after dinner?' The words were out before I engaged my brain, and could not now be retracted. She practically licked her lips with delight and leapt out of her chair. 'Great. See you about seven.'

Without a backwards glance, she strode out of the room with her handbag over her shoulder, anorak folded over her arm. My mind spun. What the hell had just happened? No wonder poor Kate had found herself railroaded about the couch issue.

A vicelike pain crushed my head and I futilely massaged my temples. Shocked by how rapidly the conversation had deteriorated, and how manipulative Miranda had been, I questioned what I should do. Decision made, I lifted the phone and rang reception. Jinty answered and I asked if Miranda Stevenson had left the building.

'Yes, though she spent ages looking at the posters on the waiting room walls before she left.'

'I need you to highlight her name so she's not booked in for me again. She's a neighbour and I've explained to her it's unethical.'

Without demanding any further explanation, Jinty agreed and I could hear tapping on the keyboard already. 'Sorted.' She was nothing if not efficient. I thanked her and quickly typed up notes about the consultation. Then I closed the tab, as if not seeing them meant they could be forgotten.

Unthinkingly I called my next patient in and for the remainder of the afternoon, had no opportunity to reflect on anything else.

My surgery ran late due to an unwell baby who had to be

urgently referred to the Royal Belfast Hospital for Sick Children, and it was well after five before I finished. The poor mum had been distressed and required gentle handling. I was totally spent by the time her partner arrived to whizz them into the scary experience of hospitals.

The silence of my consulting room was soothing as I finished my patient notes, and shut down the computer. Echoes of the day wavered and twirled.

The calendar.

Miranda's complex medical history.

Her chilling, complacent expression as she got the better of me.

A shiver brushed my spine. The last thing I wanted to do was spend any time in her company. How I rued suggesting the visit, but she'd bulldozed my feeble attempts to deflect. There was no way I was going home to make dinner now, Tom could order a takeaway and have it ready for me arriving home.

I rootled about in the drawer, retrieved my phone and rang him. But his mobile rang out and went to answerphone. Fury pounded until I remembered I could track him. Quickly I checked the tracker app to find his car outside the gym. Obviously, he'd forgotten I'd been at work and we'd need dinner. As usual, he'd assumed I'd sort it, and his dinner would be on the table when he arrived home from a workout. He probably expected his slippers to have been warmed and me to greet him wearing skimpy lingerie and a lascivious smile.

Crossly I rang my favourite Chinese takeaway and placed an order. I didn't care what Tom wanted; he could have chicken curry which he didn't much like. My attitude was foul and I needed to take it out on someone. He'd be my punchbag tonight.

I switched off the lights and walked down the corridor to the waiting room. Everyone had already left; reception was deserted, the back office in darkness. I went into the staff room to get my coat and the sound of a stifled giggle reached me. Disconcerted and as quietly as possible, I followed the noise. Light spilled from one office, the only place the giggle could have originated.

My boots creaked a little and I wished my breathing wasn't so laboured as I made my way down the corridor which ran parallel with the one I'd just come from. Before I reached the room, a husky voice spoke, followed by a girlish titter. The door was slightly open and I could see part of the room, although it was doubtful they could see me.

Jake's feet were up on his desk, crossed at the ankles, hands clasped behind his head. His top button was undone, his grin wide.

On the other side of the table, Bronagh too had her feet on the table, head thrown back, chest thrust forward. She was fiddling with her vape.

Instantly offended, I shrank back, terrified they'd spot me lurking in the darkness. My impulse was to sneak shamefully outside without alerting them to my presence, but something hardened. It may have been the result of a difficult day. Or the sneer on Miranda's face at my inability to refuse her.

I crept back along the corridor, then hit the light switch. Bright fluorescent lights beamed and I blustered down the corridor as my boots protested loudly. When I reached Jake's office, their feet were on the floor. I halted at the door, as if surprised to find them.

Jake's awkwardly cleared his throat. 'Vicky, you're late tonight.'

'Yes, it's been a long day rounded off by a very sick baby.'

Bronagh smoothed a peroxide strand into place, and simpered, 'Are you all right after everything today?'

I nodded and managed a tight smile. 'Yes, I'm fine thanks.' A beat. 'I'll be off then. See you tomorrow.'

Jake smiled vaguely in my direction, but his attention had already strayed back to Bronagh, as if she was more important. I stalled by the door, thrown off-guard. The ensuing silence dismissed me and I left with a limp 'Bye.' Each footstep slapped against the lino, my limbs tense.

So much had gone wrong since Bronagh had joined the practice. She'd weaselled her way into a position of authority and now expected to be treated with respect. Her brazen, pushy attitude had won her few friends, apart from Jake and the male partners, who'd been duped by her pretty face and flirtatious manner. They were blind to her vapid, inane personality.

Hurt mingled with resentment.

As I drove down the deserted streets to collect our takeaway, I deliberated what, if anything, I could do about it.

CHAPTER TWENTY-EIGHT

Jake and Bronagh were still on my mind as I parked near the Chinese takeaway on the main street. Jake's attention sliding past me onto her burned vividly. In an effort to feel better, I placed a quick order online, which sheared off the worst of my stress. When I exited the heat of the car into the frosty air, my breath was a frozen cloud and although gritted, patches of the footpath were still icy underfoot. Walking required my full concentration; one wrong step and I could end up in a heap on the ground.

Impatience simmered as I reached the foggy, warm takeaway. The queue was long and my mouth watered at the appetising smell of curry. Ten minutes later I finally reached the counter and paid in cash. The order wasn't ready, I'd have to wait. A kaleidoscope of the day mashed and churned as I leant against the wall, hands in my pockets. I focused on the tinny music blasting from the speakers in an effort to repair my tattered nerves.

Once the food was ready, I plodded back to the car. My phone vibrated and I glanced at it before driving off. Tom had received my earlier message and only now was offering to order a takeaway. I threw it on the passenger seat without replying.

The sleepy village welcomed me and at the bottom of my street, I scowled at Miranda's house. There would be one chance to nip this in the bud. Tonight she would meet the other Vicky, the one I was usually at great pains to conceal behind the meek and mild charade.

The gloves would come off to unleash the claws beneath the velvet.

With a grim smile, I swung into my driveway and stormed into the house. Tom looked up from where he lounged on the conservatory sofa, and offered a half-baked apology. The carryout was thumped onto the breakfast bar and I bashed around in the cupboards for plates. He said nothing until I'd slammed and banged my annoyance away. When he reached into the fridge and extracted a bottle of wine, I lifted my chin in agreement. Wine on a school night was probably a bad idea, but might make me feel better.

We sat at the breakfast bar and I spooned the food onto the plates. A pang of guilt at Tom's wince when he unboxed the chicken curry. I savoured the wine before swallowing, and once my throat had lost its dryness, gave him the précised version of my day.

The calendar was omitted, but I told him about the visit from Miranda. Naturally I couldn't and wouldn't divulge her confidential medical history, but spoke in coded terms. Emphasised my overriding uneasiness for Kate and how entangled she'd become with an unstable friend and neighbour. A sudden realisation struck me with an almost physical force.

Miranda *was* unstable.

Therefore I had to ignore the impulse to wade in with all guns blazing and tread discreetly, yet still warn her off. There was no reason to be afraid of her, for she was basically a lonely woman with limited social skills. I could handle her.

Buoyed by a second glass of wine and my belly full of food, I changed out of my work clothes into jeans. Tom had assumed his usual position on the sofa in the sitting room to watch sport on the television. With a shout I was going to visit Miranda, I zipped up my padded jacket and slammed the door. I was still unsure how to approach her, my earlier plan of attack having shrivelled and died.

On the short walk down to her house, anger brewed again which propelled me on. I'd enough on my plate without this. As I walked onto Miranda's unkempt driveway, my pulse beat erratically and I acknowledged how nervous I was. Dazzling exterior lights blinded me, and I blinked repeatedly to dislodge white flashes, rang the bell and waited.

Miranda leapt forward to wrench open the door within seconds. 'You're late by fifteen minutes.'

I clamped my teeth to kill my sarcastic response.

'Come in then, or you'll let the heat out. Do you want a cup of tea?'

'No thanks.' A fusty smell hit me when I stepped inside the dingy hallway and I instinctively scrunched up my nose. The sole light came from a dim table lamp, at direct odds with the brilliant glare from outside. She beckoned me to follow her and I trudged into a cramped room which faced the road. She took the armchair by the window and waved me on to an overstuffed chair beside a brick fireplace, which housed an electric three-bar fire. Her chair was set at an angle, apparently positioned to give a bird's-eye view of the street.

When she didn't offer to take my coat, I slipped it off and laid it on the arm of the chair. The material was threadbare, the corduroy worn. The smell was less pervasive in this room and I scanned around. Busy floral wallpaper above a lurid green dado rail, stripes beneath. A clutter of twee ornaments. Wide-screen television. Basket of wool and knitting needles. Perhaps she was nothing more than a lonely woman who craved company and was inept at recognising nonverbal prompts.

Within five minutes, I'd revised my opinion of her. Along with poor social skills, she was downright nasty with a side of malice. Laura. Annie. Even Kate didn't escape the occasional snide comment. Mostly she complained about being excluded, rebuffed by Laura and Annie. The insinuation I too fell into this category. I squeezed my nails into my palms and suppressed the instinct to retaliate. She prattled on about what a great friend Kate was and how excited she was to be included in the Book Club. Her voice faded when I didn't as much as murmur in response.

My attention was taken by the one photo in the room, high on a shelf.

A selfie. Miranda clung like a limpet to a worse-for-wear Kate. Both cradled large glasses of wine, faces blurred. My stomach clenched as Miranda droned on about Kate's deteriorating marriage. Kate and David's marriage was solid, and if there'd been cracks, it was not up for discussion with Miranda. Outraged, I abruptly stood, her mouth dropped open and she rose to face me, shoulders squared. A dark energy filled the room.

I invaded her personal space, got too close, and all the time I smiled and kept my voice low and slow.

'Please do not leave any more gifts in my back garden. Do not book an appointment with me in work again. And do not assume because you are Kate's friend, you're my friend.' It was hissed, yet sugar sweet. She could take it as the veiled threat I meant, or one acquaintance speaking superficially to another.

When I stepped back, I dropped my head to the side,

artificial smile in place. My eyes were locked on hers, until she nodded once.

'Was there anything else you wanted to chat about?' A shake of her head and I lifted my coat. It would be rammed straight into the washing machine when I got home. 'Great. Nice talking to you. Will I show myself out?'

She may have answered, perhaps not. I'd already reached the hall and turned the key in the lock. I anticipated a hand on my shoulder, or the door to be barred, but neither happened. The gentle breeze outside had never been so welcome, and I inhaled its clean fragrance deeply. Without a backwards glance, I stalked out of the drive and onto the pavement.

My impulse was to jog away, but I kept my stride long and unhurried, and ignored the blood banging loudly in my ears.

Her possessive chatter about Kate had been vexing, and if I were a good friend I'd warn her to be careful. To put some distance between them. So instead of making my way to the sanctuary of my house, I darted down Kate's drive and rang her bell.

The house was brightly lit and I could see straight down the hall into their kitchen. Shadows shifted, but a few minutes passed until David appeared. He was pale, but his eyes lit up when he saw me. When I asked if Kate was about, he gave a quick nod and invited me in.

'Kate, Vicky's here.' He shouted upstairs and Kate's answering call floated down. 'Go into the living room. Would you like coffee?' David was a gem, a bighearted man who radiated goodness.

I declined coffee and followed him into the living room. As ever, it was untidy with cushions on the floor, cup stains on the coffee table and the remote protruding from the back of the sofa.

But it had something Miranda's house lacked.

A family's love.

It was in the very fabric of this home. From the shoes abandoned in the hall, to the photos on every wall. Smiling, happy faces on the sports field, on beaches, in woodlands.

And at its centre was my friend, who entered the room with a tired smile and smudges under her eyes. She sank onto the chair opposite, and I filled her in about Miranda's visit to the surgery and determination I visit her. She pressed her lips together as I briefly explained what Miranda had said, though I hid some of it along with my nervousness. It would help no one to repeat the jealous nature of Miranda's conversation, nor her feverish manner.

When I finished talking, Kate paused before saying, 'Thanks for speaking to her. She can be quite forceful and trips me up a lot. I'll try and stand up for myself from now on.' She flopped back against the chair.

The sense much was being left unsaid lay heavy between us, but Kate clammed up when I explored further. Half an hour later, I gave her a hug at the front door. Cold air swirled around us so I didn't linger. Her face was tense, which was quickly replaced with a bashful smile as she wrapped her arms around her body. Before I reached the end of her drive, the front door was shut with a firm thump.

Her words about 'trying' to stand up for herself bothered me most. Did Miranda have a secret agenda in befriending Kate?

If so, what could it be?

Something gnawed at me on my return home, but it was hazy. A memory or an image which swam out of reach. I reassured myself I'd done my duty in warning Kate, but I wasn't confident anything would change. Tom was still prostrate on the sofa and I called hello, stripped off my coat and put it directly into the washing machine. It needed to be disinfected of the stale, unhealthy odour of Miranda's house.

A grain of satisfaction at standing up to her warmed me, and

I lay beside Tom, curled myself into the crook of his arm and kissed his spiky jaw. His aftershave was clean and fresh and my senses awoke. Desire throbbed as I ran my hands along his stomach and down his thighs. His response was restrained until I kissed his earlobe and he released a soft moan.

It wasn't until much later I worked out what had niggled.

Lying on Miranda's side table in her hall beside the lamp had been a brochure for the Mourne View Hotel. Where the Book Club had spent a night before Christmas. I recalled mist enshrouded mountain peaks, Prosecco bubbles and a crowded dance floor. The mistaken belief I was secure in my marriage and my friendships.

There was a slim possibility Miranda having the brochure was a complete fluke.

But alarm bells clanged so loudly, I was positive there was nothing coincidental about it.

CHAPTER TWENTY-NINE

I packed away my uneasiness about Miranda as best I could after my visit to her house, reluctant to worry about something I had little sway over. We'd no plans for another Book Club get-together in the near future, and a hiatus would probably be for the best, at least until we saw how the land lay with Miranda. Each morning when I woke, I'd envision a grotty plastic bag on my doorstep, or a flash of red in my garden, but relief flooded daily when neither materialised.

Despite the stormy weather, I braved the windswept, rain-drenched evenings to get my steps in and clear my head. I'd taken to scurrying past Miranda's as dread crawled along my skin, head down, scarf over the lower half of my face. Fortunately only my footsteps reverberated, rather than the expected holler of my name.

After our dire consultation and my visit to her house, I initiated a conversation with my colleague Gloria about Miranda. She was her registered GP and I'd seen from the notes how frequent her appointments were. Naturally I had to be cautious and not be too forthright about my curiosity, but what I gleaned from our conversation proved my alarm wasn't unfounded.

What I could do about it, was less definite. Arguments thundered in my head until I decided the best course of action should be to watch and wait. For I assumed she wouldn't back down without a fight. Someone like Miranda wouldn't take kindly to being excluded or challenged. My exhilaration at defying her hadn't lasted, as I waited on tenterhooks for her next move.

Kate replied to my tentative follow-up messages with curt replies. No, she hadn't seen Miranda since Monday night. Yes, she would distance herself. No, she didn't want to meet for coffee. None of this was out of the ordinary. Sporadically Kate would back off, and put a barrier between us, usually when stressed. My good intentions to watch out for her took a back seat as life got in the way.

My mum left a rare voicemail on Thursday morning. Unemotionally she instructed me to visit next Saturday afternoon at three o'clock. I was to come alone as there was something she and Dad wished to discuss with me. She gave no indication what it could be and I gripped the phone tightly as I replayed the message. My plans for an early dinner with Tom and the girls for his birthday would have to be rearranged. It never entered my head to refuse the directive.

The atmosphere in work was in turns troubled, then tranquil. Troubled when Jinty and Bronagh shared the same space, tranquil when one of them was elsewhere. The calendar never reappeared and I didn't probe Jake about it. At lunchtime the following Monday, his hot stare singed me in the staff room, and a frown darkened his features. He coloured at my quizzical glance and my smile went unreciprocated. My stomach jolted as he pivoted away and paced out of the room.

Misgivings about our friendship skyrocketed quickly.

I agonised whether he still valued my opinion. He now rarely sought my company, either in work or out. Two voices merged each time I walked past his office, the door ajar, forewarning intimacy. His messages had tapered off, and I argued with myself before texting him. When I scrolled back through my mobile, I found he'd not messaged in a week.

Nothing since the calendar incident.

Doubts rattled around my mind and I became increasingly agitated. Before I left work that day, I made up my mind to speak to him, or my night would be ruined. I waited until the end of the afternoon session, then marched down the corridor to his office. Outside the room I forced a smile and gave three firm raps on the door. When he called me in, he was engrossed in his computer. A harried smile and a request to 'hang on a minute.' He indicated I should sit down and I nearly swung my feet up on the desk like Bronagh had done.

Decorum won and I clasped my hands neatly in my lap. When he raised his head, colour had once again bled across his face.

'How are you?' His words were clipped.

'All right. How are you?'

'Fine. Is there something I can help you with?' His coolness caused the base of my spine to dampen.

'Jake, what's wrong?' I twisted my wedding ring anxiously. So much for being in charge.

His bright blue gaze searched my face, then it dropped to the pen he rotated between his fingers. 'There's been a complaint from a patient and I'm conducting an investigation. Until then, I'm sorry but I can't say anymore. It's crucial I remain impartial.'

'A complaint about me?' I stammered.

A nod of the head.

'Written or verbal?'

'Written. I have to follow procedure and will speak to you officially about it in time.' His tone was gentle now. 'This is a horrible situation, but I must follow the procedure thoroughly.'

'Can you tell me what it's about?' There was no need to tell me who'd made the complaint, it was patently obvious. Miranda. What had she concocted? A complaint tarnished a doctor's reputation, no matter the outcome of an investigation.

I wanted to throw a hissy fit, but had to appear calm and unflappable. Jake couldn't meet my eye, and I backtracked. 'Don't tell me. I can guess who made the complaint, but I've no clue what it could be in relation to.' At least, there's nothing professional it could be related to.

'I'll speak to you officially about it later this week, but, Vicky, please don't worry. You're held in high regard here.'

Little consolation, however I thanked him and prised myself out of the chair. I wanted to demand he stop this ludicrous witch-hunt, but managed a fleeting smile before I closed the door. With sweaty hands and the beginnings of a headache, I scarpered down the corridor to the seclusion of my consulting room.

My heart thudded in my chest as I retrieved Miranda's notes to remind myself what I'd written after the appointment last Monday. In the health service, if it's not documented, it didn't happen. I prayed I'd been thorough, but a kernel of apprehension settled in my gut. The notes had been written in bad temper, and I could've revealed my testiness.

Thankfully, they were simple and concise.

I apologised to Mrs Stevenson and explained as we are neighbours and occasionally socialise together, it would be unethical to treat her today. An alternative appointment with Doctor Corrie was offered but refused. No medical issues were discussed with the patient.

Head in hands, I concentrated on slow breaths to help settle my nerves. Worry trickled away as I grew increasingly infuriated with Miranda's cunning. She'd taken our measly personal relationship and used it to bludgeon my professional reputation. As though she was a woman scorned. It was a reaction out of proportion with my puny attempt at standing up to her.

My instinct was to confront her at home, however the longer I considered it, I realised it was a terrible idea as she could allege intimidation and her vindictiveness seemingly knew no bounds. I mulled it over as the surgery quietened outside my door and the rain beat a gentle tattoo on my window. As the sky darkened, I resolved the best way to get back at her was to ensure she was dropped from Book Club. To isolate her from the group she was single-mindedly determined to be part of.

There was no time like the present; my campaign would begin today. I sighed away my sullenness and reached for my mobile. The homepage was brilliant with notifications, but none required immediate attention. Eventually I opted for separate messages, rather than a general one on the Book Club WhatsApp, meaning I could tailor them individually, and each of my friends would suppose they alone were being trusted with my problems.

To Laura:

> Something awful has happened in work today regarding Miranda. Will you be home for a chat later?

To Annie:

> I really need to discuss something with you. Will you be in later?

To Kate:

How are you today? Would it be OK if I popped in on my way home, there's something I wanted to run by you.

Laura answered to say unfortunately she was staying in Belfast with Sam, but could ring me later.

After a few moments, Annie replied she would be home after six and to call over any time.

Impatiently I gnawed my nail. No answer from Kate, although the grey ticks turned blue so possibly she was formulating a reply. I couldn't sit and wait on her; the practice would be locked up for the night soon.

There was still no response from her by the time I arrived home. Had Miranda wormed her way in and lied about me to Kate? I recalled our conversation last Monday, when Kate had acted as maddened with Miranda's behaviour as I'd been.

But what if I'd been mistaken, and she was firmly on Miranda's side? Worse, what if the whole Claire debacle had made her view me differently? Think less of me?

A sudden buzzing from the phone prevented me from trundling down the path of self-recrimination. Kate had replied. As I read it, my heart skipped a beat.

Sorry, I'm not feeling well, so tonight doesn't suit.

No suggestion about another catch-up. No interest in finding out what I wanted to discuss with her. Disappointment washed over me before resolve took hold. Miranda was not going to wreck my friendship. I'd overcome much tougher opponents over the years. She was foolish to underestimate me.

She'd taken the pliable pretence of me, and assumed I had no depth nor substance.

Which would be to her cost.

CHAPTER THIRTY

It was Tom's last night at home before he left for a long-haul trip. Apart from one overnight flight in the past week, he'd been home every day, and I was champing at the bit to be Tom-free for a few nights. Although by nature self-absorbed, he could sense my unhappiness on my return home from work and over dinner I clumsily disclosed I was under investigation following a complaint. His fork clanked onto the table as his mouth dropped open.

'Jake wouldn't confirm it, but I think Miranda's the patient in question.'

A flicker of dismay crossed his face. 'What exactly do you know?'

'Not much yet, except Jake is following procedure and he'll speak to me later in the week. I don't know what she's accused me of.' My mouth was so dry, I was having difficulty swallowing the chilli con carne. 'I can't stand this! She's been a thorn in my side for weeks and now this.' The last word caught on a sob and then Tom was beside me, stroking my hair and telling me it would be all right. I leaned against him and took solace from his solid presence. For too long I'd dealt with everything on my own, to share my problems was novel, and I luxuriated in it.

'I'm sure the investigation will show no cause for concern. She's goading you.'

I nodded against his chest, raring to believe him.

'I'm going to ring Laura later, after I've been over to see Annie. Kate doesn't want to meet up, which is a worry. I'm afraid of what venom Miranda's been dripping into her ear.'

Tom stepped away and retook his seat opposite me. 'Kate's been your friend for years. She's unlikely to take the side of someone she's known for five minutes.' I wanted to believe him, but the memory of Miranda's savage expression panicked me a little.

I wanted to curl up with the curtains pulled and retreat from the world, but forced myself to go over to Annie's house after dinner. Perfunctorily I checked the street, but it was empty. Lights glowed from hushed houses, the moon peeped out from behind a cloud. The howling of the wind was the only sound.

Matt, Annie's husband opened the door, greeted me good-naturedly and showed me into their living room. They had no children, just a new unruly rescue dog called Roger, who barked excitedly, jumped around and chased his tail. Despite myself, I giggled. Matt adopted a stern tone, belied by his dancing eyes and beaming smile. He was a headteacher with a passion for motorbikes and rowing. Annie spent many hours complaining about her husband's hobbies, but his firm muscles and rugged good looks more than compensated.

Annie came into the living room, took one look at me and coiled her arms around me in a hug. Matt subtly disappeared into the kitchen with Roger, having offered to make coffee.

'What on earth's the matter?' Her nose crinkled.

Stumbling over the words, I told my sorry tale about

Miranda and her strange behaviour. Keen to see how she reacted, I surreptitiously studied her, chin dipped to my chest. She shook her head once or twice, but otherwise gave no indication she knew anything about Miranda's vendetta. Matt carried in two cups of coffee and I drank deeply as my throat was like sandpaper after I'd offloaded.

He left us alone and Annie didn't speak immediately. The silence was broken only by Roger's muffled barking from the kitchen. The suspense increased. What if she took Miranda's side?

However I needn't have worried, for when she began to talk, I learned she'd felt pressurised into agreeing Miranda could come to Book Club, and was herself progressively alarmed by her influence over Kate. 'What are we going to do?'

The *we* warmed the depths of me.

'I don't know. All I can do is wait for the investigation and hopefully it will clear things up professionally. As for personally...'

The next half hour was spent discussing our next moves, and when I left, I was relieved Annie was in full agreement with me.

I should've gone straight home, but couldn't bring myself to. The craving to pound the streets was too great and I didn't fight it. I needed headspace to work through my uncertainties which multiplied by the day. My mind was a riot of worry, which in turn left me unable to think clearly or make good decisions. For there was no question, my recent decisions were dubious at best, destructive at worst.

Living life under a microscope. Persistent hassles and doubts. Inconsistent friendships. A vulnerable marriage. The issues I faced appeared insurmountable as rain fell and wind blasted. I blended into the shadows and appreciated the darkness. For a time I was invisible.

Until too soon it came to an end and as I made for home, my worst fears were realised. A figure at the window, scowl searing. Hands on hips. The reproach inaudible.

I sneaked past with my chin tucked into my scarf, unable to hide, caught in the spotlight. My mind crowded with recriminations. The risks I took outweighed the gains and now I'd been spotted, my presence noted.

In my pocket my phone vibrated and I retrieved it as I neared home. Laura was free to talk now. But my voice was lost, choked by alarm, and so I messaged back with numb fingers to ask we leave it for another time. Relieved to be safely back home, I unlocked the front door and rushed inside.

Tom was upstairs packing for his work trip and I shouted hello. My coat was wet, my face cold, and I went into the utility room to strip off my outer clothes. As I was about to leave, Tom appeared and began to rummage in the drawers.

'What are you after?'

'I'm looking for my New York baseball cap. The navy one with the red letters.' One by one he pulled caps and hats out, and soon they were stacked on the countertop in a haphazard pile.

'Here, let me take a look,' I snapped, irritated with his fumbling. 'You'll have everything out in a minute.'

He never faltered though, as the drawer was emptied. No sign of the cap he wanted. Everything was shoved messily back in and he hauled open the one below.

'Tom, why don't you have a look in the cupboard by the window. I'm sure it was hanging on a hook in there.'

Ignoring my suggestion, out came hats, scarves and gloves and landed in a heap on the floor as he cursed. No cap. He was about to replace everything, when he crouched down low and reached into the very back of the drawer.

'What's this?' he scrabbled around and tugged on something I couldn't see.

'Probably something that fell down from the top drawer.' Annoyed, I tried to move him out of the way, but he wasn't budging.

'Ah ha!' He pronounced and with a flourish, brought out a green woollen hat. A puzzled look as he fired deep red.

'Not your baseball cap then.' I busied myself with tidying everything back into the drawer.

'Is this your hat?' he asked brusquely.

'It's an old one of Alex's. Why?'

'Nothing really.' He paused. 'I knew it wasn't one of yours, you don't usually wear green.'

'Like I said, it's one of Alex's old ones.'

We eyed each other warily until he dropped the hat back into the drawer. Then he swivelled and opened the cupboard I'd suggested a few minutes ago. The atmosphere was electric. I stiffened, ready for the onslaught. He reached in and pulled out the baseball cap with a soft exclamation.

In a strangled voice I asked, 'What's so special about that hat?'

'This?' He brandished the baseball cap.

'No, the green one.'

I sensed what he was thinking, or rather who he was thinking of. The rigidity of his face gave him away. He could dismiss it, but his embarrassment spoke volumes.

It reminded him of Claire.

The urge to confess waned before it reached my throat. He didn't deserve to know what tortured and haunted me. Not while his brain and conceivably his heart were still recuperating from his tragic love affair with my friend. His jumpy movements, tight jaw and burning face gave it away.

I smiled stiffly and walked over to caress his cheek. The heat of it scorched my fingers, but I kept my voice steady and light.

'Are you okay?'

A faint, 'Fine, just a bit harassed getting sorted for my trip.'

I leaned forward and kissed his neck, trailed my fingers over his biceps and told him I'd miss him.

Throughout, indignation and pain shrieked in my head.

And a green glower burnt my eyelids as she spat out the reason she'd cheated with my husband.

CHAPTER THIRTY-ONE

Tom had recovered his equilibrium after unearthing the green woollen hat and made love to me with his now customary intensity. He was so predictable. I tolerated it, as I always did. He could commandeer my body, but never my mind. I woke from a fitful sleep when the alarm clock beeped and it was still dark outside. He eased himself out of bed with a groan, before disappearing into the en suite. I burrowed beneath the duvet and turned my back, disinclined to see the grooves on his face, nor hear the forced jollity in his tone. Something shadowy had settled in his expression after he found the hat last night. Something I could guess at, but would never verbalise.

Before he left, he walked around the bed to give me a kiss. His breath against my ear tickled, his chin was soft from his shave. A promise of love, to which I responded with 'me too.' No silly cap ritual today, no fond farewell at the door.

Now fully awake, I listened to his footsteps on the stairs and his low call for Keiko. When he shut the front door, she bounded onto the bed and coiled herself into the crook of my knees. It was still early and I could doze for at least an hour, but the temptation to scour the house for the iPad was irresistible. I stroked Keiko and apologised for moving her, before I leapt out of bed, blood pumping with expectation.

A wasted, futile hour of searching later, my temper was frayed and I was no further on. Nowhere in the bedroom was left unchecked, unless I ripped up the carpet. Agitated as I was, I dismissed it straight away. While showering, I persuaded myself the time spent searching hadn't been pointless, I was one step closer to finding it. My thoughts glided onto work and the looming shadow of the investigation. The worry of it fidgeted and writhed, always present, never resting.

As I ate breakfast in the kitchen, morning television blared to distract me. With the last mouthful of toast, I resolved to treat the investigation with the distain it warranted. My notes corroborated that I'd been compassionate and professional. No matter what Miranda blamed me for, my behaviour had been impeccable during the consultation.

When I arrived at the practice, I pasted on a smile and greeted my colleagues with my blandest façade. Non-confrontational would win the day. Gossip and chatter was upbeat as a new reality show was discussed at length and I giggled along with them, though reality TV didn't hold my interest.

Then Bronagh arrived in the staff room in a cloud of perfume and wearing a grouchy expression. The very atmosphere cooled as one by one my colleagues exited the room, rather than include her in the conversation. Gloria and I were left with her, and I opted for pleasant. Two-faced, but pleasant.

'Morning, Bronagh.'

'Morning, Vicky.' Her glower was blistering.

'How are you?'

'Were you out for a walk in Castlebrook last night?'

'Yes, I walk most evenings, no matter the weather, especially after a tough day in work.'

Pouting, she replied, 'Yes, I've seen you a few times.'

I sipped my coffee before replying. 'Well, I do live in the village.' A short laugh. 'There's limited routes I can take to get my 10,000 steps in.'

She blew out her cheeks. 'True, I suppose.' It seemed she would say more, but instead stalked away.

Gloria sniffed loudly beside me. 'She has a face like thunder, seems you shouldn't be walking around your village without The Boss's permission.' Her ironic nickname for Bronagh always made me smile. We chatted together for a few more minutes, before we went our separate ways.

Jake came to find me before lunchtime for an official discussion regarding the complaint. He took the chair at the end of my desk, and I crossed my legs to stop them jiggling. The basis of the complaint was my 'condescending manner', 'lack of empathy' and 'unprofessional behaviour'.

'Condescending and unprofessional?' I rolled my eyes.

'That's what she alleged.' His smile was rueful. 'There's no evidence of any wrongdoing, Vicky. Your notes clearly documented why you couldn't treat her, and she declined to be seen by an alternative doctor. Jinty states you rang her after the patient left your room and requested it be highlighted on the system that she shouldn't be allocated to you in future.'

'So there's no basis for the complaint?'

'There is no basis, but unfortunately there's something else.' He avoided eye contact and stared out of the window. 'She says you've been loitering outside her house.'

Assuming this was a joke, I chuckled loudly. However his expression was grave, so I knew it was true. Indignant, I exclaimed obviously I never loitered outside her house, we lived on the same street, so if she'd seen me it was by chance.

'Unfortunately she says she can back it up.'

'What has any of this to do with the quality of my work? How can this be incorporated into an official complaint?'

He thrust out his chin. 'It can't, but I needed to update you as she may take it further.'

I flinched as though struck. 'What do you mean?'

For the next five minutes Jake talked me through exactly what Miranda had claimed. As expected, I'd been completely exonerated of any misconduct following his investigation, and a letter would be sent to her with the findings. Unfortunately if she was unhappy with the result, she could contact the Northern Ireland Public Services Ombudsman to investigate further.

Jake reassured me there was no scope for such an inquiry, but she was within her rights to request one. Once we'd exhausted the discussion about the formalities, he revisited the allegation I regularly lurked outside her house.

Perplexed, I explained about her overfamiliar attempts at friendship; turning up unannounced with a bag of books, leaving the cake and hiding in my garden while Tom and I talked in the car, demanding I visit her at home. She may even have left the bunch of roses on my doorstep.

I finished by saying, 'This is because I refused to socialise with her and told her I didn't want to be her friend.' The childishness of it all made me defensive.

Rather than placate me, Jake's reaction was unhelpful. 'I agree it's a little strange. The main problem is, she says she can prove it.' He frowned at my look of dismay and continued. 'The thing is, I've seen you regularly out walking around the village. In my street. Past my house. When it's dark and stormy and most people are indoors out of the bad weather. Last night, for example. It was pouring and windy and yet there you were.'

I bristled and replied, 'I make no secret of my walks. There's nothing alarming about them. I do not "loiter" outside houses. I didn't realise walking in the rain broke the law.'

Instantly his colour drained and he snapped, 'Of course it doesn't break the law. What I mean is, it could be thought of as a little strange by some people.'

'Do you think it's a little strange?' The seconds ticked on.

He studied his hands. 'No, *I* don't. Not really.'

Emphasis on the word 'I' riled me and I held on to my temper with difficulty. There was no need to ask who did consider my harmless walks suspicious. I tried to come up with a suitable retort, but my mind was a vacuum. Brain fog made an appearance at a most inopportune moment.

Jake rose and shoved his hands into his pockets, his habitual pose. He scuffed a toe on the lino and cleared his throat. 'I'm sorry if you're upset, that wasn't my intention.'

I shifted away from him, wanting to remain unemotional, but failing. He had upset me, I shouldn't have to hide it from him. 'Well I am upset, both about the complaint and the other suggestion. I'm sorry if my walks have put you in a difficult position.' I wasn't remotely sorry, but allowed my voice to wobble.

'It's all right. No real harm done.' He shrugged off my apology and the sting of his dismissive gesture hurt.

He left with a quick smile, his parting words echoing with menace.

No real harm done.

All I'd done was walk the village streets in the dark, and now my intention had been misinterpreted, had been included in a formal complaint in my workplace and in addition had caused a rift with my friend.

No real harm done. I was sick to death of it all. Sick of hidden agendas and sneaky accusations. Fed up with people who leeched and sucked my goodwill. Weary of subterfuge.

One thought sliced through the din in my head.

Jake was my friend. Now he'd begun to doubt me and believe some of the unsavoury things I'd been accused of. Our friendship was crumbling and I could do nothing to stop it.

A stabbing pain in my chest caused me to double over, and I gasped for air.

Throughout, the rain pelted the window and my phone flashed a warning.

At last the pain diminished and with unsteady hands, I checked my mobile and tracker app.

Tom's car wasn't at the airport as it should have been.

It was parked outside an unknown house in Belfast.

CHAPTER THIRTY-TWO

By the end of the work day, an impeding migraine floored me. Zigzag lines flashed in the periphery of my vision, forewarning a brutal headache. I swallowed pills with a slug of lukewarm water and rang Jinty. I'd two patients left; a regular with poorly controlled diabetes and a woman with a rash on her face. It would be difficult to assess them with disturbed vision, but I was too afraid to cancel them at short notice.

No other doctors had a free slot, which left me no option.

Half an hour later the diabetic patient had been referred to the specialist diabetes nurse and the lovely woman with a bad case of rosacea left the consulting room, grateful the cream I prescribed would help.

My sight had cleared, replaced by a headache which drilled into my head, and nausea which rolled over me in waves. I longed to get into bed and pull the duvet over me, but had to drive home first. As quickly as possible, I typed my patient notes, then switched off the computer and made my way to the staff room. Jinty raised her eyebrows at me until I explained about the migraine and her face screwed up in sympathy.

'You're very pale. Get yourself off home and don't come in

tomorrow if you're still unwell.' She was familiar with my debilitating migraines, and I appreciated her kindness.

There was no one else around as I trudged down the corridor towards the staff exit. Jake's door was open and before I reached it, voices drifted out. I should've walked past, but my name was mentioned as I approached the doorway.

Keep going, screamed my brain.

No way, was the response.

Eavesdroppers never hear any good of themselves. Everyone knows it. As I slowed and ground to a halt, I ignored reason, and heard most of what was said. Chunks were too muted, but it was enough to make me question everything and everyone. I no longer knew who was on my side or had my back.

'You had no choice but to be honest, as difficult as it was.'

Jake's response was too indistinct to hear.

'I'm glad you called her out, it's been going on too long.'

'It was horrible; she was fuming about it.'

'Don't tell me, she gazed at you with those chocolate brown eyes and you apologised.' A repressed titter followed by a deep laugh from Jake.

My stomach knotted at his duplicity. They talked on, but I could listen no longer. As noiselessly as possible, I crept down the corridor and into the car park, glad of the dim light as I slunk to my car. Inside I leaned my arms on the steering wheel as tears pooled.

Betrayal by Tom was nothing new.

Betrayal by Jake cut like a knife.

Was he the friend I'd believed he was?

Minutes passed while I digested this new and deadly insight while paranoia ran rampant. My trust had once again been hurled in my face. What if I'd put too much faith in our friendship from the beginning, and he'd simply humoured me?

Kept me onside. I cringed at the notion he may never have been the friend I'd supposed.

At long last the staff door opened and Gloria exited first, head bent towards Jake. From the obscurity of my car, I observed them both. So innocent. So banal. Something deep inside me curdled as Gloria raised her hand in a wave and climbed into her car on the far side of the car park. She drove off as Jake stood under a light to read his phone. Expression veiled, he swiped the screen and I ducked as low as possible to avoid attracting his attention.

I shouldn't have worried, he was too enrapt in his mobile to see me. A few minutes later he popped it into his pocket and made his way back into the surgery.

My heart hardened towards him. Bruised but not defeated, I drove home and wondered what I could do. But my head throbbed and sickness churned, leaving me incapable of working it out. I needed to lie in a darkened room and allow the painkillers to work their magic.

Relieved to be home, I locked the front door behind me with a click. I didn't even have it in me to race around the house closing blinds, but headed straight upstairs, peeled off my clothes and crumpled gratefully into bed. Keiko joined me on top of the duvet, and her soft purrs relaxed me. A short time later, sleep claimed me.

When I woke a couple of hours later, moonlight filtered through the slats of the blinds. Although not completely improved, my headache was a little better. I stretched my legs and my stomach growled in protest. All I'd eaten was an insubstantial sandwich at lunch, and I longed for hot buttered toast with marmalade and a mug of frothy coffee.

My handbag was still on the bottom stair and after I'd closed the blinds and hall curtains, I carried it into the kitchen, withdrew my mobile from its depths and waited for the toast to pop. It was then I remembered Tom's car had been outside the house in Belfast. When I checked the tracker, it hadn't moved. I lost my appetite and the toast no longer appealed.

Rashly I rang him, as I was in no state to drive into Belfast and confront him directly. The mobile rang out and went to answerphone. Frustration crackled, I sank onto a chair and resisted the urge to throw the phone at the wall. Instead, I made another call which was answered and my mindset improved. I buttered the toast and made coffee, which I carried into the conservatory. The floor lamp cast dim light over me, too bright and my headache would remerge with a vengeance. When I'd finished eating, my decision had been made. Irrespective of how I felt in the morning, I'd phone in sick tomorrow and spend my time wisely.

First I would search the house for the iPad and study its contents fully.

Next I would drive to the house in Belfast where his car was.

Finally I would confront my husband and demand to know why he'd lied to me. Again.

If he asked me how I'd found his car, I'd invent the excuse someone had spotted it when they were driving past and informed me. I was adept at inventing a good story, after all, my life was one long role-play.

Fatigued by the migraine, my disappointing day and more qualms about Tom, I opened the back door to let Keiko outside for a night of prowling. The damp air held the fragrance of woodsmoke and I inhaled deeply. In the distance, pinpricks of light twinkled on a hillside road and I remembered Claire, secluded in the hills on her own.

Misery sapped my already depleted energy as I returned indoors. After I piled the dirty crockery into the dishwasher, I plodded upstairs, where I climbed back into bed after swallowing two strong painkillers without brushing my teeth nor cleansing my face, craving the oblivion of sleep.

However my phone buzzed again. A message from Jake.

> I'm sorry if you were upset earlier.

Unable to devise an appropriate answer, I switched the phone off without replying. Rather than gaining respite from sleep, my brain was hypervigilant with negative thoughts which zipped around uncontrollably. It was after midnight before I dozed off, no further forward.

Next morning, the beep of the alarm dragged me from an unpleasant dream where I was drowning in quicksand. I'd forgotten to reset it last night, but needed to advise work I wouldn't be in. The headache still thumped although the queasiness had subsided, so I took yet more tablets and washed them down with water. Then I messaged both Gloria and Jake to notify them I was unwell and would be taking the day off. Appointments would need to be cancelled or rearranged, and I kept my messages short and factual. No promises whether I'd return to work tomorrow; it would depend on how I was feeling later.

The mobile began to vibrate as I set it on the bedside table. Tom's name flashed bright. After the briefest hesitation, I picked up.

'Hello?'

'Hi.' My lips were thick, my voice reedy.

'Sorry, I had a missed call from you when I was in the air. Is everything okay?'

'Where are you?' Petulance spilled out, but I couldn't stem it.

'New Delhi.' The cacophony of noise suggested it was true, but still I doubted him. His words tumbled over each other, some getting lost in the tsunami of background sounds. 'I had a complete nightmare yesterday morning. Ashley asked me to give him a lift, but when I arrived at his house, an engine light came on and I had to leave the car there. Robin whinged she'd be left without a car if he took theirs, so she ended up driving us both to the airport. My car's still in front of their house in Belfast. Could you ring the AA and get it sorted?'

Relief like cool water poured over me. There was a simple explanation after all. My heart broke a little for our precarious marriage as I told him of course I'd sort it. When he hung up, I was almost giddy at my lightened load. My headache was manageable, the nausea mild. If I snoozed for another couple of hours, I'd be refreshed and well enough to consider everything.

Before I fell sleep, the offensive words I'd overheard yesterday spun around my head. Words which chipped away at my self-belief and eroded my faith in friendship. The text from Jake hadn't helped. Conversely, it deepened my bitterness.

Jake wasn't altogether to blame, for he was easily lead by a pretty face and devious words. Our friendship was a testament to that.

But I laid fault exclusively at the door of the person I disliked more intensely anyone else.

Who'd tried to belittle me, and damage my reputation.

And no one could chastise me for my actions, nor the result.

CHAPTER THIRTY-THREE

I dozed on and off for a couple of hours, and woke as insipid daylight peeped through the blinds. My head still ached and a sweaty sheen coated my skin, leaving a faintly acrid odour. I needed a long soak in the bath and something to eat.

Then I remembered I had two days to play hunt-the-iPad. If it was in the house, I'd unearth it. I buried the worry Tom had removed it and even now it was in his car. Or New Delhi. Or in a skip somewhere. In reality it could be anywhere. My good form spoilt as I contemplated never finding it.

With a faint moan, I propped myself up against the headboard and grasped my mobile. Why was it always the first thing I reached for? Like wearing a hair shirt, it scraped and rubbed me raw, but I wore it anyway.

A message from Gloria:

You poor thing. Hope you feel better soon.

I snorted, replied my thanks and read Jake's. It was similar, but with an addition:

Sorry to hear that. Hope it wasn't because of
our meeting yesterday. If you're well enough,
we could have coffee after work on Friday?

I sniffed with annoyance before replying. There was no chance of me having coffee with him on Friday; I'd much rather wallow in wretchedness a bit longer.

After breakfast, I ran a bath and while waiting for the tub to fill, systematically searched the entire en suite. No iPad. The girls bedrooms were next on my list. I poured scented bath oil into the water, and sank under with a soft groan. Soothing music played from my phone to relax me. The luxury of an unexpected day to myself lifted my mood.

There was my unfinished list in the kitchen drawer; I'd take some time to see what else could be ticked off this week.

The arranged visit to my parents' was on Saturday afternoon. Even if I was at death's door, it would be impossible to cancel.

And then there was the excruciating issue of Miranda.

I remained in the bath until both the water and my contemplations cooled. The headache was a dull throb, the queasiness minor. There was no guilt about taking a sick day; I'd not missed work in three years. And I was sick. Sick of my predicament.

Dried and dressed, I went downstairs and opened the blinds. Keiko watched me from the windowsill in the conservatory and wound around my ankles when I let her in, mewing her impatience at having to wait for food. Once fed, she strutted off to find a warm spot in the sunshine.

By lunchtime, I'd completed most of the items on my to-do list, and had carefully searched Alex's bedroom for the iPad without success. Except for an ancient girlish diary hidden at the back of the wardrobe, there was nothing. I pushed it back under the heap of old shoes and moved on to Flora's room.

Undoubtedly it was shameful to ransack my daughters' private spaces as though they were nothing. My woeful excuse was it was due to a tired, overwrought mind, ignorant to how far I'd waded from the right route. Ultimately though, I had to take full responsibility. For there was no iPad, but there was something worse, which caused bile to burn the back of my throat.

My fruitless search was almost complete when I recalled Tom's initial hiding place behind the dressing table in our bedroom. There was a chance my not-very-imaginative husband had replicated it in another room. My fingers groped around the back of the dressing table, which was too heavy for me to pull out. Nothing. Next I groped behind the bedside table. Flushed with success, I yanked something out.

However it was not the anticipated iPad. Instead it was a bundle of folded notes, roughly tied together with a navy ribbon. Naturally I shouldn't look. I should put them back without invading Flora's privacy further, but I didn't. Conscience suppressed, I untied the bow and opened the first sheet of paper.

It was a hate letter, full of spite and animosity and signed by Bryony, Flora's friend from school.

Horrified, I glanced through the others. There must have been a dozen, different writing, different pens. Calling my daughter names. Ugly, repellent names. Some signed by many names, some unidentified.

Déjà vu.

I clutched my stomach as memories engulfed me.

A different school.

A different victim.

A howl escaped my lips as I rocked back and forward on my knees, the carpet burns unnoticed.

My daughter had been bullied and I'd had no idea. She was pretty, smart and popular and I'd been complacent she could never be a target. Swiftly I rose and charged to the bathroom, where I retched my misery. My poor, lovely daughter who'd been unable or unwilling to talk to me, through the last difficult year in school. I'd been diverted by my own life as she wilted and shrivelled into a waif. Who'd dismissed my sporadic queries as stress of A2-levels and I accepted her explanation without delving beneath the surface.

I wailed my shame and guilt, which rebounded coldly back at me in the tiled bathroom.

So many regrets. For being unsuspecting of her suffering. For being a neglectful parent. For being self-absorbed and selfish.

I pictured Flora with her warm smile, razor-sharp cheekbones and wicked sense of humour. Dark circles. Saturday nights alone at home watching movies she'd loved as a young teenager. Withdrawn and silent as she observed her phone, biting her lips, eyes brilliant.

How could I have been such a terrible mother she never told me. I wrapped my arms around myself on the hard tiles as I whimpered aloud and chastised my failure as a parent. And then the slow dawning. Perhaps the spiteful notes were merely the tip of the iceberg and much worse had been sent in a private, online world only Flora had access to. How relentless it must have been for her each time her phone buzzed.

Surely she was thriving now, happy and content studying journalism with English at university. Adamant she wouldn't go to Queens University in Belfast, she'd stated she wanted to spread her wings at the Ulster University on the North Coast and we'd accepted her choice at face value. None of her friends were going there. Now it made perfect, hideous sense. With the benefit of hindsight, I understand her reluctance to come home at weekends or socialise in Belfast over Christmas, except with Alex. A crumb of comfort she'd moved on and left it in the distant past.

Then I recalled another victim of bullying who'd exacted her warped revenge many years after the events and how the fallout had impacted and fragmented my family.

For the first time since the middle of December, I allowed myself to consider my teenage behaviour. My despicable, horrendous behaviour towards someone weaker and defenceless. Humiliation overwhelmed me, from my centre to my extremities. Now the cool tiles were welcome and I lay until I became stiff and sore.

The iPad would wait. I needed to contact Flora and offer to drive to the North Coast. To hold her in my arms and see for myself she was flourishing now. I'd never be able to admit I'd found her stash of hate letters, but would make certain she knew how loved she was and the door of communication was pasted open, never half closed.

My own situation paled into insignificance beside my need to prove myself a good mother and I hauled myself into a sitting position using the side of the bath. The headache was back, more invasive than before. Perhaps I deserved it. For being a poor mum and a generally rotten person.

This reality check singed in its ferocity and undermined the persona I'd created and portrayed to everyone.

Perfect, pretty Vicky who disguised the truth from everyone, including herself.

Signing heavily, I walked on aching legs into the bedroom, where my mobile lay on the bed. Then I rang Flora. It went to answerphone, but I left a message suggesting I drive up to visit her on Friday. I was sorry I hadn't seen her for a few weeks and told her I loved her. Which in itself was not unusual, but over time had become a formality. The extent of my despair was hidden by a cheery tone, but each syllable was heartfelt.

My mission to find the iPad was temporarily forgotten as I anxiously waited for her to contact me. I reclined on the bed in the dim light, with the phone clamped to my chest. Each vibration caused a rush of fear. Around an hour later, Flora messaged to say she'd love me to visit on Friday after her last lecture. Tears welled as I replied.

Guilt assuaged a little, I resumed my search. A cursory browse through the spare room revealed the iPad in the bottom drawer. Not hidden. Instead it unashamedly lay on top of a woollen throw with the charger beside it. I lifted it out and switched it on, though my heart wasn't in it, still preoccupied with my earlier find.

When I checked it, there was nothing new.

No rogue emails. No proclamations of love, or lust, from an unknown woman. No incriminating photos or videos.

I switched it off and replaced it where I'd found it, knowing there would be a time when the impulse to explore it would win, but for today, I'd done enough snooping.

It was time to move beyond this. To condemn it to the past. Either I trusted him, or I didn't. No one was forcing me to stay with him. It was my choice, one I could change at any time.

For now, I was staying. Despite the pain and the lying. My own purgatory.

In love with a man who was faithless. Haunted by past deeds and bad memories. Condemned forever to chase rainbows. And to be plagued by demons.

CHAPTER THIRTY-FOUR

Next morning my headache had lifted and the nausea mostly gone, but I rang in sick anyway. A GP must be fully well and able to concentrate on their patients; feeling under the weather would do them a disservice. This was the worst migraine I'd suffered from in months, probably as a result of the strain I'd been under. After a night of hurtling emotions and poor sleep, the rising of the sun brought a chink of light. Rather than race out to work, I had a self-indulgent morning, filled with daytime television and calorific stodge.

In the late afternoon I was ready to visit Kate. It could be put it off no longer. Her car was in the driveway, the curtains open an inch, so she must be home. Once I'd rung the bell, I glanced around as I waited. The flower beds were a mass of dead plants and decaying leaves. A broken terracotta pot lay on its side, clumpy soil a hardened mound on the path. Discarded garden tools rusted in a heap by the side wall. The neglect disturbed me, for image is everything and the scruffiness of her home had become more pronounced over the past year. Kate and David's children were teenagers now and required less attention. Also, Kate didn't work and not for the first time, I wondered how she filled her days.

It was several minutes before she answered the door with a vague smile. Her hair was dishevelled, sweat bottoms stained. The odour of burnt toast greeted me.

'Oh, hello.' A whiff of the raw garlic she chewed to manage menopause symptoms drifted over.

'Hi, could I have a quick word?'

Her gazed skimmed past me and I stopped myself from turning round to see what she was staring at. A shiver caressed my skin. Perhaps Miranda had magically appeared in Kate's garden, summoned to provide backup.

'Yes, come in.' Kate stepped back to allow me pass, and firmly shut the door. Thankfully Miranda didn't materialise indoors either.

I unzipped my jacket, but she didn't offer to hang it up, so I awkwardly kept it on, despite the stifling heat. Silently I followed her into the kitchen and barely suppressed my gasp of astonishment. The place was a tip, much worse than merely untidy, it resembled the aftermath of a hurricane. Clothes and shoes on every surface, dirty dishes toppled in the sink and on the countertop, the floor sticky underfoot. The burnt toast smell was pungent and charred black flakes littered the worktop.

Her glare was a challenge as she sized me up. 'Do you want coffee?'

'Lovely, thanks.' I met her dare head on.

'What's up?' Her tone softened a little.

I dived in as she busied herself making coffee. When she sniffed the milk, I didn't blink, but hid my disgust behind a fixed smile.

'I really need to chat to you about Miranda. Have you spoken to her this week?'

A loud sigh. 'I speak to her most days, so yes, I know about the complaint. She was very unhappy after your appointment.'

Her words hit me like a slap. Kate had known about the complaint for days, but chose not to speak to me about it. For the first time in our long friendship, I was thrown off-balance, unsure whose side Kate was on. Previously I could've counted on her to support me, no questions asked, loyalty unyielding. She'd been the one person who wholeheartedly cheered for me, and excused my occasionally less than stellar behaviour.

'What did she say?' I accepted the proffered mug and trailed behind her into the living room. Another bomb site. The television had been silenced and an ancient rerun of a soap played on. Half full mugs of cold coffee dotted the coffee table. It crossed my mind Kate could be depressed. The unkempt house and garden, drawn demeanour, unwashed hair and clothes. If I hadn't been so distracted with my own issues and been a better friend to her, I would've enquired how she was. Asked why the curtains were closed at lunchtime. Queried whether she had worries which overpowered her.

Obsessed by my own agenda and to my later shame, I didn't ask, but left her to navigate it on her own.

Instead I took off my coat and sat down on the one free space, an armchair by the fireplace.

'It would be best if I don't say too much until Miranda gets a written response to the complaint.' She didn't look at me, but observed the television, where Angie and Den were having a row.

'Kate!' It spewed from me. 'You don't believe I've done anything wrong, do you?'

She shrugged, as if to dismiss my difficulties and our friendship.

'How could you? It would have been unethical of me to

treat her, against my code of conduct.' A plea to relax the stony expression. 'She wanted to discuss your marriage.' I'd planned to keep that card up my sleeve until later, but her vacant expression chilled me.

'She's a good friend; there's nothing wrong with what she said.' Totally emotionless.

My jaw dropped at her comment. I was banging my head against a brick wall, so lobbed my last grenade. 'She's made a complaint I've been lurking outside her house.'

'Well, have you?' Her voice was weary, not horrified as I'd predicted.

'How can you even ask?'

Again a shrug of dismissal. My temper rumbled.

'You've been one of my best friends for years, hers for a few months. And yet, you're taking her word over mine?' I sounded unhinged, but no longer cared.

'I'm not taking sides. I'm neutral in all of this. Please don't pull me in and expect me to choose one of you. Miranda has done nothing but be nice to you.' This was a new Kate, one which equally appalled and alarmed me. 'All she did was try to be included and be your friend, but for some reason, you've taken against her and put me in a very difficult position.'

I set the mug on the coffee table with a thump, between a pair of dirty socks and the remote. Dismayed, I stood up and mustered my composure. 'I'm sorry you feel that way. I assumed you knew me well enough to know I'd never be unprofessional and frankly I'm shocked you've given these accusations credence.'

Rather than cry, which was Kate's default reaction, she met my eye and said, 'Do you hang about outside Miranda's home hoping to intimidate her?'

My fragile composure cracked. 'For feck sake. Of course I

don't. You're sure Claire is hanging about outside my house as well.'

A hesitation. 'I'm not so sure it's Claire. I think someone's been wearing a hat like Claire's, that's all.'

I could've bitten my tongue off for mentioning Claire, so pulled on my jacket while expecting a plea to stay. However, she said nothing and it hung between us. Without another word, I thundered out of the room, inadvertently kicked a hockey stick on the hall floor and almost tripped over. The fresh air cooled my temper and I gulped it ravenously. I'd walk off my stress. When I reached Miranda's house, I couldn't resist taking a gawp. The curtain in the front room twitched and I straightened my shoulders, refusing to give Miranda the satisfaction of seeing me upset.

An hour passed before I arrived home and it wasn't until I'd stripped off my coat that I remembered I was off sick. If a patient had seen me, it would leave a bad impression. Terrible in fact. I scuttled inside, locked the door and reprimanded myself for allowing my temper to lead me into doing something stupid.

Laura was a calming influence, I needed to speak to her soon to put my mind at ease. For I was in unfamiliar territory with Miranda's dogged determination to make me notice her. Like a wayward toddler, any attention was better than none.

After I texted Laura, I settled down to scour social media. The photos, posts and reels smoothed the edges of my very frazzled nerves. When I clicked on Instagram and checked Tom's account, there was no new activity. Relieved, I inspected the most recent photos on my friends' feeds and amused myself by leaving comments.

Laura had posted a photo of a white tipped waves breaking over a harbour wall.

Annie's latest post had been of a fundraiser for her breast

cancer charity. Dressed in a pink tutu and wearing a head bopper, she scaled a muddy climbing wall. My smile lingered until I clicked on Flora's last photo and anguish once again overflowed. It had been taken after her exams, her pallor unmistakeable. How could we have missed her unhappiness?

But as was my tendency, I became engrossed by another post, another photo. This one was of two entwined shadows, one tall and broad fused with the smaller, slimmer one. Taken at the top of a hill, the backdrop of green fields extended to a sliver of sparkling ocean in the distance.

The caption, 'Happiness is a walk with my fav.'

Without giving myself pause for thought, I added a comment. A spiteful, unkind comment which produced a bubble of happiness.

The next couple of hours were spent on the sofa with a frothy coffee and a new thriller. Amazingly the beeping of my mobile didn't distract me, I was too absorbed in the devilish doings of a serial killer.

When I tore myself back to reality, I reached for my phone and checked my messages.

Flora confirmed when and where we'd meet in Portstewart tomorrow.

Laura bolstered my confidence. I wasn't out of order about Miranda. She was at fault, I was above reproach.

Tom would be home late tomorrow night, thanked me for dealing with the AA and let me know that Robin would drop him home after getting him and Ashley.

As usual, I couldn't hold my phone without checking social media. Blithely I scrolled through Instagram, until horror wrapped its tentacles around my heart as my gaffe boomed and bellowed.

There was no way to know if my comment had been read or viewed, but it mocked me in black and white. My first mistake.

Rapidly I deleted it, as the pressure tightened. How stupid of me not to change profile before commenting, I'd always been so careful. So circumspect. One impetuous error could potentially cost me dear.

I had to hope I'd deleted it in time.

If not, I could be in serious trouble.

CHAPTER THIRTY-FIVE

The next day I drove an hour north with the radio blaring loudly. I'd had a disturbed night as my carelessness fumed and snarled. Although there was no obvious comeback, I catastrophised incessantly, certain my house of cards was on the verge of tumbling down around me.

To my relief, Flora shone with contentment in her new life at university. We lunched together in a seaside café which afforded the perfect view of Portstewart Strand. Although the middle of winter, the café was busy and there was a long row of cars parked at the foot of the sand dunes. The paint was chipped and dulled on the iconic 'DANGER Do Not Swim Near Rocks' sign on the beach steps, the nearby lifeguard hut unoccupied.

Over fish and chips, I delicately raised the subject of her school friends. She played with her teaspoon and flatly replied she'd unfriended them on social media and never contacted them. I allowed the silence to be filled by the voices around us and scrape of cutlery on plates.

'I'm good, Mum, stop fretting. Those bitches are my past, not my present.'

I should've dug further, but her glower was firm and I reluctantly changed the subject. After I paid the bill, we walked two miles along the Strand between choppy waves on one side, high dunes on the other. With the salty tang on my lips and stiff headwind, we didn't talk much, but when we reached the Barmouth, she playfully insisted we scramble onto the black rocks and walk out to the lighthouse.

Across the shimmering water, the Inishowen Headland of County Donegal was cloaked in low-lying cloud, while the Mussenden Temple stood proud on the cliffs looming above the sea.

Happiness spread as we took selfies with wide smiles. Her trauma seemed to be behind her, leaving no obvious marks. Later, I dropped her off at her halls of residence and two girls waited for her on a low wall. They jumped up as she reached them, and their giggles delighted me as they walked away together without a backwards glance.

The drive home was a slow one with poor visibility and a diversion on the dual carriageway. By the time I reached Ballyrevy, I was completely spent. Worry about Flora had dwindled with each passing mile, surpassed by unpleasant thoughts about Miranda, work and the growing fissures in our disintegrating book club.

It was nearly five o'clock and streaky orange daylight split the darkening sky. The streets were thronged with schoolboys in rugby kits, black blazers slung over bags, or fresh-faced girlfriends' shoulders. New drivers with R-plates crawled down congested roads near the school, and I inched my way past them towards the practice.

The surgery car park was almost empty, with a handful of cars. Jake's was one. Light spilled out of reception, and adjacent consulting rooms, meaning that people bustled about inside. I didn't want to be spotted by my colleagues, so parked on an adjacent side street, which gave me a clear view of the surgery, but concealed me in the deepening gloom. The hostility of my meeting with Jake still disheartened me, and I argued with myself if I should speak to him in person. As the engine ticked and cooled, I sent him a text.

> If you're free on Sunday afternoon, could I come over for a quick coffee?

A flutter of anticipation at the three rolling dots, but the reply never came. Instead the screen remained blank where his answer should be. For the next half hour, I monitored the surgery entrance with one eye, the other glued to my phone, as I willed it to flash with his response.

Dusk fell and streetlights flicked on, dim yellow light cutting through the blackness. An elderly woman lumbered out of the practice, swollen legs and cumbersome gait supported by a walking frame. A middle-aged man barely made it outside the front door before the red tip of his cigarette glowed brightly.

When Jake's car was the last one in the car park, I could wait no longer and recklessly chose to go and find him. Halfway across the deserted street, voices reached me from the direction of the staff entrance. Jake wasn't alone. My heart jumped, I slunk back into the shadows and watched as they made their way to his car. Her trill laugh pierced the silence, a possessive hand placed on his arm. The sickly sweet aroma of peach wafted over in the cool air.

Undercover of the shadows, I tracked the car as Jake drove them both towards the high street. Empty of emotion, I trudged back to my car and crept inside. I was used being in control and resented this loss greatly. Truthfully, I couldn't understand it. For most of my life, people had prized my friendship, craved it. Miranda was a case in point. Those who were included in my friendship group had been prudently chosen.

Then Claire had broken ranks to exert her retaliation and smash my self-confidence.

Now Kate was a loose cannon, on the cusp of picking Miranda over me.

And Jake, the one platonic male friend I'd ever had, was proving himself increasingly unreliable.

It hurt. The sneakiness and disloyalty. I could only be expected to shoulder so much before I snapped. Really it wasn't my fault, the decision I reached as condensation formed on the windscreen and my fingers ached from compressing the steering wheel. I started the engine and drove straight to the supermarket.

It didn't long to get the ingredients I needed and I added a bottle of Prosecco to the basket. Tom would be home later, with his deception and lies. If I drank a couple of glasses before he came home, it would erode the fierce ache of hurt. After a short hesitation, I added another bottle. There was the summit with my parents tomorrow, my reward would be a glass of something cold and refreshing after.

Before I left the car park, I made a phone call. It rang out and I tried again. No answer. In temper I flung the phone onto the passenger seat and it bounced onto the floor. With a curse, I drove home, mind already elsewhere. On the way I passed the end of Jake's street, which irritated and offended in equal measure.

Where once I would have casually called in for coffee and a chat, self-doubt forbade me. As I drew level with my beautiful home, the Monoblock drive, landscaped garden and pristine paintwork had never been so unwelcoming. I recognised it for the superficial façade it provided.

On the exterior and to the uninformed, we had it all.

On the interior, we were splintered and peeling, while darkness submerged the light.

I slammed the front door and walked through the house, snapping the blinds shut. Jake's failure to reply smarted, and again I was unsure how to act. No doubt he would respond at some point, but it gave me little comfort. Usually he texted back quickly and this prolonged delay was new and most unlike him.

Activity had always shaved off the excesses of my anxiety, and I itched to pound the pavements. Although determined not to change my routine because of criticism, I cowered from further accusations of loitering. Then courage swelled. It was half six; Tom would be home in around an hour. To hell with them all, I was going for a walk.

Up and down familiar streets I marched, wrapped in many layers to ward off the chill. Except for a lone dog walker in the park, I met no one. The freezing night air and exercise worked their magic and my tension was allayed with each step, until my phone buzzed in my pocket. I withdrew it and read Jake's message. Sunday would suit him around four o'clock. After I'd replied I would see him then, a smile played about my lips.

With renewed enthusiasm, I turned for home. At the end of my street, I crossed the road to avoid walking directly in front of Miranda's house. I didn't glance in her direction, determined I could weave my magic and my friendship with Jake would be restored.

Tom arrived home not long after me, with dark stubble and tired eyes. He embraced me in the kitchen, his kiss brief. Mundane chitchat and a bottle of beer later, he said Robin had complained continually on the drive from the airport. It gave him a new appreciation of how accommodating I'd always been of his job and necessary spells away from home. I spontaneously kissed him before he went to shower, antagonism thawed for a time.

While he was upstairs, I made arrangements to see Laura on Monday evening. It had been too long since we'd caught up on each other's news. She suggested inviting Kate and Annie as well, but the memory of Kate's vacant look was too harrowing, so I declined and explained I preferred to see her alone.

When I checked social media, I was relieved to see my earlier comment hadn't provoked a reaction and I relaxed. Presumably if anyone had seen it, they'd have responded. I poured myself a glass of bubbly and planned the next few days.

Above me, Tom's footsteps thumped around in the spare room, which was unusual. Unless he was going to check the iPad. Giving myself no time to consider, I tore out of the kitchen and up the stairs. When I reached the room, he sat on the edge of the bed in semi-darkness, head in hands, though he turned when he heard me.

'What's wrong?' A pang of fear.

'I'm sorry, sweetie.'

'Sorry for what?'

'I can't believe I jeopardised us again. Our marriage. Our family.' His face was careworn.

'What do you mean again?' Had he done something stupid on this trip?

'With Claire. We have so much and I almost threw it away. There's something wrong with me. It was all for nothing.'

My feet moved across the room and I knelt on the carpet in front of him. Words careered around my head, but I couldn't express them. Instead I leaned my forehead against his and we sat together.

When he began to talk, I listened. Really listened to what he said. No interruptions with bad temper nor questions. I'd never fully understand his compulsion to push boundaries or stray, but it would be hypocritical of me to rebuke him. In my own way, I was putting our marriage at as much risk as he had.

And if I crashed and burned, he'd have to pick up the pieces. The temptation to confess my own story was great, but it glided away before I uttered it.

The truth was laid bare between us that Friday night.

The almost truth.

And as a result, I slept better than I had in weeks.

CHAPTER THIRTY-SIX

The late winter sun hung low in the sky on the morning of the visit to my parents. When I woke fragments of my talk with Tom whispered to me, and I smiled at the memory. We were finally beginning afresh, with a greater understanding and acceptance of our sullied past.

Tom climbed out of bed with the mumbled instruction I should lie on; he'd bring me breakfast. As I nibbled on the toast and marmalade he'd carried up, the progress we'd made in resolving our differences last night delighted me. It was as if the walls which had been constructed from spikes and wire between us were disintegrating. Even facing my parents in the afternoon couldn't wipe the smile from my face.

I should've known it wouldn't last and the sunny morning would blend into a turbulent afternoon, that a bitter wind was already blowing.

Tom kissed me at the door before I left for the city. The worry lines faded. A sighed 'I love you,' before I exited our cocoon and embarked on the drive alone.

The earlier sun was blotted out by thick cloud which settled on Cave Hill, high above Belfast. Occasionally optimistic rays of watery sunshine would perforate through, then were obliterated. The congested motorway and city streets whizzed past and I hummed to myself. Memories of our candid talk and the aftermath flashed. We were finally laying the ghosts of his affair to rest.

When I arrived at my parents' house at exactly 2.55, I experienced a twinge of dismay at the prospect of dealing with them. Although I'd try not to let their digs bother me, I reverted to childhood in their presence. One steely frown or negative comment and my self-assurance crumbled. In anticipation of seeing them, my stomach flipped.

Within a minute, Adam drove in behind me. No Natalie nor Zander today. Another smidgeon of foreboding. They'd never summoned us without our families before. I watched in the rear-view mirror as my brother unfolded himself from the car and lifted a hand in greeting. He straightened up, strode over and opened my door. As he leaned down his smile was uncertain.

'Hey, sis. Do you know what this is about?'

'No idea.' I climbed out of the car and squinted up at him. Three years younger and five inches taller than me, he was a handsome man who'd always been there for me when the frigidity of our home grew intolerable. I grasped his hand and smiled encouragingly.

'Once more unto the breach then.' He grinned down at me and we rang the bell at exactly three o'clock.

My mother opened the door within moments, as if she had been hiding behind it with a stopwatch to ensure we entered at precisely the commanded time. Her smile didn't reach her eyes as we kissed her cheek and she lead us down the hall towards the lounge. Dad was in his usual leather armchair, today no unfinished book nor half-moon glasses. Instead he nursed a whisky, which was extraordinary so early in the day.

Adam and I sat at either end of the sofa and after a cursory offer of coffee, which we both declined, my mother neatly seat beside Dad. I stifled a giggle at the impression we were about to play table tennis across the walnut coffee table.

Two hours later me and Adam left the house together, shell-shocked. Silently we hugged before we got into our respective cars. The drive home passed me by, my mind consumed with my father's blunt words.

I have been diagnosed with advanced cancer.

My emotions were perplexing and varied; I hated my father, but I loved him too.

Years of failing to get a compliment or word of praise. Of fierce demands I could never achieve. Cold stares and malicious lectures.

And yet I'd assumed one day we would build bridges and smooth over our disagreements.

Now we were running out of time to make amends and as the bomb exploded, his taut jaw and puckered brow provided little leeway for reconciliation.

Sobs erupted from me as I wailed my heartache, which pealed around the car. His prognosis was guarded, dependent on how he responded to treatment. In his usual intransigent manner, he'd laid out his wishes in a firm, matter-of-fact way. My mother had sipped a sherry, face caked with powder, hand shaky. She was shrivelled and small, like all fight had leaked from her. Most unusually he hadn't snarled as I questioned him. Hands which wrung together were the solitary sign of his edginess.

I fell into Tom's arms when I arrived home and spluttered the news. He hugged me tight and rubbed my back as if I were a child. We held each other for long minutes, as I answered his questions to the best of my ability.

'I always thought your father would live forever.' Tom moved away and offered me a drink, but I declined.

'It sounds so stupid, but I know what you mean.' If you could prolong life through force of personality and willpower, Dad would never have surrendered to illness.

Mind blank, I went upstairs. From the back of the drawer, I plucked out yoga leggings, a T-shirt and trainers. They were designed for indoor classes, but would do. A lightweight top, then I tied my hair in a low ponytail. With a shout to Tom I was going out, I slammed the door. My face lifted to the moon and the rain as I inhaled the clear air, and did some stretches. The tumult in my head could be silenced only by exercise.

I walked onto the pavement and began to jog.

The tyrant of my youth had been confronted with his own mortality. The shadow he'd cast over my life had been long and bleak, but now it would lighten and shorten. The burden of his expectations and inevitable disapproval would become as nothing, an illusion, relegated to history.

The run was painful as my lungs burned and muscles cramped. It had been too many years since I'd eaten up the miles on the pavements and running tracks, my stride sure and long. Now I was middle-aged and relatively unfit, despite my walks and sporadic exercise classes. Fulfilment now was in the release of pent-up emotions and the expunging of nightmares, not the chasing of medals or winner's podiums.

On the way home I slowed to a plod and gulped desperate gasps into my protesting lungs. The rain was a deluge, as grief fought an inner battle with the promise of freedom. My clothes were soaked as I stopped outside Miranda's, hands on hips, guzzling air. It was a natural resting spot, under the streetlight. The fine mizzle slanted downwards, artificially yellow in the soft glow. My heart rate gradually slowed and the cramp in my muscles lessened as adrenaline spiked. My first run in decades. Not pretty, but happiness surged through me.

I studied Miranda's house, the external lights unforgiving

and cold. If she spotted me, I no longer cared. She could do her worst and it would never be enough to bring me to my knees.

Exhausted from my run, I dawdled past Kate's house with its broken outside light and dented car. Inside my fickle friend hid from conflict as her life hurtled around. Gentle and impressionable, she was a natural prey for stronger characters.

When I reached home, the gushing torrent of sadness at my father's news had become a trickle.

I was resolute and determined.

I was my father's daughter.

I would survive, and may ultimately thrive.

Tom's face reflected his surprise I'd gone for a run, but he stretched his arms out wide before pulling me tight against him and rubbing my back. From time to time, I'd confessed how much I missed it and he'd questioned my resolution to abandon it completely. My reasons were intricate and not easily fathomable.

Perhaps it was a natural reaction to being confronted with my father's news.

Or possibly it signalled a fresh beginning without his tirades to drain my peace.

Whatever the reason, I hungrily consumed the steak and chips Tom cooked as I showered. Originally I'd planned a birthday meal out with the girls, but had cancelled when my parents had summoned me. Instead I'd booked a table at one of our favourite restaurants in Belfast on Tuesday, his actual birthday. Unfortunately it meant the girls couldn't join us, but my parents' decree had to be obeyed.

After dinner we watched a movie together on the sofa in the living room. Although grief ballooned when I recalled my father's news, I listened to the comforting thump of Tom's heartbeat and savoured the strength of his arms around me.

For a short time, I put everything aside and focused on the present.

But as Tom dozed off, I squirmed out of his embrace and turned the volume of the television down, but didn't switch it off. As quietly as possible, I went into the kitchen and retrieved my mobile from my handbag. I sat at the breakfast bar, with a glass of Prosecco which fizzed in my mouth.

Methodically I skimmed the notifications and messages, read posts and left comments. Repetition of the familiar took the edge off my worries.

Then I removed my list from the back of the drawer. One item left to tick off. One I had written weeks ago, but never acted on. I perused my scribbled note and sucked the end of my pen. My plan had been laid, the wheels ready to set in motion.

It was the final step in a path I'd chosen many months ago. Or rather, the path which had been chosen for me. I had debated and vacillated, first one way, then the other. As time had passed and the path became increasingly rocky and onerous, I'd run out of options. A fire raged inside me, leaving me incapable of choice.

One last thing and everything would return to normal.

My marriage intact.

Friendship restored.

Obstacle defeated.

<h1 style="text-align:center">CHAPTER THIRTY-SEVEN</h1>

Almost inevitably after my father's news, I had a restless night where I dreamt I was swimming in a race wearing a weighted suit. No matter how hard I swam, I sank to the bottom as the jeers of the crowd and bellows from my father badgered me. I woke with a start, and tasted terror on my lips. My skin was clammy, the dream too vivid to dismiss quickly. It took over an hour before I fell back to sleep.

Next morning wisps of the dream remained, and my vision blurred. Over the years I'd sporadically dreamt of competing, but usually I won. Not this time; I'd thrashed about but my opponents had broken free, and only splashes on the water's surface remained.

Tom's side of the bed was empty, and I was grateful I could cry alone, without meaningless words of comfort or inept back rubbing. Perhaps I would never get to the bottom of my convoluted emotions regarding my father, or possibly it was simply too fresh.

At last my sobs subsided and my mind recoiled from grief. I hoped for a stress-free day with minimal obligations, and mentally ran through my short to-do list.

Ease my tired, throbbing legs with a long soak in the bath.

Visit Jake in the afternoon.

Cook a leisurely dinner for me and Tom.

Routine Sunday relaxation before the frenetic work week.

After the bath, I went downstairs to find Tom hunched over his phone at the table. Straight away he set it face down, screened it with his hand and raised virtuous eyes to me. 'I left you to sleep on. You thrashed around all night.'

'Thanks.' I had no energy to confront him about my doubts. 'I had a bad dream.'

'About your dad?'

'About drowning.'

'Oh, sweetie, you poor thing.' Instantly he rose, enveloped me in his arms and rubbed my back.

Rather than soothe, this time it irritated. I stepped away and popped some bread into the toaster. 'It's fine. I'm fine.'

He then disrupted my plans with the suggestion of a beach walk, which he presumably believed would stop me from moping. I glanced out of the kitchen window to find the rain had cleared overnight and the morning was dry and sunny. So I agreed, though thought *As long as it isn't Ballydunn beach.* The memory of our day there tainted my guardedly optimistic outlook. However, I smiled thinly when he suggested a different beach with a seaside café. Our vow to move on lived to fight another day.

Decision made, we dressed in warm clothes, waterproof coats at the ready. I offered to drive and Tom good-naturedly agreed. Before we left the house, he hugged me and stroked my hair. His familiar smell and wide chest made me feel small and cherished, and my hands dropped to his butt to pull him closer. We kissed and I was tempted to scrap the walk and lead him by the hand upstairs.

Sanity prevailed and we held hands on our way out to the

car. I never glanced around for prying eyes, my attention fully on the road as we left the village behind.

Tom fiddled with the radio, searching for music we both liked, then we sang along like teenagers. The car ate up the miles as we sped towards the Irish Sea and by the time we reached the coastal road, contentment had settled beneath my ribs.

We drove through seaside villages with sheltered harbours, past sheer cliffs and seaweed strewn rocks. Wild swimmers braved the freezing water along with bodyboarders, and Scotland rose from the misty horizon as scanty clouds raced across the sky.

Before we reached the beach car park, Tom muttered quietly and reached down into the footwell. Disinterested, I glanced over as he groped about at his feet and with one hand braced himself against the dash.

'What's up?'

'There's something caught under the seat. It's half out, but has got stuck.' His words blasted a warning, for immediately I knew what it was.

'Don't worry about it now,' I barked. 'It's probably something that rolled out of my handbag.'

With a grunt of satisfaction, it broke free and out of the corner of my eye, I saw him lift it up. Small, black, solid. Fear pulsed as he examined it. Excuses filled my head, but failed to reach my lips as I indicated right and pulled into the first empty space. Sudden silence as the radio cut off and the engine faltered.

He turned to face me. 'Why do you have a burner phone?' His nostrils flared.

'Don't be daft, it's not a burner phone.' Playing for time, my brain rushed to invent a reason for my second phone. But it was completely blank and I couldn't produce one credible excuse.

'I'm not stupid.' Too late I recalled he was the expert at deception. Abruptly he pressed the button and to my horror, the screen illuminated immediately. There was no pin code, no face ID. After all, it was a secret, there was no need to protect it from anyone. Usually it was concealed in the depths of my handbag.

Horror tightened my chest as I recalled flinging it down in anger when my call went unanswered on Friday outside the surgery. The phone had bounced off the passenger seat and onto the floor, but in my upset, I'd forgotten to retrieve it. Too perplexed by Jake's slyness to think clearly, and rather than return it to the inner pocket of my bag, I had left it lying under the seat. Now my husband watched me through narrowed eyes as I desperately tried to make up a reason for having it.

Before I could speak, he began to scroll through it.

It didn't take long, for there was no internet connection on this most basic of phones. No messages had been sent, its sole purpose had been to make calls. The log displayed one number, rung multiple times. Tom's knuckles were white, to match the pallor of his face.

'Whose number is it?' His words landed heavily in the oppressive atmosphere of the car.

My arm shot out and I tried to wrestle it from him, but he clamped it firmly and I couldn't loosen his hold. Maddened, I flung myself back against the car door as I panted loudly.

'Give me the phone.'

'Whose number is it?' Slow and deliberate.

'It's a work phone.' A believable lie had finally come to me as I rubbed my temple furiously.

'That's not what I asked.'

His face was unreadable now. I refused to answer, but stretched out my hand, as if he would calmly pass the phone over and we'd continue merrily on our walk.

Without speaking, he paused at the number, then poked it angrily.

'Please.' My voice broke. 'Give me the phone.'

His head swung from side to side and he clutched it tightly. Sickness swept over me as the seconds ticked over. I could hear the ringtone clearly.

Once. Twice. It was answered on the fourth ring.

A woman's breathy voice. 'Hello.'

Tom's answering hello.

'Who is this?'

Tom paused, bewilderment palpable. No doubt he'd been expecting a man to answer and the female voice had thrown him. I grabbed the phone from his open palm and disconnected the call in one swift move.

Then I snapped, 'I told you it was a work phone. That was Jinty the receptionist. No big deal, except now I'm going to have to explain why my husband was ringing the poor woman on a Sunday.'

'But why do you have a work phone and why did you get angry when I found it?' Confusion contorted his face, but I seized the chance of escaping the noose.

'You've no reason to doubt what I've said.' Attack was my best option and I ploughed on ruthlessly. 'We're not all up to no good, some of us have boring, dull lives and the biggest drama is a walk on the beach on a cold day.'

I held my breath as his cogs turned. Finally, after interminable moments, he nodded. 'Okay. There's a rational explanation.' He smiled and I tightly smiled back.

Reaching over, I lightly stroked his jaw. 'Did you really think it was a burner and I was up to something?'

He huffed a little before replying. 'I was just a bit suspicious why you had a second phone, I'm sorry to have doubted you.'

I contrived reluctance as he placed a gentle kiss on my lips, unyielding until he apologised again. Only then did I relax. He'd come dangerously close to prising open my deepest secret, my darkest obsession.

With a final kiss, we exited the car and strolled along the windswept beach. We chatted together and I concentrated on filling his mind with nonsense so he'd forget the mobile.

Forget the precarious moment I'd protested my blamelessness.

Forget why I had a phone with one number, but multiple calls.

When we reached the car park after our walk, I suggested coffee in the beachside café and he agreed with no dispute. Hopefully the memory of the phone had dissolved, replaced by golden sand and thunderous waves.

My unprincipled, gorgeous husband, who'd spent so long concealing his own discretions, had underestimated me.

And my aim to decimate.

CHAPTER THIRTY-EIGHT

We arrived home from our walk and coffee in the beach hut in companionable silence. Tom hadn't mentioned the mobile again, and I'd buried it in my coat pocket. It was useless to me now. I'd break it and cut up the SIM card when he was occupied elsewhere. Then I'd replace it with a new one in the next few days. I was due to change it anyway: I'd used this one since the beginning of January, which was longer than I usually held on to one.

Once I'd changed into more presentable clothes and scrunched my hair into a messy bun, I was almost ready to visit Jake. A slick of lipstick, a brush of blusher and layers of mascara. Painstaking no-make-up make-up to enhance my looks and imitate midlife radiance. We may be platonic friends, but he was still a male and therefore susceptible to good looks.

A pretty face allows you to get away with so much, for people expect an attractive exterior to equate to an equally attractive interior. Which of course can be a misplaced assumption, and shockingly I'd weaponised my looks to my advantage over the years.

Tom had assumed the position in front of the television with the remote and I gave him a chaste kiss before telling him I was going to visit Laura. If he'd been observant, he would've recalled her car wasn't in the driveway, but as usual, he never questioned me or my whereabouts.

My friendship with Jake was my guilty pleasure, private yet essential to my well-being. As fundamental to me now as breathing. It had relieved the banality of my life and added fire and spice, which had been sadly lacking for years. There was a slim possibility Tom would disapprove of me having a male friend, therefore I'd hidden it from him. There was no possibility of him understanding not all male/female relationships ended in sex. As weeks of lying had slipped into months, the opportunity for honesty had passed. What he didn't know wouldn't hurt him.

I trudged down the street, alert for anything out of the ordinary. The nape of my neck prickled as I passed Miranda's house, certain she tracked each step. The prickling stopped when I reached Jake's street and contentment fluttered. He was bound to use today to apologise for his brusqueness last week, his reserved manner, his biting behaviour.

His car was in the drive and I inched past it to ring the bell. While I waited for him to answer, I glanced around the street and inhaled the woodsmoke aroma of a nearby bonfire. There was no one around, the street was empty and quiet. Jake answered the door with a cautious smile and invited me in. Silently I followed him into the kitchen, where he offered me coffee and I took my usual seat at the table, though he was clearly preoccupied.

Politely he enquired if I was feeling better, and initially I was bright and cheery. However, conversation which usually flowed, stalled, and the silence was broken by the clang of a spoon and the fridge door closing. In a wooden voice, I asked if he was all right. An intense blue stare and from nowhere, apprehension uncoiled. A brief *'Fine,'* followed by an inclination of the head that we should move through into the living room. My footsteps slapped along the tiles as coffee sploshed over my wrist, scalding it. I was too unsettled by his frosty expression to say anything, and unobtrusively massaged the sore area.

When we reached the sitting room, he flopped onto his gaming chair with a soft groan, then relaxed his defences. A sip of coffee, before he spoke in a stilted tone. 'I'm sorry if I seem a bit worked up. Something unsettling happened earlier.'

I raised my eyebrows and waited for him to continue. When he broke the silence it was as though he'd changed the subject.

'I should probably have cancelled you coming over, but I didn't want to go into work tomorrow without having cleared the air between us. Again, I'm sorry if I annoyed you when I spoke to you about Miranda Stevenson's allegations. I've sent her a written response explaining my findings, so hopefully it will be the end of it.' His manner was gruff, his face closed.

My chin jerked up in the approximation of agreement, though I suspected he'd more to say.

'Regarding the other accusation, well, I believe you when you said you don't hang about outside her house. I mean, why would you?' His snort of laughter sounded more like a yelp of pain. 'But so many odd things have happened recently, things no one can really explain.' His eyes roamed the room until they fixed on one of the black framed photos on the mantelpiece.

Words raced to fill the silence which grew lengthy, but one false step could cost me dear, so they stuck in my throat. He began to speak, but a noise from the hallway interrupted his flow.

The click of a key turning in the lock. The front door creaked. 'Hello' trilled a girlish voice.

He tenderly replied, 'Honey, we're in here.'

Heels clacked on the floor tiles and a slim figure filled the doorway as the cloying scent of perfume drenched the room. Blond hair, fine features and a blood-red pout. Stilettos and a short skirt.

'Hi, Vicky.' Indifferent.

'Hi, Bronagh,' my response.

She strode over to Jake and kissed him full on the lips. His hand cupped the back of her head as he pulled her close. I could've been invisible, my presence redundant as they whispered sweet nothings into each other's ears. Bitterly I gawked at the photos on the mantelpiece, to avoid their overt display of affection.

One photo of them in evening dress, him smart in a tuxedo, she beautiful in a red strapless dress. His arm protectively around her narrow waist, she clawed his other hand.

The other was a selfie of them both on top of a mountain, her left hand held aloft to draw attention to her solitaire engagement ring, a sliver of river far below.

This woman had inveigled and snaked her way into the affection of my friend. She'd coaxed him away from me, downgraded me in his affections and eroded the bonds of our friendship. His betrayal had been absolute when he'd asked her to marry him, then against my advice, promoted her in work. Throughout their relationship she'd diminished our friendship as second rate and manipulated Jake with her beauty.

And the whole time I'd pretended I was happy for him. For them. However jealousy and rage bit and snarled, and gradually I lost my sense of reason.

I'd worked hard to make him see sense, that she wasn't good enough for him. To gently persuade him she was narcissistic, selfish and demanding. But all I'd succeeded in doing was push him into her slim, tanned arms until she'd taken up residence in his mind and his heart and I was relegated to the sidelines.

Hand in hand, they disappeared together into the kitchen leaving me alone with my envy and burned wrist. My possessiveness was so intense I couldn't swallow the coffee and banged the mug onto the table. Her muffled snigger reached me and I recalled the remarks she'd made last week when I'd frozen in the dark corridor and listened to her mock me. What had pained me most was Jake's reply. He too had laughed at me, making me ludicrous for putting my faith in him.

Before my rage boiled over, they came back into the room and Bronagh sat on the sofa, took off her stilettos and tucked her feet under her. It was so compact I could feel the heat rise from her. She sucked on her vape and exhaled the sickly cloud of peaches. I fixed a smile, prepared my excuses and made ready to leave.

Then she addressed Jake. 'Did you tell Vicky what happened this morning?'

He shook his head and Bronagh sighed loudly. 'I got another phone call from the withheld number. My stalker.' Her eyebrows disappeared under her fringe and I affected surprise, though the harshness of the word caused my skin to itch.

'What happened?'

'This time he spoke. Said hello. I asked who it was, but of course he said nothing.' Flecks of spittle flew out from between her artfully sculpted lips. 'I bet it's the same person who broke my car window, posts unwanted gifts and comments daily on my socials. And of course, sent that awful email with the photo of me and Jake on the works night out. He must have been seated close to us and we never realised.'

'How awful.' Sedately I reached for my mug and this time the coffee slipped seamlessly down. 'Did he say anything else?' I feigned concern, for Tom had said nothing incriminating and it was impossible to have worked out who'd called her from the burner phone.

Bronagh said no, and Jake interjected. 'Poor baby has been so traumatised by everything.'

Poor baby. I wanted to vomit. His poor baby was a scheming fishwife. I lowered my lashes to conceal the full extent of my loathing, and chose my words with care. 'It's been so tough for you, I'm not surprised you've been traumatised. Has anything else happened?'

A private look was exchanged and my heart stilled. Evidently they were keeping something from me. After an age, Bronagh cleared her throat. 'Nothing much except they sent me a copy of *Admin for Dummies* and fake tan remover pads. The usual nastiness.'

'And you thought they were outside your flat again a few times.' Jake's voice cracked.

It had always struck me as strange how although they were engaged, they'd never lived together. This house was so determinedly Jake's, whereas Bronagh shared a flat in Ballyrevy with her sister Simone. Allegedly her parents disapproved of living together before marriage, something I found difficult to believe with someone whose morals were as low as Bronagh's. I patted her forearm in a show of sympathy and tried to work out what was not being said.

I prodded and encouraged, but they disclosed nothing of substance. The hint of plans, the taunt of ventures new. It had been years since I'd been so blatantly excluded and superfluous. When my fragile ego could take no more, I drained my cup of cold coffee and said my goodbyes. Jake looked as if he was about to speak, but Bronagh's head shot from side to side, and he said nothing. Instead he studied his nails.

A scream of frustration built in my throat. The atmosphere

thickened as my battered mind went into overdrive. The silence lengthened and grew stale until I unsteadily got to my feet and smiled vaguely, as if unwitting they shared a secret which deliberately excluded me. Self-entitlement oozed from Bronagh's smug expression.

Neither asked me to stay, nor showed me out. Her giggle escorted me into the hallway, and it took immense willpower not to slam either the door or my fist into the wall.

Hands shoved into my pockets, I stepped into the twilight. The dull glow from the streetlights accompanied me as I marched along, and the damp air cooled my tantrum. I couldn't go straight home, not with my emotions so delicate, nor temper so volatile.

Therefore I skirted the park and crouched low through the hole at the very back of the hedge. The grass was flattened from my many walks, and pale moonlight guided me to my usual hiding place directly behind Jake's bungalow. From this vantage point and through the branches, I could see straight into his kitchen.

It made me feel close to him, as he pottered around, made dinner, drank coffee and the like. However the main reason I did it was because I could monitor when Bronagh visited, which saved me from parking outside her flat and guessing where she was. She'd almost caught me once when I'd dropped my guard and parked too close. But I'd learned quickly and over the months, had become quite the expert in surveillance. When she'd spotted me on the Lisburn Road, I'd had my excuse at the ready. Lunch with Alex in the very café where she and Jake 'happened' to be with friends.

To term it *stalking* was offensive.

I wasn't stalking her, not in the true sense of the word.

I was simply scrutinising her as she dissected my friendship with Jake, piece by piece, day by day.

It had become an addiction, something which simultaneously amused and caused extreme pain.

My natural dislike of Bronagh had melded into something darker when she'd stolen my friend.

There was no question in my mind. I was as much a victim as her.

CHAPTER THIRTY-NINE

When I tired of watching Jake and Bronagh in the kitchen, I was almost ready to face Tom. Almost, but not quite. The knowledge they'd hidden something from me, cut deep. With any luck it was inconsequential, like a holiday, but I knew that potentially it could be significant. Worst-case scenario, they'd set a wedding date. Bronagh's jaw had tensed when Jake almost spoke, and her eyes had flashed a warning. He'd been close to sharing, until she'd clicked her fingers and he'd clammed up. The memory of it jabbed me, and my stomach churned with worry about the unknown.

As I plodded back along the hedge, I pulled Claire's green woollen hat from my pocket and fingered it. She'd inadvertently left it in my car when I'd driven the Book Club to the Mourne View Hotel in early December. Before I learned of her affair. Before she confronted me with my teenage behaviour. The bobble had got tangled under the seat and I'd never returned it, predicting it could come in handy, and it had indeed proved useful. When Tom had produced it from the drawer in the utility room, my pulse had hammered like a drum as he studied it before accepting my fictitious tale about it being an old one of Alex's, despite faint traces of Claire's perfume clinging to it.

When news had broken about Tom and Claire's affair, my main hope had been to gain sympathy from the others. There could be no margin of understanding for Claire's reason, no compassion shown. The germ of an idea had come to me as the reality of my situation had sunk in.

To make Claire more treacherous and myself more of a casualty, I'd given the impression she continued to stalk me. I needed someone to fall for my tall tale, and Kate had been the obvious choice. She'd always hankered to be my best friend and to my shame, had been easy to manipulate. Therefore I'd regularly walked in the field behind our houses, wearing Claire's distinctive hat, and always made sure Kate spotted the mysterious figure. As I'd hoped, she'd assumed the role of the horrified friend who believed someone was hanging around the fields, and bought the notion I was being watched. By Claire. An easy target who was helpless to defend herself. The day she'd been outside the coffee shop had been chance, nothing more, like the time she'd driven past us in Ballydunn.

The crescent moon afforded dim light, and the field was in semidarkness as I opened the gate as quietly as possible and nipped through. Once I tugged the hat down low, I slowly walked over the soggy grass and the wet blades soaked the hem of my jeans. Every light in Kate's house was on. Swathed in blackness, I watched her son Luke help himself to food from the fridge until Kate appeared to playfully chase him away. Once she was alone, I turned on my mobile's flashlight and swung it around to attract attention. She spotted it, and peered out of the window, hands cupped to see better into the shade.

Suppressing a chuckle, I strode off in the direction of my own house. Another one for her overactive imagination. Then I switched off the flashlight, doubled back on myself, removed the hat and thrust it into my pocket. I'd leave it for a while before I walked up our street, in case Kate appeared outside to hunt shadows. I meandered up the unlit country road for a few minutes, until my phone vibrated. My plan had worked. Kate's text conveyed her excitement.

> There's someone in the field again!!!

My reply was immediate.

> Are you sure? Please don't go outside by yourself

It took her several minutes to reply.

> Yes, I'm certain. Don't worry, I won't!!!

Kate's fondness for exclamation marks in her messages generally made me smile. She really was a sweet person. Happy she'd once again fallen for my dupe, I retraced my steps and turned onto the street. A quick recce confirmed no one was hanging around. Miranda's house was in darkness. No curtain twitching. No bright exterior lights. Her car was parked in the usual spot in front of the garage. I hurried on.

Once I arrived home, I called hello to Tom. A sleepy answer, as I whipped off my coat and popped my head around the sitting room door. Keiko lay curled on his lap, and both appeared to have been dozing. I offered to make dinner and to get him a beer.

'Lovely. Thanks, sweetie.'

It rankled a little he didn't ask how my afternoon had been, but I suppressed my annoyance and retreated into the kitchen.

There I extracted a beer from the fridge and presented it to him with an unenthusiastic smile.

Music played as I prepared the veg and wrapped Parma ham around chicken drumsticks. Tom loved a Sunday roast, though I had minimal interest with both girls at university. A roast dinner for two was a little sad compared to our previous roasts for four. However the tedium of cooking helped reduce my lingering apprehension.

When the food was in the oven, I became engrossed in Bronagh's social media posts. I left a few comments, fastidiously ensuring there was no repeat of the disastrous day I'd made the scathing remark from my own account. That was the closest I'd come to catastrophe before the business with Tom and the burner.

She'd blocked *Bea Goode* but my new guise, *Summer Rose*, had up to now been on her best behaviour. With a few well-chosen, acerbic comments tonight, Bronagh would once again be at the mercy of an unknown internet troll. A few months ago I'd purchased a VPN for my iPhone, which increased security and reduced the risk of being traced. I'd been relieved how straightforward it was to stay undetectable; all it took was a little homework and planning.

My mind wandered as I scrolled.

The burner had been perfect for my anonymous calls, and I'd got such a buzz when she ranted down the phone to an unresponsive caller. Afterwards, worry had always seeped from me.

Selecting the unwanted gifts had given me a laugh. When she'd yapped about needing to lose a few pounds after Christmas, I'd got extra-large gym wear delivered. The self-help book and fake tan remover wipes could be construed as helpful. My favourite had been the photo calendar. It had taken time to snap all the photos, but had been worth it in the end.

And of course, when I'd taken the money from petty cash, I'd donated it to charity. I'm not a thief.

Primarily I'd wanted to unnerve her, not frighten her. Not really. Make her wonder who detested her and why. The problem was, it took ever greater stakes to get the same level of satisfaction. After months of escalating behaviour, I no longer knew when enough was enough and when a line had been crossed.

But as usual, I reminded myself it was her fault. Hers and sadly, Jake's. They were complicit in keeping something from me and it hurt. Like a physical pain, deceit wrapped itself around me, and squashed my happiness.

Where once sending unwanted gifts and making crank calls had been enough, now it left me unfulfilled. Sadly I had to acknowledge my plan had failed. Rather than drive her away from Jake, it had pushed her closer to him. Brought out his protective side. It was transparent where his loyalties lay.

With her, not me.

Self-pity swept through me as jealousy's stranglehold tightened. His friendship had meant so much, but she'd usurped me and it had become devastatingly plain our friendship was one-sided. In the blackest hours of the night, I agonised he'd barely tolerated the older woman who'd exaggerated a good working relationship and fashioned it into something it wasn't.

For friends didn't lie to each other and keep secrets.

Friends made time for each other, supported and backed each other.

They didn't gossip about, laugh at, humiliate nor demoralise.

The oven pinged, which startled me and hauled me from my reverie. Despondently, I lifted out the food and served it on two plates. I carried Tom's through on a tray with another beer and he thanked me without lifting his eyes from the television.

Sighing, I left him to it and sat at the kitchen table. My appetite had gone, so I pushed my food around, weighed down with negativity.

Why had I chosen this course of action? How I had become mired in this messy situation which was sure to end badly?

When guilt unfurled, I recited the reasons for my choices.

My ability to separate my conscience and my activities was astonishing, and slightly scary. For I was a fundamentally good person who'd dedicated her life to helping others. The lengths I'd been forced to go to were out of my control. It was Bronagh's fault. She'd given me no choice.

Tom carried his tray into the kitchen and didn't comment on my barely touched food. He scraped the leftovers into the bin and stacked the dishes in the dishwasher, chittering rubbish.

'I'm going to have a quick shower.' I pecked him on the lips and hoped he wouldn't remember I'd already had a long soak in the bath this morning. My mind was spiralling and I ached for solitude.

Nonchalantly he helped himself to another beer from the fridge and headed off to the living room. Dispassionately I tracked him. He may look like an Adonis, but could be mind-numbingly dull at times.

Upstairs, I checked his iPad. The battery was flat. Which was an inconvenience, but not a tragedy. When he was next away with work, I'd charge it and have a quick peek. The burning desire to read his texts and scour his Instagram had died when confronted by Jake's betrayal.

Tomorrow would bring its own sorrows, but if I approached it correctly, I could find out what Bronagh and Jake had been hiding from me. All it would take was a friendly tone and subtle questions.

Sudden optimism bloomed. Before the end of the day, I'd have uncovered their secret.

CHAPTER FORTY

Awake before the alarm beeped on Monday morning, I was confident I'd devised a way to get Jake to spill their secret. While I breakfasted in the kitchen, buoyant music played from the speakers and my foot jiggled along. Undoubtedly it would be a busy day and hopefully by home time everything would be back in its proper place.

Optimism bubbled during the drive into Ballyrevy and brewed while I chatted to Gloria in the staff room. She was sympathetic to my migraine and admonished me for working too hard. Then a wave of excitement swept the room as loud gasps competed with chatter.

'What's going on?' I asked Gloria, who blushed and bit her lip.

'I'm not sure.' Her bland smile fell flat.

Ants crawled over my skin. 'You're a partner, you must know what's happening.'

'I can't say anything,' she hissed. 'Not until I'm given the go-ahead.'

Exasperated at being excluded from the heated discussion, I tapped Jinty's shoulder. She swung round, eyes shining.

'What's everyone talking about?'

'Jake and Bronagh have handed in their notices, they're leaving at the end of the week!' She could barely contain her excitement.

'What?' My vision clouded. 'Is it true?' I pivoted back to Gloria, who cleared her throat. 'Why? How can they leave so quickly?' My voice was high-pitched, but I was incapable of lowering it.

'They approached the partners and asked it be kept quiet for as long as possible. Under the circumstances.' She meant the peculiar happenings. 'They both had two weeks annual leave left, which meant a shorter notice period to be worked. Needless to say, we aren't exactly impressed as Bronagh has recently been promoted.' The stain across her cheeks had deepened to an ugly red, and her tone became conspiratorial. 'Didn't Jake say anything to you before the news broke?'

All I could manage was 'No' in a croaky voice, which betrayed my upset. She placed a comforting hand on my forearm, which I resisted wrenching away with difficulty, dangerously close to losing my cool. Either I would cry or squawk my torment.

Jake's treachery pained my heart. He could've forewarned me, but instead had secreted it from me, and left me to find out with everyone else. Conversation around me quietened and faces glazed as my fantasy collapsed around me.

He loved Bronagh and our friendship meant little to him.

Somehow I kept my face still and my chin up despite the shock which surged through my body.

When Bronagh strutted into the staff room a short time later, her arrogance and loud giggle inflamed further. 'It seems we surprised you all.' She flipped her hair and dissolved into giggles.

'Have you another job lined up?' Jinty brazenly demanded.

Bronagh's smile vanished and her gaze slid away to the left. 'Not yet.'

It rang false, and I detected a lie. She didn't want anyone to know, so she couldn't be followed. Dismay replaced astonishment. This had been carefully planned for some time. The thunderbolt revelation had simply been announced sooner than they'd predicted.

Jake came into the room behind her and slipped an arm around her waist. He winked at her and the corners of his lips turned up. Then he said something into her ear and she stroked his face tenderly. They didn't care what people thought and were immune to the smirks. Jake made eye contact with me then, but I looked away, unable to affect either enthusiasm or enjoyment. The weight of their dishonesty was a heavy burden to bear.

Unable to witness their show, I strode from the room, ignored my name being called and blindly groped for my consulting room door. The air singed my lungs as I buckled onto my chair, and the ground rose to meet me. I laid my head on my arms to settle the wooziness as the walls closed in. Hysteria hovered as I processed it all.

Jake and Bronagh were leaving. Going somewhere unknown. I inhaled slowly, counted my breaths and steadied my nerve. When my sight cleared and palpitations eased, I could think lucidly.

This was nothing but a blip. It would be easy to ascertain which practice they moved too, after all, Northern Ireland is a small place and GP practices communicate regularly.

I leaned back in my chair and prayed Jake wouldn't come to find me. The news needed to sink in, to become real before I could decide on the best course of action. It was then I remembered the last item on the to-do list in my kitchen drawer.

One I had written weeks ago, but delayed carrying out. Now they'd pushed me too far. It was time.

Jake didn't come to find me all morning and I avoided the staff room. At lunchtime, I strolled around the park, disinclined to get involved with planning their leaving lunch on Thursday. Jinty had emailed staff with instructions about gifts, organising food and buying *Sorry you're leaving* banners. Although glad to see the back of Bronagh, my colleagues were genuinely sorry Jake was going too. He was hugely popular and considered fair, as well as being exceptional at his job.

He made everyone feel special, which was both a talent and a failing.

A talent, because everybody felt valued by him.

A failing because some people made the mistake of assuming they meant more than a mere work colleague.

Furious with us both, I paced along the path beside the river and relished the sudden downpour. Rain soaked my clothes and stung my face, but I didn't care. Muddled emotions chased around my head, and I was afraid to return to the surgery until I'd worked off my nervous energy.

I was furious with myself for having read more into our connection than Jake had meant.

Then I raged at him for knowingly abusing my friendship and trust.

When I arrived back at the practice, my anger was controlled and I chatted normally with Jinty. If Jake came to find me, all well and good. If not, I wouldn't seek him out.

The afternoon surgery was agonisingly slow, face after face, ailment after ailment. At the end of the day, I had no idea who I'd seen, what I'd prescribed or notes I'd documented. When the knock came, it came was soft and hesitant. I steeled myself and called him in.

His mouth was a thin line, eyes skittish. It gave me no

pleasure, but I wouldn't make it easy for him. Indeed I was entitled to be dazed by their news, to show some degree of hurt. It would be odd if I didn't.

'Hello.' I pointed towards the chair usually reserved for patients, and he sat with a frown.

'Hello. I wanted to talk to you.'

'Really, what about?'

He inspected his fingernails. 'I'm sorry we didn't confide in you about leaving yesterday. We didn't want the news to get out and preferred no fuss.'

'You owe me nothing, Jake.' I was glad my tone was firm. 'You clearly had your reasons for keeping it a secret, so it's not a problem.'

Quietly he replied, 'I'm sure you understand why we didn't want it to be general knowledge. We were afraid Bronagh's stalker would find out and cause trouble.'

I almost recoiled but didn't betray myself with even a shudder.

The silence between us grew uncomfortable and I filled it with inane words. Finally the burning question. 'Have you new jobs lined up?'

His gaze flittered away and my stomach lurched. He wasn't going to tell me. He didn't trust me. What remained of our friendship shattered into minute shards. I scrambled for my dignity, murmured not to worry and of course I understood, as my blood pumped in a phrenzy around my overheated body.

The scales had fallen off and it was bitterly obvious.

When they left, they wanted no one to know where they were going, bar the partners who'd write their references.

The resounding silence crackled between us until with a final smile, he rose and turned his back, leaving a cold void where our friendship used to be. I scolded myself it wasn't an impossible situation, that I knew where Bronagh lived. It would be easy to follow her and find out her new place of work. It was ridiculous of them to suppose no one would find out.

Then uneasiness washed over me. Possibly I'd not been convincing enough.

What if Jake or Bronagh suspected my role in everything? Or one of them had seen my single lapse, the vicious comment from my real Insta account, and put two and two together?

I massaged my temples and comforted myself I was catastrophising again. If they doubted me, they'd have confronted me before now. The simple explanation was they were being overly cautious.

Certain I was safe, I texted Laura to cancel meeting up and suggested we rearrange. She replied it wasn't an issue and we'd catch up soon.

Absorbed by my own problems, I was a poor friend. Incapable of seeing beyond my obsession, powerless to control it. Again I derided myself. Then my internal voice reminded me I wasn't used to being cast aside and should be kinder to myself, acknowledge my bruised ego. Coming so soon after Tom's infidelity, this was a step too far.

Really it wasn't fair to expect me to bounce back as if our friendship had counted for nothing. Resolute and determined, I switched off the computer. Bronagh had instigated them leaving. She was to blame.

And therefore, she deserved everything that was coming.

CHAPTER FORTY-ONE

Silence echoed throughout the empty house when I arrived home from work. Keiko had greeted me at the front door and shot into the gloom past my feet. Tom was elsewhere, presumably at the gym. Although my mind swarmed with other things, I checked the tracker. As expected, his car was outside the leisure centre. One less thing to torture myself with.

Before I changed my clothes, my attention was taken by the darkening sky through the kitchen window. From force of habit, I closed all the blinds. Miranda could be hiding amongst the trees, planning her next move. She'd become a paltry nuisance when faced with the awfulness of the day's news, but I couldn't shake the feeling of being watched.

I trudged upstairs, stripped off my work clothes and caught sight of myself in the full length mirror. Dark rings under my eyes, deep creases lined my face and silver threads streaked my hair. Who was I?

The cowed daughter.

The wronged wife.

The vengeful friend.

Once my self-confidence had brimmed over, now I was wrecked with self-doubt.

Bronagh had ruined everything, driven a wedge between me and Jake. My goal had been to sabotage their relationship, to make him doubt her. All I'd wanted was to get my friend back.

Aggravation ebbed away, replaced by despair. Exercise beckoned, so I dressed for a run and tied my hair out of the way. For the first time in years, I considered cutting it into a bob. Then I snarled as Bronagh came to mind. A bob would be too reminiscent of her. My route would take me past Jake's, to see if her car was parked outside. If it was, I'd sneak behind his house and watch as they laughed at me and connived their next escapade.

An hour later, I arrived home to find Tom cooking pasta and singing tunelessly along to the radio. The endorphin rush from exercise always cheered him up and I reached my arms around him, inhaled the scent of his shower gel and hid my expression. His skin glowed, muscles bulged and I fleetingly chided myself for getting distracted by another man.

My dreams were vibrant that night, and when I woke, a sweaty sheen coated my skin. A sliver of moon pooled on the bed, the single beam of light in the blackness. The dreams faded, but left a pit of alarm in my gut, and it took a long time for me to doze off again.

Next morning I presented Tom with his birthday gift and informed him a table was booked for dinner at his favourite restaurant. A grin split his face when he ripped open the paper to find a new Tudor watch. Unquestionably he believed I'd deliberated long and hard before purchasing it, but he would be wrong. I'd chosen it online because I was lazy and disinterested, and the shop delivered to the house.

All day in work I kept to myself and avoided both Jake and Bronagh. Sandwiches were eaten at my desk, I sneaked into the unoccupied staff room to make coffee, and left promptly at five o'clock. It was almost unheard of to finish on time, but I'd worked through lunch to get ahead of referrals and notes.

Not one person sought me out.

No one asked if I was okay, or why I was missing from the usual morning and breaktime chitchat. Disillusionment left me tetchy.

My temper simmered on the drive home and I longed to put my feet up in front of the television. However I had to drive into Belfast as it was Tom's birthday, and behave as if everything was rosy, not grey and desolate. Fatigued both by emotional duress and poor sleep, it crushed me that no one cared.

Tom was already dressed in chinos and an open-necked shirt when I arrived home. His hair was damp, and he'd nicked his chin shaving. My annoyance decreased and I resolved to be on my best behaviour all evening. It wasn't Tom's fault I was unhappy.

'I'll change out of these clothes and then we can leave.' I lightly stroked the nape of his neck.

He nodded and I tramped upstairs, absorbed in my phone. Bronagh posted a nauseating reel on Instagram which teased adventure ahead. My lip curled and I took pleasure from ordering food she wouldn't eat and getting it delivered to her flat. My prepaid debit card meant she wouldn't be able to trace it. I toyed with creating chaos in work before she left, like I'd done with the mountain of envelopes and messing about with the staff meetings, but satisfied myself with the scheme already planned.

Content for the time being, I dressed in a flattering shirt dress and high boots. A slick of pink lip gloss and I knotted my hair into a neat bun. It was incredible that my façade was calm as my emotions tossed and turned.

Tom ran his hands over my curves and nuzzled my neck

when I reached the bottom of the stairs, and I playfully batted him away. We made our way out to the car and I noticed a flash of red on the street nearby. Miranda stood under the streetlight at the end of Annie's drive and peered over. I raised a hand in greeting and her resulting scowl made us laugh. I no longer cared if it provoked or infuriated her.

The drive into Belfast was tedious, visibility poor as spray splashed the windscreen and the wipers screeched. Fortunately we were going against the traffic, and I found a parking space easily in the Cathedral Quarter multistorey car park. We held hands under an umbrella as we walked towards the restaurant and Tom was chatty, moaning about his next long-haul flight, claiming he wanted to change to short-haul. It may have been remorse or what he supposed I needed to hear.

When we reached the restaurant, a tide of noise flooded out to remind me how much I enjoyed the city. Raucous, vivacious, boundless activity. No one could be bored with all the city had to offer.

The middle-aged waitress showed us to a table in the corner and soothing music played from hidden speakers. The décor was chic and minimalistic, with quirky paintings on the charcoal grey walls. A candle flickered between us and we ordered sharing plates of tapas. My mobile vibrated persistently, so I slipped it into my handbag. Tom switched on the charm with the waitress, who blushed at being shown attention by my handsome husband. If anything he'd grown more attractive with age. Less attractive was the knowledge he delighted in it.

My cheeks ached with the effort of smiling and by half nine I was ready for home. Tom was tipsy, having consumed most of a bottle of Rioja on his own. I'd toasted his birthday, but otherwise he'd downed glass after glass, which loosened his tongue. After dinner he insisted on an Irish coffee with his cheeseboard, and I bit my lip to stop myself yapping at him to hurry up.

At ten o'clock I flagged down the waitress and asked for the bill. Tom left an ostentatiously large tip, but I knew better than to dispute it when he'd been drinking. Unsteadily he weaved his way through the tables to the exit and I trailed behind. When he knocked against the door, I glossed over my impatience with a short laugh.

The waitress disappeared into the cloakroom to find our jackets and Tom leaned against the wall, hands in his pockets. Then I remembered the umbrella was still on the floor under our table, so I gave his arm a gentle tap and explained I'd go back and retrieve it. A dismissive nod and I squeezed past the waitstaff to our table. The cacophony in the restaurant thundered and suddenly I longed for fresh air and space. I groped on the floor, my fingers quickly circled the umbrella and I reminded myself we'd soon be home and I could find refuge with my mobile.

I made my way to the front door to where Tom was waiting, my coat over his arm. He held out my jacket with a smile when I dangled the umbrella in front of him. As I reached over for my jacket, his eyes slid past me and his face drained of colour.

Instinctively I swung around and came face to face with Claire and her husband Will.

Will's brown stare was glacial, as Claire shrank behind him. He loomed over her, much slimmer since the last time I'd seen him in early December. Claire was a tiny waif in high boots and a burgundy wrap dress. Face ablaze, I stammered hello, though I wanted to bolt from the restaurant and never look back.

Good mannered to a fault, Will managed a hoarse hello, eyes frozen on Tom. I glanced at Tom and was horrified to find his features had softened as he licked his lips. Fright compressed my chest as it became blindingly obvious.

Despite his protestations to the contrary, my husband had cared for Claire and feasibly still did. The noise in the restaurant receded at the sound of my heart breaking all over again.

She didn't speak, but rested a tremulous hand on Will's forearm and looked away. Those striking green eyes which haunted my sleep and roared their condemnation.

Trapped between Tom and Will, I swiftly sidestepped them both and jerked Tom's arm. There was no possibility of small talk nor reconciliation. I staggered into the nippy night and Tom spoke quietly behind me.

'That was awkward.'

'Hmm.' I couldn't speak, could visualise nothing but the tenderness of Tom's face as he'd gawked at Claire.

'I'm sorry. I didn't know they were back together.'

Our footsteps reverberated in the empty car park, as lights sputtered off and on, first dark, then light. Silently I unlocked the car and opened my door. However Tom gripped my wrist and twisted me around. Good sense reminded me he was drunk, to let him say his piece and fight this another time.

But my temper exploded and I pummelled his chest furiously with my free hand. Hopelessness made me weak and my legs trembled as he wrapped his arms around me. My hair came loose from the bun, he tucked a tendril behind my ear and mumbled apologies.

A minute passed as my agony gushed and jarred. Unsteadily I said, 'It was bound to happen sometime. Seeing her, I mean. It wasn't your fault.'

He expelled alcohol fumes over me and tried to kiss me, but I withdrew from his embrace and stepped away. He had the grace to look shamefaced and I shook my head sadly.

Just when I'd allowed myself to believe we were on more solid ground, I'd been proven wrong.

All it had taken was a brief encounter to expose how vulnerable we still were.

CHAPTER FORTY-TWO

On the drive home from Belfast, Tom unbelievably snoozed before we reached the outskirts of the village. Or at least pretended to, in order to avoid further discussion. Once the initial shock of seeing Claire wore off, embarrassment replaced it and swept freely through me.

She'd been terrified, rigid with uncertainty. Will's expression had mirrored hers, but also conveyed his anger. Which in itself was new, for he was usually even-tempered and slow to rile. They must be working on their marriage, and I was genuinely glad. She'd jeopardised everything for what had amounted to very little, with far-lasting effects. In much the same way I was. Again we had more in common than we knew.

The next morning Tom groaned in pain and with a glimmer of contempt, I chucked a box of painkillers at him. When we'd arrived home, he had morosely helped himself to Scotch and drank it in the semidarkness, listening to music. His face impassive, emotions hidden, I'd stormed upstairs alone. The aftershock of our evening would hang around, no matter how hard we tried to bridge the gap between us.

In work I buried my true feelings, fibbed to Bronagh I would miss her and her shoes wouldn't easily be filled. And so on. Lying compliments throttled honesty. All day I avoided Jake and remained holed up in my consulting room, hoping he'd stay away. My pain was too fresh to playact with him.

Tom was nowhere to be found when I arrived home, which gave me ample opportunity to bake the cookies I'd volunteered for the leaving lunch. After I changed out of my work clothes, I returned downstairs to prepare the ingredients I'd bought in the supermarket previously and stored at the back of the cupboard. I was a rotten baker and usually relied on the village bakery, however these cookies would have my own special twist. A little extra flavour. A morsel of zing. With one eye on the door to check Tom didn't interrupt, I bashed and whisked, mixed and folded. Prep completed, I tidied the worktop and watched them bake through the oven door, afraid they'd burn if neglected.

Before they were ready, Tom arrived home with a bunch of wilted flowers he'd purchased from the village garage. A murmured apology, a sloppy kiss and the assumption of automatic forgiveness. Our unstable relationship unfolded as before, and I permitted his excuses, though my heart toughened. Pleased with himself and his oh-so-clever gift, he offered to make me coffee and asked what was in the oven.

'Cookies for Jake and Bronagh's leaving lunch tomorrow.' I was prickly, but he failed to notice.

'Who's Bronagh?' Asked over his shoulder.

I swallowed my frustration, and replied she was a work colleague who was leaving for pastures new. He should've recognised the name, but had minimal interest in my work, or workmates. Which was both advantageous and infuriating. Tom lived expressly in Tom-land, paying minimal attention to anything which did not directly affect him.

The oven timer pinged, I removed the cookies from the oven and set them on the worktop to cool. They were a bit overdone, but didn't look awful. They'd have to do. Tom reached for one, but I good-naturedly swatted his hand away, before I relaxed and offered him one with a crispy crust.

'Very nice.' He spoke through a mouthful of cookie. 'There's an unusual taste. Have you added something extra?'

'No, it's my terrible baking.' My laugh was sharp as I rubbed my temple.

'You always rub your temple when you're lying.' He grinned at me. 'Did you add booze so they'll be stocious during afternoon surgery?'

'Ha! Wish I'd thought of it.' Tom knew nothing about baking or that alcohol gets burned off during the process, but I humoured him, then suggested a takeaway for dinner, unable to face cooking when my mind was elsewhere. Though I could justify it, an unaccustomed spasm of guilt took me by surprise.

I consciously put it out of my mind and asked Tom to ring through an order to the local Indian takeaway. It would be an hour before they could deliver, which left time for a jog to see if Bronagh's car was outside Jake's. If it was, I'd have a quick peek from my viewpoint behind the hedge to calm my nerves.

Sure enough her car was abandoned on the kerb outside his house, and I spent ten fruitful minutes observing them in the kitchen. Jake rarely closed his blinds, which was really very fortunate. Bronagh sat in my usual chair at the table, and I was surprised my blazing daggers didn't puncture her skin. Any reservations I had, melted.

Next morning I carried my precious cookies into the surgery and set them on the table beside bags of crisps, bottles of sparkling water and a variety of traybakes. Neat triangles of sandwiches were stacked in the fridge, along with cocktail sausages and sausage rolls. A cake nestled inside the walls of a white cardboard box. '*Sorry you're leaving*' banners had been stuck to the walls with Blu Tack and I wondered if they were cheering their departure or remorseful to see them go. The staff had excelled themselves and Jake's grin was wide.

He came over to speak to me before my first patient arrived, but I laughingly protested I needed to catch up on emails. Upset scurried across his face, but I refused to chitchat. It would be difficult enough to keep my emotions hidden later, when they were presented with their leaving gifts and cards.

The morning was interminable, each patient an imposition, each referral a chore. At long last it was half twelve and we gathered in the crowded staff room. Chatter, laughter and anticipation tinged the air. I stood guard near the table, nervously observing, quietly watchful, too on edge to eat much. My paper plate was piled high with food, however the squashy tomatoes had bled into the white bread, leaving them soggy. Finally, Bronagh waltzed in, stilettos tapping, lips pouting. She filled her plate with sandwiches, though hardly nibbled them.

My shoulders ached with tension as I lost heart. Possibly she had no appetite and would leave the rest of the spread untouched.

Then she reached forward for one of my cookies. Slowly she raised it to her lips, but before she could bite down, an involuntary holler burst from me.

'Bronagh, stop!'

Her head swung round and she halted with the cookie halfway to her mouth, an expression of shock on her face. Around us the room quietened in response to my exclamation.

Good wrestled evil and ultimately, good won.

It was the culmination of many weeks despair, and yet I stopped her from eating my peanut-laced cookies, painstakingly prepared with her allergy in mind. Wisdom surpassed my need to harm her.

'I'm sorry,' I gibbered. 'I'm worried there could be traces of peanut in the cookies. Tom ate a packet in the kitchen last night when I was baking them and I wouldn't want you to risk them.' My voice died as she dropped the cookie as though poisoned.

Jinty saved the day by exclaiming how lucky it was I'd spotted Bronagh in time, and my colleagues agreed. But a tingling sensation on the back of my neck caused me to glance over my shoulder. Jake's penetrating stare was pinned on me. Lips compressed, his scowl was unmistakeable. My smile was timid and when it wasn't returned, anxiety soared.

Did he suspect?

Deliberately I swivelled away from him as warmth spread across my chest. The babble quietened as Gloria banged a spoon on the table and made a short speech wishing them all the best for their new beginnings. A toast was raised and the cake cut, gifts handed out.

Almost as if it were a wedding.

Afterwards I didn't dawdle, but dashed back to my consulting room, where I shut the door and flung myself into the chair. The memory of Jake's tense expression bored into me. My hands trembled as I replayed it all, and I was certain he had doubts. I'd have to speak to him before I left today, to suss out if my worries were unfounded or very real.

At five, my last patient gathered up her belongings and exited with thanks. Minutes passed until the expected knock at the door. I steadied my nerve and called him in. Whatever had darkened his expression earlier had been replaced by a dry smile. He didn't take a seat, but rested against the door in his familiar position. A pang of nostalgia quickly extinguished when he cleared his throat. His fierce blue glower burned intently as he dived straight in.

'It was lucky you noticed Bronagh and your cookie. You know how highly allergic she is.'

'Yes, thank goodness.' My tone was casual. 'I suddenly realised there was a small chance the cookies could have been contaminated.' Not so small a chance since I had crushed the peanuts into powder and intentionally added them to the mixture.

He rubbed the toe of his shoe along the lino and scrutinised me. Instinctively I rubbed my temple, until I recalled Tom's flippant remark about it signifying a lie. My hand dropped onto the table as the silence grew toxic between us.

'It must be strange not having to come into work tomorrow,' I prattled, desperate to thaw the cold atmosphere.

'It is.'

'Well, good luck with everything. I look forward to hearing all about it.'

He didn't respond, but folded his arms across his chest. The deadly hush told me everything I needed to know and my eyes smarted.

He might not know exactly what I'd done, but he had suspicions.

Fear clawed me.

Without another word, he left me alone and scared in my room.

Our friendship in ruins.

My heart in pieces.

CHAPTER FORTY-THREE

I spent a sleepless night as the leaving lunch fiasco rebounded in my head. Bronagh's look of dismay when I shouted her name. Jake's quiet fury. The deafening silence as he'd turned his back on me. Though I soothed myself there was no harm done, I recalled the lines etched between his brows and downturned mouth.

Tom slept the sleep of the innocent beside me and I dozed off sometime after four. I'd forced myself to speak to Bronagh before I left work, wrapped her in a hug and wished her the very best, though the words had obstructed my throat. I wished I could hiss and spit my true feelings, but years of withholding emotion held me in good stead. Naively she thanked me for being a good friend and I smothered my mirthless laugh at her gullibility.

Friday morning dawned cold and overcast, and mist blanketed the hilltops. A headache had settled behind my eyes, which were gritty and dry. Tom was on standby but unfortunately the phone hadn't rung, and his guilty conscience insisted we spend the day together. A walk by the sea, followed by lunch. I unwillingly agreed, although would have preferred to focus on my phone and social media. To check if Bronagh slipped up and leaked her new place of work or make sure I didn't miss a message if Jake contacted me.

No such luck.

Tom stifled me, and was attached like glue all day. The walk he suggested was on a beach halfway between the village and the North Coast. We had lunch at a neighbouring café, taking a table by the window. My heart constricted with guilt as Flora appeared. That was why he'd been so insistent we eat there. I berated myself for my selfishness and concealed my discomfort with a laugh. Lunch was lovely, Flora happy, Tom self-righteous. And throughout, my phone vibrated face down on the table, and it took all my willpower not to grab it and tear into the toilets.

It was getting dark by the time we returned to the village. Light drizzle gave the world a soft glow, and I anticipated going for a run. Then I would hide behind the hedge and watch my nemesis as she laughed and conversed with Jake in his kitchen.

However Tom was sulky at my suggestion of a jog, and moaned so much I gave in and watched television with him in the living room. An old movie played as displeasure gushed and impatience nipped. Thankfully my prayers were answered when his phone rang and he learned he would have an early flight to Doha in the morning.

Ecstatic at the prospect of a day alone, my smile was genuine. I could endure him for another few hours, then tomorrow would be spent doing exactly what I wanted, with no demands.

Next morning, I woke refreshed and more positive. It had been dark when Tom slipped out of bed and I kept my back to him as I counted down the minutes till he left. Freedom was tantalisingly near.

As soon as the front door closed with a thud, I reached for

my mobile, unable to resist. Surprisingly Bronagh had been completely absent from social media since Thursday, after an effusive post about her leaving present. There'd been no mention of her brush with death, nor future plans.

The idea took hold I should visit them and make amends. Buy them a present and take it around to Jake's. Surely a good friend would mark their leaving with an individual gift, rather than give a few pounds to the collection.

Buzzing with sudden energy, I practically ran downstairs to make coffee and reflected on what I should buy.

A plant? Too boring.

A picture? Then I remembered Jake's bare walls.

Coffee mugs? With something cute like 'Best Friends are Forever.' Insincere, but it had potential.

There was a gift shop in Ballyrevy, there was bound to be something appropriate. My good humour evaporated with each bite of toast. Bronagh no longer being in my work place would be a nuisance, as I'd have no opportunity to spoil her work, or keep one step ahead of her plans. Immediately I was furious with both her and Jake. For their duplicity and their coupledom. For deceiving me. Really they didn't deserve a present, they deserved my temper and my disappointment.

A shower diluted my nerves, and as I dried off, I reverted to my original idea. I'd buy a gift and take it around after lunch. The last thing I wanted was to visit too early and catch them half naked. My breakfast soured in my stomach.

I spent a bad-tempered twenty minutes selecting a present, which would imply sadness, but in reality meant nothing. *You are dead to me* matching tumblers piqued my interest, but I opted for *I'll never find better colleagues than you* ones instead. Ten more minutes were wasted choosing an appropriate card.

My spirits were lower than they'd been all week when I reached home. Their deception rubbed raw and I was tearful as

I unlocked the front door. I set the tumblers and card on the breakfast bar and rifled in the drawer for a pen. Tempting as a red pen was, they might recall the condolence card had been signed in red ink, so I chose a black one. As I deliberated what to write, I chewed the end of it. It didn't really matter, but I had to maintain the pretence of being distressed at losing them both.

Finally it came to me.

Thank you both for being not only colleagues in a million, but such great friends.

I rummaged in the drawer for a gift bag, having forgotten to purchase one in the shop, and glanced at the clock. Eleven o'clock, too early to turn up unannounced at Jake's door. I made another coffee and settled on the sofa in the conservatory to scroll through my phone.

There were several messages from Book Club I'd missed. I'd become so self-involved over the past few weeks, my friends had been relegated to the bottom of my priorities. Sheepishly I read them.

Annie had been back to the breast clinic after finding a lump. Thankfully she'd been given the all-clear, and I texted an apology for my lack of reply and to express my delight.

Laura was excited about a long weekend to Edinburgh with Sam at Easter.

Kate had been whinging about her kids. No mention of Miranda, nor David. Just the usual litany of complaints about her children.

Normal everyday stuff, which had become irrelevant as my fixation with Bronagh had grown. Keiko jumped up on my legs and I absent-mindedly stroked her while considering everything. For too long I'd defended my behaviour as reasonable, convinced I'd been the injured party. Rarely and usually in the wee hours of the night, I had doubted myself, troubled I was taking it too far. Afraid she would learn I was behind it, and would turn Jake completely against me.

Ultimately though I'd never been uncovered. Until now. A flashback of Jake's steely glare chilled me. Did he suspect me? Nerves fluttered as I recited it was too insubstantial, not provable. Our relationship and the situation was still salvageable.

Once again I scrolled through my mobile.

Bronagh's lack of posts was glaring. Nothing since Thursday. Worry burrowed deep. It was time to go to Jake's house and confront them both, this state of limbo was unbearable. Before I left the house, I cleaned my teeth and applied some make-up. Plaited my hair, dressed in flattering skinny jeans and a loose top.

I pushed my feet into boots, lifted my coat and slammed the door behind me. A subdued sun split the clouds and I hurried down the street, keen to get this over and done with, then I could regroup and plan my next course of action. The street was empty except for some children on scooters, whom I avoided crossly. Once I reached Miranda's house I defiantly glared at her front window, and imagined her ogling as I threw my head back.

Down the path I strode, until I reached Jake's street. From this viewpoint I could see no cars in his drive. It was empty. Instantly I was incensed, having expected them both to be there, and once again I rebuked myself for having assumed, not checked. A hesitation, then I lifted my phone out of my pocket and walked on. I'd message Jake, to find out what time they'd be home so I could return with their gifts. When I formulated a light-hearted message, I pressed send.

By now I'd reached his house and could see something was different. It took a few moments to realise what it was. The vertical blinds in the front room were missing. Perhaps Jake had opened them to allow in more light. I continued walking until I reached his driveway. Something else was wrong, but I couldn't put my finger on it. Then the slow realisation; there were no curtains at the bedroom window.

Unable to stop myself, my feet carried me down the driveway until I reached the front door and rang the bell. No answer. A glance over my shoulder to establish no one was around, then I stepped onto the path which ran along the front wall.

When I drew level with the living room, I gasped aloud. The room was empty. No furniture at all. What on earth was going on? I continued down the path until I reached the bedroom window. Again the room was empty. There was no furniture, clear shelves and blank walls.

Horror overwhelmed me as it became horribly clear.

Jake had moved out.

Without telling me, nor confiding where he was going.

The enormity of his deceitfulness gradually sank in.

My last chance to redeem myself smashed around me.

CHAPTER FORTY-FOUR

I stumbled home from Jake's empty house, mind reeling.

He was gone.

He must've moved out yesterday when Tom had driven me miles up the coast for our walk and brunch with Flora. I hated Tom then, for interfering in my life and leaving me lost in a sea of regret without a lifebelt.

Where could Jake have moved to? How could he have left without telling me? His betrayal struck me like a physical force.

Unable to think straight, I wondered if I should drive to Bronagh's flat to speak to her. Maybe she'd slip up and reveal their plans. Spots flashed before my eyes as I searched for my car keys in the drawer. My fingers closed around them and I gave myself a severe talking to. It would be a terrible idea to storm over and make a fool of myself.

All was not lost. I was one step ahead of them, despite their best efforts. They wouldn't get rid of me so easily. I must be reasonable and clearheaded, not irrational and rash, which could lead to disaster.

I sagged onto a kitchen chair and took a few deep breaths. I hadn't got to where I was today by allowing emotions to cloud my judgement. Alarm tamped down, I checked my phone. My last message to Jake was unread and unanswered. I questioned my next move. A text to Bronagh would be best, to let her know I had a present for her and to suggest I pop over with it.

It took three attempts before I was happy enough with my message to press send. Ten minutes later, she still hadn't replied. To occupy myself, I scrolled through social media. First I checked Bronagh's Insta. My heart plummeted.

This account is private.

There must be some terrible mistake! She was addicted to social media and her follower count: she'd never resort to that. Next I checked Facebook. With mounting shock, I realised she'd unfriended me and removed her public *About info*. Apart from her cover photo and updated profile pictures, I could see nothing. A growl of dejection escaped.

Hands trembling, I checked the work WhatsApp group. Both Jake and Bronagh had been removed.

My vehemence grew.

Could I send her an email? Without pausing for thought, I sent her a brief email but it pinged back as the email could not be delivered.

Unable to process things coherently, I resorted to ringing her. The number I'd called so frequently over the past months was as familiar to me as my own, and I got it wrong on the first attempt. When I tried again, the same mechanical message played.

The number you have called has not been recognised.

Realisation dawned. She'd blocked me. My head was jumbled, I could neither accept it, nor understand. There was one last thing I could do and after that, I'd have exhausted all options.

I must go to her flat. If she wasn't there, her sister probably would be and hopefully I could speak directly to her. Fake concern. Feign friendship. Then I'd learn Bronagh's plans without drawing attention to my reasons.

Logically I was in no fit state to bang on the door of the flat and make small talk, but had to do something. Ideas swirled and churned, but nothing made sense. Coherent thought had been superseded by panic and dread.

Two things I was certain of; I must not reveal I knew Jake had moved out, or that Bronagh had blocked me.

Simultaneously frightened and enraged, I cursed aloud.

It wasn't fair. It was selfish of her. Totally uncalled for.

Righteous anger teemed through me as I drove into Ballyrevy. I swerved potholes and puddles, swore at inept drivers and parked a short distance from her flat. Common sense prevailed and I waited until my anxiety dropped a notch before I exited the car. A glance in the mirror to check I didn't appear feral. My smile was a grimace, which gave me a slightly manic look. I exhaled and tried again. Not great, but it would have to do. Hysteria threatened again. I needed to do this now and could delay no longer.

I bolted over to the block of flats and pressed the buzzer. Too late I realised she might question how I knew which apartment was hers, but I'd fabricate something if asked. A disembodied voice answered, similar to Bronagh, but it wasn't her.

'Hello?'

I barely controlled my cry of annoyance. 'Hello. Is Bronagh in?'

Loud breathing before a woman's voice asked, 'Who is this?'

'My name's Vicky, I work with her. Worked with her, I mean. I have a gift for her.'

'Bronagh's not here.' Was she being obtuse on purpose?

'Oh, I see. Will she be back later?' My tone was tart.

'Maybe. Wait a minute and I'll come down.'

I stepped back from the door and peered up to Bronagh's first floor flat. I'd sat outside often enough to watch her flit from room to room, cook herself food in the poky kitchen, watch the television.

The door was opened by a shorter, courser version of Bronagh. She was nowhere near as pretty and lacked the distinctive blonde hair and inflated chest. Her path through life would be a tougher one than Bronagh's, without the advantage of good looks. She leaned against the door frame and crossed her arms. Bushy eyebrows raised, she silently observed me.

I knew her name, where she worked and that she watched daytime telly when she came off nightshift. She had a casual boyfriend who tended to visit when Bronagh was elsewhere and had a habit of cooking wearing nothing but an apron. Thankfully I remembered in time, I was a stranger to her.

I forced a smile. 'Hi.'

No answer except a scornful glare. I held up the gift bag with a small laugh.

'I've a present for Bronagh.' She made no attempt to reach for it, which nettled me greatly.

Finally a slow drawl. 'Bronagh mentioned you. I didn't think you'd turn up here.'

'What do you mean?' I snapped, all pretence at cordiality snuffed out.

'Bronagh told me you fancied Jake and about how you chased him. We had such a laugh about a middle aged woman hassling my gorgeous sister's fiancé.'

'Jake and I were friends, nothing more. I'm happily married, I didn't chase him!' My voice sounded pitiful, the fire within me doused.

'Ha! That's not exactly how they described it to me.'

I backed away, afraid of the acrimony in her face and truth

of her words. 'Will Bronagh be home later?' I stuttered, unwilling to drop it.

'No, she won't. And before you ask, I'm not telling you where she is.'

The door slammed in my face and I was left open-mouthed. Self-pitying tears pricked my eyes as I wheeled around before indignation swelled.

'Bitch.' I rang the buzzer again and again, but it remained unanswered.

Finally she leaned out of her living room window above me, and shouted down. 'If you don't stop ringing the buzzer I'm going to phone the police. Now, get lost.' The window shut with a bang before I could reply. It was like a bucket of icy water had been thrown over me. What if a patient had seen me? What if she really did ring the police and I was carted off for disturbing the peace?

I scuttled back to the car, shut the door and hyperventilated with mortification. Bronagh had told her I fancied Jake and they'd laughed at me, refused to believe we were nothing more than friends. And if her sister Simone was being honest, he'd laughed along with them. My sight misted over as my humiliation intensified. When at last it settled, I drove off without a backwards glance. By the time I reached the outskirts of Castlebrook, my rose-tinted glasses finally shattered.

I had foolishly read more into my friendship with Jake than there ever had been.

We'd been work colleagues who got on well, nothing more. It had taken on a life of its own as it intensified in my head until I thought of him as my best friend. In my mind, he'd replaced my female friends and become closer than my husband.

A ghastly realisation; had Tom strayed with Claire because I'd become infatuated with Jake, determined to wreck his relationship with Bronagh? Had their affair continued for over a year not because Tom was adept at deception, but because I'd ignored the warning signs and dismissed him as clingy?

My face burned when I recalled it was usually me who invited myself for coffee at Jake's.

Me who messaged first.

Me who resented Bronagh's presence from day one, when Jake's eye's had widened and he'd gaped at her as though she were a goddess.

Possessiveness had stabbed as their relationship had grown and mine had floundered through neglect.

I parked in front of the house and switched off the engine. The car cooled as self-recrimination abounded. Drops of rain hit the car and I numbly watched them trickle down the windscreen, until they became a deluge. Soon rain drummed on the roof of the car and still I sat on.

For the first time, I took stock of my behaviour. Over the past months it had become increasingly questionable, progressively more despicable, leaving Bronagh afraid and paranoid. Shame crushed my chest. My friends and family would desert me if they learned what lay behind the mask.

I'd always prided myself at helping others, caring for the underdog in an effort to wash the sins of my teenage years clean. And yet, I'd sunk lower and acted more appallingly than I ever thought possible. Perhaps it was unforgivable. At last I acknowledged my actions had been illegal.

How could I ever have justified it to myself?

I started the engine and reversed out of the drive.

There was only one person I could unburden myself to.

Who would listen without judgement as I confessed what a truly awful thing I'd done.

CHAPTER FORTY-FIVE

When I arrived home, the house was in darkness and rain fell continuously from the heavens. I parked on the drive, clambered to the door and scrabbled with the lock. Keiko barrelled out from beneath a bush and straight into the hall, crying for food.

It was as if nothing had changed. The fragrance of jasmine still hung in the air from the candles I'd lit at breakfast. Rubber gloves were folded beside the sink, my charger lay on the breakfast bar.

And yet, so much was different.

Or it was me who was different.

I'd driven high above the village to Claire's home, which hugged the side of the Antrim Hills. The scene of many happy Book Club get-togethers, when the five of us had gossiped over copious glasses of wine. Barbeques in the hut, play dates when our children were small, weekend breaks to foreign cities.

The wind had buffeted me as I exited the car and I'd forgotten how blustery it always was up here. The road to the coast shimmered far below and headlights twinkled in the gloom. When I rang the bell, Claire had answered after a few moments and a look of dismay tore across her cheeks. A pause, when our shared history rumbled between us, then she'd mutely stepped back to allow me to enter.

I followed her into the front room and gratefully accepted her offer of coffee. My eyes whizzed around when she disappeared into the kitchen, to allow both of us to catch our breath. The view of the valley through the floor-to-ceiling windows was stunning, and in the distance Cave Hill towered above Belfast. No wonder she'd withdrawn here when her life imploded. When she returned, her face had regained some colour and she sat on the sofa opposite me.

Our conversation and my admission of poor behaviour was something I would analyse for hours to come. Her eyes had narrowed and mouth tightened as I'd falteringly confessed my latest sins. Naturally, I couldn't admit to everything, but glossed over the worst of my actions to pretend it wasn't quite as awful as it really was. An admission of complete guilt was dangerous.

When I finished speaking, I primed myself for the attack. A barrage of insults. A bawl of horror. However rather than deride me, she made a comment about menopausal madness, Laura's favourite excuse for bizarre midlife behaviour.

'Why did you tell me?' she asked later, as I rose to leave.

'You of all people would be least likely to judge my mistakes.'

She grinned suddenly and with a lift of her eyebrows showed me out. Our friendship was in no way restored, but it was promising.

Back in my own kitchen, I boiled the kettle to make a cup of mint tea and replayed the day. The doorbell cut through my musings and I sighed heavily. There was no one I wanted to see or speak to, so delayed in the hope they'd leave. No such luck, the bell chimed again. Irritated, I walked into the hall to find Kate and Miranda standing at the front door, with Miranda's finger on the bell. My tenuous link with poise frayed. I was in no mood to listen to them rant and rave at me, so reluctantly opened the door.

'Kate. Miranda. To what do I owe the pleasure?' I blocked their way, as frigid air brushed my skin.

Kate exhaled audibly. 'We've come to see if we can sort this issue out. Without a fight or finger pointing.'

'Was this your idea?'

She nodded vigorously while Miranda smirked at her shoulder. Although I wanted to slam the door in their faces, I moved aside, weary to the bone. There was nothing they could say which would change my mind about Miranda, though they might try. They plodded into the living room behind me and sat together on the sofa. Kate was clearly uncomfortable, with puffy dark rings under her eyes and a tremor in her hand. She noticed me looking, so interlocked her fingers on her lap and eyed me suspiciously.

Sudden pity for her flooded through me. I could make this difficult, but she'd been my friend for years and I longed to rebuild bridges. So I allowed her to take the lead, ignored Miranda's pointed expression of thirst and settled back on the armchair. Kate's earnest words swooped and dived, and never once did Miranda's sly sneer lift from me. Finally the room fell silent.

I cleared my throat to give myself time. 'Okay. I've had a lot on my plate as you can imagine. Maybe I've been a little less tolerant than usual.' Miranda ostentatiously rolled her eyes and I wanted to snap and snarl, but continued placidly. 'As I've repeatedly explained to you, Miranda, it would be unethical for me to treat you. Your complaint has been investigated and dealt with, so it would be unprofessional of me to discuss it now. Regarding the Book Club, well, I'm afraid I'm still of the same opinion, for now, it should be the four of us.' Miranda sniffed loudly. Before she could intervene, I said firmly, 'I'm sorry, but it's how I feel.'

'Thanks for being so honest,' Kate spoke before Miranda could answer. 'You've been through a lot, but I know Miranda is distressed at being excluded. I don't like rejecting anyone, so it might be best if we leave it for a while and see how things are then.'

Oh, for goodness' sake, why can't they drop it? I thought to myself. *Who wants to be included in a group of friends when you've been told over and over you aren't welcome?*

The atmosphere grew heavy as I weighed up my options. Kate's eyes beseeched me and unease spread. Whatever the real reason for this visit, it had been at Miranda's insistence. Kate was practically begging me to accept her offer. So I gave in. Agreed to revisit in a couple of months. Pliantly smiled and nodded along, playacting. Kate deflated in front of me, as strain seeped from her.

Miranda grinned triumphantly and relaxed back against the sofa. She crossed her legs and made another comment about being thirsty. My hands curled into fists and I took no notice. It was another fifteen minutes before they stood to leave, though I could scarcely bring myself to converse. Annoyance at the imposition and the beginning of a headache made me short-tempered. Miranda was ruthless, chatting and smiling, though Kate grew quieter and more reserved. In that moment, I wondered why Kate persevered with this friendship when it had given her nothing but trouble.

At the front door Miranda smiled patronisingly and clamped her hand to my forearm. I wanted to shake her off angrily when her sticky fingers pressed too long. Kate hugged me and whispered her thanks into my ear, so low Miranda couldn't hear. When she pulled back, I caught a whiff of something sour on her breath, with a smidgeon of mint. Again I wondered what exactly she was hiding, but with Miranda's hawk eyes on us, I had no choice but leave it unasked. Something was amiss with Kate, there was no question about it. She was jumpy and nervous. I planned to visit her soon, to get to the bottom of it.

I stood in the doorway and watched as they made their way down the drive. Miranda had looped her arm possessively through Kate's and threw me a contemptuous look before they disappeared onto the street.

'Bye, Vicky,' she called over her shoulder. 'See you soon.'

I heaved a sigh of relief as they disappeared, leaving me alone on the doorstep. I was about to shut the door when the postie appeared.

'Got a parcel for you.' She wagged a long, rectangular package at me.

'Thanks.' I reached for it and glanced at the address label on the front. I'd not ordered anything recently, so wondered what it could be.

The door shut with a soft click and I returned to the kitchen, where my blank phone screen taunted me. I deposited the package on the breakfast bar, attention already drifting. I'd open it in a minute.

As I re-boiled the kettle, I mulled over the day. Claire. Kate. Miranda. Jake. Bronagh. Anxieties and worries ran amok, though I attempted to contain them. It was exhausting inside my head. I carried my mobile and the mint tea into the conservatory, where I settled on the sofa.

There I checked my messages, WhatsApp, social media.

There was no communication from either Jake or Bronagh.

Possibly by now Simone would have informed Bronagh I'd visited the flat and the three of them would snigger about the foolish middle-aged doctor who'd supposed herself to be Jake's best friend. My heart was sore at them ridiculing me, and the panicky feeling I'd experienced earlier returned fiercer than ever.

In an effort to slow my speeding pulse, I flung my phone aside and padded into the kitchen to put my cup into the dishwasher. My head throbbed and I rifled in the drawer for painkillers.

It was then I spotted the parcel which had been delivered earlier. I'd forgotten about it in my haste to check my phone. I swallowed two painkillers with a glass of water and carried the package into the conservatory. There I ripped it open and tipped it upside down to extract the contents.

The calendar I'd sent Bronagh a few weeks ago fell onto my lap.

I shook the envelope and groped about inside. It was empty. Nothing but the calendar had been sent to me.

It was open at December, at the photo of the practice car park with my car beside Bronagh's.

There was no message, no indication why it had been sent.

I stared at it, puzzled, until my sight cleared and it became dazzlingly clear.

Jake had worked everything out.

CHAPTER FORTY-SIX

A gasp of dread as I stared at the photo.

There was nothing amiss at first. A car park. Two cars parked under a window. But someone, presumably Jake, had taken a pencil and lightly circled an image in the centre of the window. It wasn't distinct, but if you studied it carefully, the reflection of a person holding a phone became obvious. Indisputably the person who'd taken the photo. It was blurry and imprecise, and the bottom half of the face was obscured by the phone. But the person had long hair and high cheekbones.

Like me.

Once seen, it couldn't be dismissed.

Without question everything had been because of me. Seemingly he'd been oblivious until the goings-on with the cookies, which had triggered misgivings. Then he'd searched until he'd exposed something unequivocal.

Petrified, I swung my legs over the side of the sofa, panting loudly. Was he going to contact the police? Or the practice partners? Would he tell Tom?

Tears fell as I held my head in my hands and sobbed pathetically. It really wasn't fair. If you broke it down into minute pieces, I'd done very little wrong. So what if Bronagh had been a bit upset, they'd mocked me and flaunted their relationship under my nose. She'd deserved it.

After a time, my emotions stopped thrashing around. There was no way to prove anything. They'd absconded together, to start afresh. If Jake had gone to the police, they'd already have knocked on my door. There was no evidence of my wrongdoing.

Somewhat placated, I ripped the calendar in half and carried it outside. Darkness had fallen, and the wind was bitter, but the rain had stopped. I glanced around, half expecting a flash of red to leap out from behind a bush, but the garden was empty. I struck a match and held it to December. If there was no calendar, there was no proof. Flames licked the page and I dropped it onto the path, where it burned until there was nothing except ash. I did the same with the rest of the calendar, then swept up the remains and emptied them into the bin.

Though I was weirdly calm as I returned indoors and locked the door, I shivered as I closed the blinds. I washed my hands in the utility room and longed for a bath, to warm up. First though, I poured a glass of brandy, which my father swore was good for shock. Remembering my father, a pain snagged under my ribs. I couldn't dwell on him when I had enough to contend with. With the brandy in one hand, and my phone in the other, I climbed the stairs and plodded into the bathroom.

As I waited for the bath to fill, I sat on the closed toilet seat and sipped the brandy. Both Jake and Bronagh were gone and assumed they'd left no trail. By sneaking away and moving elsewhere, they hoped Bronagh had been freed from what they perceived as harassment. They'd never know for certain if it had been me behind it all, especially since the evidence was now destroyed. It wasn't stalking. Stalkers were people with no self-control. No willpower. And I had both in abundance.

Really they could do their best, but they'd never avoid my attention. It was an itch within me nothing else could scratch.

I stripped off and sank under the water. A groan of pleasure, then I opened the tracker app on my phone.

Not the one I had hidden in Tom's car, but the second one I'd purchased at the same time.

The one I'd dropped into Bronagh's handbag that day in the coffee shop, when she'd whinged about peanuts to the waitress and Jake had been in the bathroom. I'd made a quickfire decision as I'd lifted it out of the way of the pram and chanced my arm.

I was amazed to get away with it, but slipping it under the hard inset in the base of the bag had been a stroke of genius, and Bronagh must never have found it. It allowed me to follow her from a distance. To monitor her movements. It was far from ideal, but it was better than nothing now they'd moved and blocked all communication. I'd invested in one with a long battery, so at least it gave me breathing space for a few more weeks.

I stared at the app and smiled to myself.

Donegal wasn't far away, not far at all.

And I'd always loved the beaches there. In fact I was going to suggest a long weekend to Tom, in a hotel up the road from where Bronagh now was.

My smile widened as I anticipated the look on her face when she spotted me walking in the village she'd scurried to.

She thought she'd been so smart, but she'd never stood a chance.

THE END

ALSO BY ALISON IRVING

Casual Cruelties

Her Best Friend's Husband

The Love We Chase

ACKNOWLEDGEMENTS

My thanks as ever to the fantastic Bloodhound team for believing in my writing and all their incredible hard work. Special thanks to my editor Clare Law, who gives the best advice and who I trust completely to make my writing better.

Andy, the man with the biggest heart and boundless patience who drives me to the North Coast and books a table at my favourite Italian 'just because'. Who backs me and boosts me every day.

Mum, you've always been there for me, no matter what, and words are inadequate to thank you. Dad, you may be gone but will never be forgotten.

Alex and Jamie, thanks for brightening each and every day.

And finally to my readers. So many of you have reached out to let me know how my stories have affected you and for that, I'm humbled and grateful. Thank you for your ongoing support and I hope you've enjoyed Vicky's story.

ABOUT THE AUTHOR

I was born in Northern Ireland and studied physiotherapy at the University of Ulster, where I met my husband Andy. After graduation we spent the next fifteen years in Oxfordshire and then Troon, Ayrshire.

On our return to Northern Ireland in 2007 with our children Alex and Jamie, I continued to work in the NHS as a physio. I retired following my cancer diagnosis in 2024.

My first book, *Casual Cruelties*, was published by Bloodhound Books in November 2023 and the follow up, *Her Best Friend's Husband,* was published in August 2024. My standalone women's fiction novel, *The Love we Chase*, was published in April 2025.

I can be found dragon paddling on the Lagan most Monday mornings, or putting the world to rights with my book club.

A NOTE FROM THE PUBLISHER

Thank you for reading this book. If you enjoyed it please do consider leaving a review on Amazon to help others find it too.

We hate typos. All of our books have been rigorously edited and proofread, but sometimes mistakes do slip through. If you have spotted a typo, please do let us know and we can get it amended within hours.

info@bloodhoundbooks.com

9 781917 705486